THE
LAST KEEPERS
of the
COVENANT

THE LAST KEEPERS *of the* COVENANT

AN END-TIME SAGA

JOHN WILLIAM SANTANA

The Last Keepers of the Covenant
Copyright © 2020 by John William Santana. All rights reserved.

No part of this publication may be reproduced, stored in a retrieval system or transmitted in any way by any means, electronic, mechanical, photocopy, recording or otherwise without the prior permission of the author except as provided by USA copyright law.

The opinions expressed by the author are not necessarily those of URLink Print and Media.

1603 Capitol Ave., Suite 310 Cheyenne, Wyoming USA 82001
1-888-980-6523 | admin@urlinkpublishing.com

URLink Print and Media is committed to excellence in the publishing industry.

Book design copyright © 2020 by URLink Print and Media. All rights reserved.

Published in the United States of America
ISBN 978-1-64753-455-4 (Paperback)
ISBN 978-1-64753-456-1 (Digital)
24.07.20

CONTENTS

Introduction 7
In Gross Darkness 9
Spokane 12
Summer Escape 18
The Covenant 25
In Realms of Light 32
Provisions of the Covenant 35
Rita's Tragedy 44
The Encounter 61
Dark Plots 76
A New Life 78
Confrontation 94
Heavy Decisions 111
No Way! 122
New Beginnings 124
Nature Gone Berserk 127
An Uncertain Future 135
A Timely Rescue 158
Into Exile 168
Meanwhile, In the Great Temple 173
Snatched from the wolves 176
A Desperate Enemy 186
The Plot thickens 188
In Babilovia 197
Relentless 199

Destruction Commeth!	202
Frustration	213
A Scary Development	215
Happy Hunting!	218
The Coronation	225
Reunion	231
The Die Is Cast	235
The Rescue	239
Homeward Bound	245
Epilogue	247
Appendix	249

INTRODUCTION

In the shadow of things to come...
This book has been written because the vast majority of people do not have an idea of what's ahead for the United States, for Europe, and for the rest of the world. If we see ourselves now in a state of siege due to terrorism, on the verge of desperation due to global warming and atmospheric mayhem, in fear of earthquakes, tornadoes and hurricanes, in expectation of pandemics of frightening disease, in morbid starvation in some parts of our world while hoarding in others, and in unrelenting violence and immorality, we haven't seen anything yet. Even though politicians, ministers, and many scientists attempt to calm nervous minds by predicting, "we will prevail," "everything is just fine," and "this too will pass," there are those who know that nice platitudes will not save us from what is to come.

Although most people don't know what is really going on, they have had the answers very close to them for centuries. In spite of the indifference, rejection, and outright loathing that many have shown toward the Bible, the amazingly accurate fulfillment of its prophecies is a powerful testimony to those who are searching for answers, and a reproach to its detractors and mockers.

From the beginning, God made a covenant with mankind that offers protection from the onslaught of evil in this life and an awesome future upon the final destruction of evil. Unfortunately, many have allied themselves with the chief perpetrator of all evil, Satan, the fallen cherub, twisting and spinning the biblical truths about God, to the end that today there is more confusion than knowledge about him and his plan for mankind.

Those who entered into this covenant in the past have enjoyed peace and protection during the most threatening episodes in their lives. You can see them across the pages of the Scriptures: Noah, Abraham, Joseph, David, Daniel, and his friends. They were Keepers of the Covenant, and the covenant kept them in their hour of greatest peril and need. In the same way, it is promised that those who abide in the covenant at the time of the end will be kept safe and secure as the world tumbles around them. (See Psalm 91 and Psalm 27:5.)

What is this mysterious covenant and what is the source of its awesome power? Why is it so crucial to be a part of it? What are the consequences of not entering into it? Why have some preachers, teachers, and theologians kept this information from us?

The story in which you are about to be absorbed is a view of the end time as predicted in the Bible, using illustrative events and fictional human characters. It foretells the spirit that will prevail as the great controversy between Christ and Satan comes to an end and how those who choose to be on either side will come to their reward. Welcome to the future!

IN GROSS DARKNESS

In the dark regions of planet Earth, six miles into its fragile crust, there is a cavern so enormous as to accommodate the presence of an innumerable horde of aliens who invaded our planet about six thousand years ago. The main cave, ornate beyond the beauty of other earthly structures, is the audience chamber of the Prince of Darkness, who rules with an iron hand the hosts of supernatural beings that make up his kingdom. Its walls sparkle with earth's most precious metals and sought-out stones. At the far end, there is a beautifully carved ivory throne, set up high above his subjects on a solid slab of the most exquisite marble. Every month, as the full moon appears, he beckons them to a council of evil assessment and planning. For many centuries he has carried on a treacherous war against his loathed enemy, the Prince of Peace, and against the human race he created.

The council was called to order, and an eerie silence prevailed as a very tall, somewhat majestic apparition with deep-set eyes took his place on the ornate throne. He wore a costly crown, a symbol of his authority, and an extravagant robe of many colors, which contrasted greatly with the simple black garments of his powerful army. The eerie silence was finally broken by a gravelly voice, loud enough to shake the walls, and powerful enough to instill fear and obedience in those who, having cast their lot with him, must now submit to his evil leadership.

"The world is quickly going into total disorder. We must rush to finish our conquest of all mankind. We have greatly succeeded thus far, but a lot of work still needs to be done. We must eliminate the last vestiges of opposition to our goals and objectives. That means that those vile Keepers of the Covenant have to go. They must be destroyed before we can succeed! They must be stopped from continually persuading other humans with their subtle arguments and their empty promises of a better life! We will succeed if we persist!"

"This ain't gonna work, either," a high-ranking demon whispered to another in the back row.

"Do I hear dissent back there? Is that you again, General Algarroba?" the gravelly voice became louder and agitated.

"Yes, it is me! Success continues to be one of your empty promises!" the angry fiend replied. "You've lied to us from the beginning! You lied about the character of God, about the laws of His kingdom, and about the nature of the Prince of Peace. You lied about the nature of freedom and have made us into slaves of your ambition and whims! You continue to lie…"

"That's enough, Algarroba! Yes! Lies, deception, these are my very best weapons!" he declared with a grotesque laugh.

"Lucifer, you destroyed everything we had previously enjoyed, and now expect us to believe that success is still possible! You never should have lied to us, to fools like us, who trusted so much in your leadership! Our doom was sealed at Calvary, don't you understand? There's no hope of ever defeating the purposes of the Prince! Wake up and smell the brimstone, Satan!"

"How dare you use that hated human appellation! I am Prince Lucifer! And only one truth prevails in this kingdom:

I shall be king! As for you, Algarroba, I will teach you a lesson of submission which you will never forget!" And raising his arm and pointing his index finger at the enraged general, he released a strange ray of power that left the angry fiend shivering in pain.

"Release me! I will submit!" The excruciating howl reverberated within the huge cavern, and the torturing flow of power was stopped.

"That's better! And now, to the rest of you, you have your orders. Dissuade with your sophistry! Deceive with your lies! Destroy with your powers! Go! And conquer!"

The myriads of demons spread their wings and streamed out of the cavern like a swarm of bats out of Carlsbad.

SPOKANE

The city languished in misery as the summer heat bore down on its inhabitants. The biggest business in town was repair and construction. Eight months before, the city had been battered by a freak combination of thunderstorms, tornadoes, and hail. The trail of destruction began west of Coeur d'Alene and ended near Moses Lake. Hundreds were left homeless and many homes and business structures were destroyed. Three-thousand and sixty-two people were injured and fifty-seven lost their lives.

Not that it was much better in other parts of the country. Some years before, hurricane Katrina had stunned everyone with the breadth of its destructive power. Since then it seemed like the very elements were at war with all of mankind. Hurricanes had increased in number and intensity every year. Many homes in southern Florida had been abandoned and its residents, weary of rebuilding, had scattered throughout the country.

New Orleans had never fully recovered, but the casinos in Alabama and Mississippi had made a comeback after the enormous waves had destroyed much of that coast.

The fires in Texas had created a new desert, and many other storms had destroyed a lot of crops in America's farmlands. Prolonged droughts had turned forests into dry tinder, setting many areas in the country on fire at any given moment, and driving food prices sky high, exacerbated by fuel prices in the eight dollar per gallon range.

In Spokane, people were adjusting to the situation as best as they could, and at least some schools were open and one college was still in operation.

"Gerry! Gerry! Over here!" Lisa shouted excitedly as Gerry walked away from the chemistry building toward the campus common. Gerry followed the sound of her voice until he saw her sitting on one of the benches under the welcoming shade of Genr'l Jackson, as the campus' oldest oak tree was known. It was unusually hot for the beginning of summer, and anything that blocked the sun was eagerly sought out.

"Hey, Lisa! How'd you do in that brain smasher? You were the first one out, so I'm sure you aced it!"

"Don't you believe it, hon. Oh, I hate that man! You'd have thought he was hired to teach chemistry, not to torment us that way. I couldn't answer half the stuff on that test, so I walked out early. Fortunately my GPA is strong enough to make up for the probable "C" I'm likely to get."

"Well, at least that was the last one for this term. Put it behind you. Let's see what we're going to do for the summer."

"I saw Rita a while ago. She said we're all meeting at Joyce's apartment at seven tonight to unwind from finals. Personally, I don't want to see a chemistry book anywhere within twenty-five miles for the rest of the year! If I read at all, it'll have to be something romantic and enchanting!" she said as she giggled. "Go ahead, laugh and smirk all you want!"

"You women are all the same. No, I'll take that back. Rita is a lot more practical and creative. I'll see you at Joyce's."

Gerry headed home with some heavy thoughts on his mind. What would be do for the summer? He should have scouted out a job during the last two months. Waiting for the last moment never worked. And with the shutting down of nine major auto plants, many businesses across the country had also been affected and unemployment was unbearably high, with thousands competing for the few jobs available. Car sales were at the lowest point ever since the price of gasoline had kept climbing beyond the reach of the average consumer.

The consequences of global warming had pushed governments worldwide to develop and distribute bio-fuels. Every country that formerly produced petroleum was now heavy into the production of alternative fuels made from vegetable sources. This, in turn, had driven food prices through the roof in the developed countries and caused massive starvation in many others. Food riots were a common part of daily life in many cities around the globe; food transportation and distribution were major disasters as truck drivers went on strikes; black markets sprung up everywhere, and food and gas theft were more common than traffic violations.

Gerry wasn't the only one facing the job crisis, either. His friends Ben and Ahmed were stuck with the same uncertain future. Hopefully the group session that night would lead to some solutions.

"Hi, Mom, how was your day?" His greeting blended with the slamming of the screen door. But Sonia only needed to hear his voice and know that her boy was home.

"I'm glad you're here early, Gerry. I didn't have time today for grocery shopping and have nothing prepared for dinner. So bake a potato or something. I have to attend my committee meeting in a little bit." Sonia was rushing to gather her stuff and walk out the door to the most important appointment of her very busy week.

At forty-two, with her petite look and charming smile, she had made a lot of friends in high places and was currently vice chairman of the city's Committee for the Enhancement of Family Life. As he watched her go across the street, he realized how badly the family life there needed enhancement, It was bad nationwide, with an unemployment rate of thirty-five percent. To top that off there was drought in the northwest, earthquakes in California, Texas and Missouri, a heat wave in the northeast, and an unusually early hurricane season in the south, all disasters together draining the dwindling resources of many government agencies, whose budgets had already been drastically cut due to the ongoing war in the Middle East.

Sonia's main concerns were in Spokane, Washington, where riots had broken out over shortages of food and gas. Even teachers had gone on strike, and there seemed a likely possibility that schools would not open on time in the fall. That would mean kids and youth out on the streets extending their havoc beyond summer.

A few minutes later, Gerry was on his way to Joyce's, with great anticipation of what they would cook up for a seemingly dull summer. When he arrived, the place was buzzing with animated conversation, occasional laughter, and of course, pizza, and beer.

"A toast to Professor Greenwald," Ben shouted, unable to contain a mischievous smile.

"How dare you offer a toast to that old coot!" retorted Lisa. "I break out all over just entering his classroom. I hope he's really retiring this year, or the college will have to shut down the chemistry department."

"C'mon, Lisa, everyone knows you're the teacher's pet!" Ben teased. That comment cost him a fast flying pillow right to his face.

"All right, now, everybody. Let's get serious and do some planning for the next two weeks. We all need jobs so that should be our first priority. I plan to hit it hard starting tomorrow morning. Let's share whatever leads we find and help each other. That way, whoever lands the first job can buy the pizza and beer next week." They all laughed as they shared ideas for their group job search.

The days passed, and Gerry became increasingly frustrated in his search. Every business and factory in town had either closed, cut back, or was holding still for any change in the economy. With all the problems worldwide, the president had called for another day of prayer and fasting. He urged the nation to go to church every Sunday and pray for relief from disastrous weather, for national prosperity, and for peace in the troubled cities. Ministers were urged to lead the people back to God, so that his blessings would then be poured upon the suffering peoples of the nations and the world.

Saturday morning found the loyal group of friends gathered around the table at Gerry's house. The mood was somber. Only two of them had found jobs: Rita was to work for two weeks helping a bearings factory to do inventory and packing so they could relocate to Dallas, and Ahmed would work three days a week in a restaurant that served the National Guard troops now camping outside of town. Business there was good, as long as the troops stayed. That, however, was uncertain, since they were continually being moved to wherever civil unrest required them.

"You know what we really need?" Ben mused rather thoughtfully. "We need to get away from here for a while."

"I think you're right, Ben. We're just beating our heads against the wall and getting depressed!" Lisa carried the thought.

"Hey, what do y'all think about going camping next weekend? We'll give this job hunt a few more days, and if things don't get better by Friday, we're out of here!" Gerry was really excited. Just the prospect of getting out of that musty city and into fresh air and starlit nights suddenly invigorated the whole group. And just in time, as stomachs began to rumble, Sonia came out of the kitchen with a large tray of piping hot enchiladas, followed by side dishes of Mexican rice, refried beans, and an awesome stack of nachos.

The days flew by, and though the friends did their best to find jobs, the situation didn't change. In fact, Rita was let go on Thursday, and Ahmed would not work again until Tuesday of the following week. So Friday, they all awoke with more excitement than disappointment as they gathered their camping gear, clothing, and food for a week. This was to be some seriously fun camping.

SUMMER ESCAPE

"I can't believe it took half of my savings to fill the gas tank and this army can!" Ben complained as he loaded a military gas container on to the niche on his Jeep. "At this rate, I may never be able to camp again!"

"So you better enjoy this one to the hilt," Ahmed replied. "Personally, I don't know if I want to come back here. The thought that something really exciting might be waiting on the other side of those mountains intrigues me. At least I don't have parents to come back to, so... who knows?"

"I'm sorry, Ahmed. I know these last two years have been very sad for you. But maybe you'll get to see your parents someday, you know... people say that the dead can appear again to see how their kin are doing."

"May your God hear you," Ahmed muttered as he finished tying down the tarp over the luggage. Just then the rest of the group rounded the corner, and after a few excited exchanges, they formed a caravan in direction toward the nearby mountains.

Their planned route took them through Coeur d'Alene and up Highway ninety-five past Hayden. Suddenly, Gerry saw an old, dilapidated sign that flashed a dim memory into his consciousness. Unwittingly, he began to muse out loud. "You wouldn't believe I used to go to summer camp by that lake when I was a kid. I had some of my best times up there. The swimming, the horses, the stories by the campfire… yeah, I had some great times there…"

"What camp?" Lisa stirred from her own wanderings. "Are you awake or just delirious?"

"Oh, never mind. It's too far a memory to go back. But I'm sure going to make up for lost time. This weekend is going to be great!"

The trip took several hours, and Ben and Ahmed carried on about the mundane events of the last couple of months, while Rita and Joyce used the time to catch up on all the sleep lost during the last week of finals.

But back in Gerry's pickup, Lisa was stirring up some concerns about their present situation and what the future held in store. Gerry was to begin his senior year in biochemistry and Lisa her junior year in premed. They had known each other since childhood, growing up in the same neighborhood. Their parents had been friends, and, even though their parents had divorced and gone their separate ways, the children had been able to hold on to their friendship.

"I'm scared of the future, Gerry. I have no idea if and when things are going to return to normal. I can't understand all that's going on in the world. It's like society, nature, government–everything's gone out of whack! I don't know if I'll ever marry, if I'll have kids, if there will be any happiness for them or for me. Just getting a job would give me some sense of security." A cloud seemed to have settled over her beautiful face, and Gerry couldn't help taking his eyes off the road to glance at her. In that moment, he realized how much she meant to him and how earnestly he wanted her to feel safe and secure with him.

"It's going to work out, Lisa; you just wait and see," he said with a gentle smile. Of course, he had no idea just how it would work out, but for now, he felt a need to reassure her.

He reached over and took her hand in his as she blushed and tucked her head on his shoulder. A peace seemed to come over her, and she soon fell asleep.

They traveled past Sandpoint, beyond Bonner's Ferry, and just a few miles from the Canadian border, they took a dirt road into the hills. An hour of bumpy discomfort led them to stop for a break in a small meadow bordered by a clump of shady pines.

"Where are we, Gerry?" Ben asked, not being at all familiar with the area.

"We should be getting close to the Kootenai River. Wait till you see it–some of the best fishing in Idaho, and some great swimming holes. But I don't quite remember which fork to take ahead. I haven't been up here since I was a kid. Any sign of life up here?"

"You know," Joyce responded, "it seems I saw a cabin set back in the woods about a mile back. Why don't we go back and see if anyone's there. I'd hate to be lost in these woods after dark, and that's not too far off."

Everyone agreed, and so they turned back, and sure enough, there was a nice-sized log house surrounded by a sapling fence. They drove up as close as they could, and stepped out just as a bearded man came off the porch toward them, followed by a friendly golden retriever. The man was about five foot, six inches, with an impressive muscular build and well-tanned skin. His gray hair spoke of an age his body didn't agree with. A few wrinkles on his face gave his age at late fifties or early sixties. He smiled as he approached the group.

"Welcome to Shiloh Homestead. I'm Guillermo Rodriguez Valentin…and who would you all be?"

Ben was the closest to the man, so he stretched out his hand as he introduced himself and the members of the group. But the man did not take his hand. Instead, he placed his hands in front of him and, interlocking his fingers, held them in front of him while holding his peace. Ben felt rather awkward at this and his voice trailed off as he spoke the last two names.

Gerry was quite puzzled by the man's apparent rudeness, until a thought suddenly struck him…a memory hidden for many years in his psyche and now triggered by this man's peculiar behavior. Looking intently at the big man, he slowly approached him, and, interlocking his own fingers in front of him, touched his own hands against his.

"Do you know what you're doing?" Guillermo pierced into Gerry's eyes with an intensity that made him more than a little nervous.

"I…I th..think so." Gerry wiped a ripple of perspiration gathering on his forehead. "It's the traditional greeting of the Keepers of the Covenant, isn't it?"

"And where did you ever learn that?" Guillermo asked, struggling to suppress an emerging smile. The others looked at Gerry with bewilderment. *What in the world is going on here?* must have been everyone's thought.

"My mother used to tell me when I was a kid about a group of people who gathered on Friday nights to study the Bible. She learned a lot of stories that she would then tell me at night before going to sleep. These people were very strict on biblical teaching and practice. One of the things she taught me was very peculiar, and that was the way they greeted each other by interlocking their own hands and touching each other's. She seemed to know what it all meant, but never explained it to me."

"Who are you? What's your name?" Guillermo was now obviously intrigued.

"My name is Gerardo Gonzalez de la Rosa, but everyone calls me Gerry. My mother is Sonia de la Rosa."

Guillermo now exploded with delight. "You are Sonia's boy?" he exclaimed as he took Gerry off his feet in a hug with the ease others would lift and hug a broom. Gerry himself was caught off guard, and felt rather sheepish in front of his friends. But now Guillermo turned to Ben and the others and apologized for his unexpected behavior. He shook hands with all of them, making the boys flinch but remembering to be gentle with the ladies.

"I'm so happy you stopped to say hello. I know this boy's mother from many years ago. I was a member of that group he referred to, and I remember her very well. How is your mother, Gerry? Is she well? Does she still meet with the group in Spokane?"

"Yes, sir, she is quite well. She is working with the city in an important position with the Committee for the Enhancement of Family life. But it's been many years since she's had any contact with Covenant Keepers. She hasn't even mentioned them since I turned twelve."

Guillermo showed a brief expression of disappointment, but then said with a cheery smile, "Say, you all must be hungry. My wife happens to have a pot of vegetable stew that's just about right for eight people. There's also fresh baked bread and we have apple dumplings. What do you say we go in and enjoy a simple but nutritious dinner?"

He didn't have to ask twice. Everyone was famished from the drive. The wife had come to the door to see what all the commotion was about, so introductions were in order.

"Elizabeth, I want you to meet a nice group of young people who happened to stop by asking directions. They look like they're ready for a good meal, so I've invited them for supper. Let's see if my memory is as good as it used to be. This here is Ben, and there's Lisa, Joyce, Ahmed and Rita. And you're not going to believe who this young man is!"

Elizabeth greeted each one warmly, and then stared a little closer at Gerry.

"I can't guess who you are, but you look harmless enough!" she said with a twinkle in her eye.

"My name is Gerardo Gonzalez de la Rosa, ma'am. I'm Sonia de la Rosa's son."

"I can't believe it! Sonia's son… what a pleasant surprise! Welcome. Please come in… all of you. Make yourselves at home." Gerry's friends quickly recovered from the slight shock over his strange greeting of and indirect connection to Guillermo and Elizabeth. They had never seen anything like it, and Ben made a mental note to ask him about it later.

They followed her into the house and discovered a clean, tastefully furnished, country home. As they washed up, the smell of the fresh baked bread and the dumplings filled the air. Once seated, the strangeness began to defrost, and conversation began to flow.

Just then, the sun began to descend out of sight behind the mountains. While the others ate, Guillermo reached for his guitar, and making himself comfortable in a rocking chair, began to sing softly a melody of gratitude and praise to the God of his personal experience.

The young people listened quietly, wondering about
the unusual couple that had crossed their path that day. Finally, the silence was broken with a casual question.

"How long have you lived here, Guillermo?" Gerry led out in the social inquiry.

"Oh, we've had this place for about twenty years. My wife and I used to come up here from Yakima every summer and enjoy the outdoors. This place always meant a lot to us. When the kids finally left home years ago, we decided to retire and come up here permanently."

"So, where are your kids now," Lisa had noticed the pictures of a handsome young man and a pretty brunette on the mantelpiece.

"My son, Rolando, is a physician who spent a number of years as a missionary doctor in the mountain region of Peru. Recently he joined a French organization known as Medicine Sans Frontieres, or, as we say here, Doctors Without Borders. He usually comes to see us at least once a year, but with all these worldwide pandemics of AIDS, dengue, and Ebola, these poor doctors barely have enough time to eat."

"Wow, that's neat. How about your daughter?"

"Well, Isabella is a school teacher and since her husband, Shawn, is a minister who gets transferred every five years to a new parish, she's lived in a few places, currently in Bend, Oregon."

"It must get lonely out here without your children or neighbors," Joyce chipped in.

"You know, it's not as bad as you might think. The beauty of the place, the company of birds and all the little creatures, the occasional visits by friends like yourselves, and the peace that comes from living in a covenant relationship make life really bearable up here. Yes, sir, life is really good here."

There goes that covenant word again! thought Ben. *I've got to know what that's all about. Strange how Gerry knew about this and never mentioned it.*

THE COVENANT

"Mr. Rodriguez—," Ben began, but was interrupted. "Just Guillermo, please. I left my government job behind with all its formalities and titles."

"Guillermo, then. I am curious about this covenant thing. Believe me, I was thrown out of whack when Gerry recognized your unique way of greeting and identified it as a covenant something."

Guillermo smiled. "I'm glad you asked, Ben. I enjoy talking to people about the covenant and its provisions for all mankind. I assume that most of you, if not all, have been exposed to the basic story and principles of Christianity, or am I assuming too much?"

Ahmed stiffened a little at this, but allowed Gerry to answer for the group.

"We are all children of various Christian denominations, except for our atheist friend here," nodding toward Ahmed. "Some of our parents are still active church goers, but our generation has kinda lost contact with our religious roots; ya' know what I mean?"

"Yes, I know just what you mean. I think every generation goes through a stage during which all values and beliefs are put through the strainer and that which has not rooted well gets sifted out. I went through all of that too. Until someone took the time to explain the true origin, meaning, and intent of God's covenant with each individual and with all of mankind. And once I understood all this, I suddenly had a totally different, positive, invigorating view of what I could become through a covenant relationship with the Creator of the universe."

"Man, that sounds so far out!" Ahmed couldn't hold off any more. "What makes you think there is such a person as a Creator?"

"Well, Ahmed, that's a fair question and a good place to start. If you read the Bible and believe that it is the direct communication of the Creator with His creatures, then a belief in His existence and in His creative power and purpose is relatively easy. For those who don't believe that way, God has provided other evidences, such as the infinite complexity of everything in nature that abolishes the numerical probability of their spontaneous appearance by mere chance. I understand some of you are studying the sciences at your school. What does a scientist do with the law of entropy, one of the principles of thermodynamics, which states that all matter goes from order to disorder? Left alone, with no outside force or intervention, how can matter go from disorder to order, to greater, more complex order, to organism, and on to higher life? If you think long enough about these things, I don't think it is difficult to conclude that all of nature has a definite design, and that design therefore requires a designer. That Designer, I understand to be God."

Ahmed thought for a moment and replied with a wan smile, "I'll have to think about that one for a while."

"Well, there's a lot more to it but going back to the question about the covenant, once one accepts the existence of the Creator, one finds in the Bible a description of who he is and what was his purpose in creating this world, its creatures, and us. Would you like me to read what the Bible itself says on these issues?"

"Well, yeah, that's okay." Ben had asked, and now could hardly appear disinterested. After all, the man had treated them very well. Just the apple dumplings were sufficient to put up with whatever religious ramblings were up next. The others probably felt the same, for they muttered their approval. Guillermo reached over to the corner table by his side and took a beautifully engraved Bible into his hands.

"Let's go back to the very beginning. The first book of the Bible, the book of Genesis, starts out telling us the story of how God created the world in six days."

"Hold it right there!" Ben interrupted. "Isn't there a place in the Bible that says that to God a day is as a thousand years? Many intelligent people believe that God took six thousand years to create the world. After all, every object and organism is so complex that it would take a long time to design and put together. So the six thousand years makes a lot of sense to me."

"Good observation, Ben. It's important to bring up these possibilities because they help us study deeper and decipher what the Bible is really saying. What that verse, written by St. Peter is saying, is that since God is eternal, time has no beginning and no end with him. For us who are mortal, limited to an average of seventy to eighty years, every precious second counts and we measure time closely by marking birthdays every year. At the end, we look back and say, 'where did time go?'

"The briefness of human time is an issue to us. But to God it is not, because he has such an abundance of time, that a day appears as long as a year, and a year to him is so small that it appears as a day. However, when God is speaking to us through his inspired word, he is aware that out time is measured, and always refers to our days as literal twenty-four hour periods, and not long protracted time.

"When God created the earth, he did so in six twenty-four hour periods. Then he rested on the seventh day. If it would have taken him six-thousand years to create, did he then rest for a thousand years? Doing what? Then he states that we are to imitate his example of rest by keeping holy the seventh day as a celebration of his creative power and works. In the fourth of the Ten Commandments, he states, "Remember that Sabbath day to keep it holy. Six days you shall labor and do all your work, but the seventh day is the Sabbath of the lord your God. In it you shall do no work: you, nor your son, nor your daughter, nor your male servant nor your female servant, nor your cattle, nor your stranger who is within your gates. For in six days the Lord made the heavens and the earth, the sea, and all that is in them, and rested the seventh day. Therefore, the Lord blessed the Sabbath day and hallowed it (Exodus 20:8–11).

"If the Lord is asking us to celebrate his creation, and he knows that our lifetime is only seventy to eighty years, how could he ask us to keep the Sabbath every week for a thousand years?"

"Well, that makes sense to me. Why can't people believe that God has the power to make things that quickly?" Rita, the quietest one of the group, spoke up. Her Spanish accent had always made her a little self-conscious, yet Guillermo's argument had made an impact on her.

"Good thinking, Rita. The Bible states it this way, 'Then God said, "Let there be light," and there was light' (Genesis 1:3). And the book of Psalms is very clear in chapter thirty-three, verses six and nine, 'By the word of the Lord the heavens were made, and all the host of them by the breath of his mouth...For he spoke, and it was done; he commanded, and it stood fast.' I mean, how long can it take to make something if all you have to do is speak? Just an instant!"

"But wait a minute!" Joyce was a little agitated. "If you say that God spoke everything into existence, how come I was taught as a child that God made man by forming him of the dust of the ground and then breathed into him the breath of life? We are such a complicated mass of cells, organs, arteries, bones, and so on, it seems impossible for us to have been made in an instant. It took brilliant scientists many years just to figure out the human genome!"

Guillermo smiled. He really like the intensity of the young. He had provoked their thinking and now was seeing brains sizzling with both curiosity and defiance. "You are absolutely right, Joyce. You've brought up a very unique instance in the process of creation. God chose not to speak us into existence. He had in mind a creature so special, so much like himself, with the special purpose of an intelligent relationship that he took his time on this one. He wanted to place a very special touch on us. He handmade every detail and designed the human genome is such a marvellous way that this creation would pass on to future generations the godlike characteristics of our Creator."

"Your story makes great fantasy, sir, but nor very good science," Ahmed broke his silence, "All religions have their fantasies. But as a future scientist, I must see observable evidence of this creative power, with reproducible results many times over, before it can be stated as fact."

"I understand your argument, Ahmed," Guillermo responded patiently. "However, to understand God and his power requires not only evidence, but also an element called faith. Faith was best defined by St. Paul when he said in his letter to the Hebrews, chapter eleven, and verses one and three, 'Now faith is the substance of things hoped for, the evidence of things not seen… by faith we understand that the worlds were framed by the Word of God, so that the things which are seen were not made of things which are visible.'

"You can search in your mind and in the physical existence of all things around you to try to figure out how they were made. After you run out of all human or natural possibilities, if you become convinced that everything required a designer and maker, you are left with only one choice, and that person is God."

"There you go again with that designer thing. Why can't you accept that things evolved on their own, progressing over millions of years?" Ahmed was getting intense with his replies.

"Okay, Ahmed, let's talk about theories of chance and probabilities. Suppose you take your laptop computer completely apart–every wire, every screw, every transistor, every chip–and place all the large and minute parts in ten random piles on the floor of a room. You close the door, and come back a million years later, open the door and look inside.

What do you think is the probability that the ten random piles will have come exactly together to form a working computer?" Dead silence. Everyone was looking at Ahmed, as if saying, *Okay, Ahmed, you got yourself into this. Let's see you wiggle out of it!* Ahmed was finally able to manage a smile. "You know, it's been a long day for me. I'm stretching out my sleeping bag under the biggest tree. Thanks for the supper, Mr. Guillermo. Good night, everybody."

Guillermo didn't want to push. They had covered a lot of territory, and overkill would be disastrous. "Say, if we push some of this furniture aside, this carpet would accommodate all your sleeping bags. That beats the hard ground outside. You're welcome to spend the night free of mosquitoes."

Everyone welcomed the invitation. Soon they were all stuffed in their bags and drifting off to sleep, that is, except Ben and Gerry.

"Say, Gerry. This guy talked about everything except the covenant thing. It's almost as if he intentionally avoided giving me an answer!"

"Hang in there, Ben. I have a feeling he's going to continue his explanation in the morning."

"Oh, no! You mean we have to put up with more religion tomorrow? We came up to these mountains to camp and have fun, not for a catechism!"

"Relax, Ben. Besides, I'll put up with a little more, just for a delicious breakfast of pancakes, eggs, sausages, hash browns, coffee, and Danish. How's that for motivation?"

"Dream on, you fool! You'll probably get grits and coffee grounds–if you're lucky!" Gerry didn't answer. He felt Lisa's toes wiggling against his through the bags. He smiled as he drifted off to sleep.

IN REALMS OF LIGHT

Across the limitless realms of space, in a city of incredible beauty described in the book of Revelation, chapters twenty–one and twenty–two as the New Jerusalem, capital of the universe, there was a flurry of activity as the clock ticked toward the third major event to take place on planet Earth. In the palace of the Eternal God, within the very throne room where He, as the Monarch of the Universe holds audience, the Crown Prince, know to humans as Jesus, the Prince of Peace carries out his daily ministry on behalf of mankind.

As Creator, the Prince brought planet Earth into being, and in only six human days, he created everything that exists on it. On the seventh day, he stepped back to revel in the beauty of his creation, and designated that day as a weekly celebration of His creative power and his love for his creatures.

But his creatures betrayed him, yielding their allegiance to a stranger–to the powerful enemy of the Prince described before, and who had been cast out of the Realms of Light along with his disaffected followers. Thus, the great controversy that had started in heaven was to continue on planet Earth. The issue was the character of God. The prize was rulership of the planet Earth.

But the Prince was not about to let Satan get away with it. He loved the human beings that he had created and determined to win them back. It took approximately four thousand years for the second major event to take place, the battle at Calvary. The prince cleared the name and character of God forever by showing God's attributes of love and justice in dying on the cross and paying for the consequences of mankind's sins. In so doing, the human race could be forgiven and restored to full communion with God. Satan and his accusations were laid bare before the universe, and the Prince won the great controversy. His enemy was now doomed to eventual destruction.

At the time this segment of the story began, the Prince was in the throne room of the universe, otherwise known as the Heavenly Sanctuary. It was so called because it was there where human beings could find sanctuary from the verdict of death imposed by sin. It was there where the Prince presented the prayers of confession and pleas for forgiveness sent up by repentant sinners, and where, subsequently, forgiveness and removal of sin took place. The Prince had been doing this work ever since his return to heaven after his resurrection, first in the Holy Place and, since the year 1844, in the Most Holy Place (the throne room).

Time was running out for planet Earth. Its inhabitants had only a short period during which to make their choices—either to be on the side of the Prince of Peace, or to submit to the Prince of Darkness. Soon mediation was to cease. The Prince of Peace would declare the forgiven as saved and the impenitent as lost. The Prince would then remove his priestly robes and proceed to His coronation as King of Kings and Lord of Lords. For the moment, he was trying to reach all who would accept him as their Lord and Saviour.

Jebosh, one of the leading commanders of the heavenly hosts of angels, was standing by at the door of the Sanctuary.

The Prince turned and called him inside. The majestic looking angel entered and bowed reverently before the Prince.

"I am at your command, my Prince. What errand to you have for me this time?"

"I want to thank you, my dear friend, for what you and the angels under your command are doing on behalf of my faithful followers. Continue to protect them from our enemies until this war is over. Now I have an additional task for you, one that you will really enjoy!" The Prince had a joyful smile on his face.

"I'm already looking forward to it, my Lord!" Jebosh responded with keen anticipation.

"There's a group of college students from Spokane that is ripe for a final decision as to who they will follow for eternity. Go and join their guardian angels. Direct them with your special skills. Watch over their souls as precious heirs in my future kingdom."

"Your request is my delight to fulfil, my Prince. I'm on my way!" Bowing deeply and reverently, Jebosh headed for the door of the temple. Once outside, he pointed his impressive wings backward, and went into flight at a speed beyond human calculation.

PROVISIONS OF THE COVENANT

Saturday morning found everyone in a lazy mood, chitchatting avidly, but still lounging in sleeping bags. Guillermo, however, had been up for a couple of hours and was busy in the kitchen whipping up whole wheat pancake mix, scrambling eggs with chopped veggies, and sizzling hash browns on the grill. The aromas of good cooking permeated the house, and the young brigade started to crawl out of their bags and wash up for breakfast.

"What'd I tell you last night, Ben? You can wait for the grits and coffee grounds if you want. I'm going after my pancakes and scrambled eggs," Gerry grinned at his friend.

The girls, of course, took over the bathroom, so the boys went out into the forest. Soon they were gathered around the table wolfing down an abundant stack with butter and hot maple syrup.

The conversation was lively and soon turned to what was currently happening in the world. The news that week had focused on Europe. Everything there was in turmoil. Unemployment was at an unheard of rate of forty-two percent, and growing. There were continual protest demonstrations and public transportation had come to a halt due to strikes against government wages. Mail was at a standstill, sanitation workers were on strike, garbage had stacked up in huge piles in the cities. Rats and roaches had multiplied by the tons, and crime was rampant everywhere. Back here, in the States, the situation was heading in the same direction.

Unemployment had already reached thirty-five percent and was still rising. The same greed that had driven gas prices in the past, was now determining the price of bio-fuel. It had risen to such an extent that truck drivers were on massive strikes, and food began to get scarce. Black markets were now thriving and people were hoarding what little they could get against a worsening crisis. The government wasn't happy with the situation, but there was little it could do, since the police force was facing the same wants with their own families.

"What does all this mean, Guillermo? Is this the beginning of the end? Or should we expect this situation to improve and for peace and prosperity to return?" Lisa was suddenly finding it difficult to swallow her tasty breakfast. Her parents were still very deep in debt and were struggling to pay everyone off while they still had jobs. If they lost those jobs, they would be at the mercy of ravenous creditors.

"I don't mean to alarm you, my young friends. But, yes, I believe we are seeing the beginning of the time of the end. Things will get very much worse before they get better. But there's also very good news. For those of us who survive the final crisis, things will be infinitely better, even beyond your wildest dreams!"

"Now you have me really intrigued, Guillermo. You mean to tell me that you know what is really happening and how it's going to end? I've got to hear this!" Gerry was eagerly leaning forward with both elbows on the table in violation of mother's table manners.

"Well, I'll be happy to share what I know with all of you. But I can't do it until I finish explaining what we started last night about the meaning and history of the covenant. If you don't understand God's covenant, it will be more difficult for you to put the pieces of the historical puzzle together."

Uh oh! thought Ahmed. *Here we go again!* "Say, guys, I came up here for some serious fishing. Now, I know there are some beautiful fish down there waiting for my bait. So, I'm out of here! See ya'll later!" With that, he rose from the table and headed out the door and to the jeep for his fishing gear.

Guillermo followed him to the door and, placing his hand on Ahmed's, shoulder, said with a patient smile, "There's a whole school of fat trout in a pool about a quarter mile down from that big pine down there. Have a good time."

Everyone else quickly folded up the sleeping bags and moved all the furniture back into place.

"Okay, Guillermo, let's have it!" Ben was ready, on the edge of the sofa, with Joyce sitting on the carpet, leaning against his knees, both seeming to enjoy the closeness.

"Now where did we leave off? Oh yes, we discovered last night that God decided to create creatures in his own image for the purpose of friendship and fellowship. When he made mankind, he provided everything they needed for a happy existence. The very best food, a beautiful garden for shelter, and the delightful company of all the perfect animals previously created. But his greatest gifts were his love, life, freedom to choose, an identity and laws to regulate and enhance their relationships.

These gifts have passed on from generation to generation, from God to our first parents, from them eventually to us, from us to our children, and from them to our grandchildren for generations to come. In the best of human relationships, there is the passing on of life, the expressions of love, the freedom we allow our children to choose for themselves, our family name, and the rules and regulations that govern our homes and our relationships. Take any of these away and family relations become bitter and estranged."

"You know, I never thought of it that way," Gerry mused. "Those five things you have mentioned just about cover everything you want to get in a relationship."

"That's right, Gerry. And we call these God's five Provisions of the Covenant. They constitute God's side of this agreement. But there's another side, and that is how we respond to these provisions. It cannot be a covenant unless at least two persons enter into it."

"Man, what can we possibly give God in exchange for all this? We don't have his power, we don't have his resources, and we can't even see him. What kind of relationship can a man or woman have with God?" Lisa seemed puzzled by these cosmic ideas.

"Well, Lisa, this is a spiritual relationship. You cannot see or know God face to face because His person is so sublimely glorious and powerful that if you saw Him, you would be extremely overwhelmed. Moses wanted to see Him in person, but God told him that if he saw Him he would die. We find that story in the Bible, the book of Exodus, chapter thirty-three and verses eighteen to twenty-six.

"Instead, God would like for us to simply respond to His five provisions with five responses of our own. In Deuteronomy, chapter six and verse five, He asks first of all, that we love Him with all our hearts. To place Him first and foremost in our thoughts and to think ahead of time on how our words and actions will affect our relationship with Him should be out first response. To worship Him exclusively as our Lord and Creator is the second thing He asks. The first four of the Ten Commandments, as given in Exodus twenty, verses one through eleven, deal with this exclusive loyalty, which keeps us from giving the allegiance due Him to anything or anyone else. Loyalty is essential for the uniqueness of a relationship.

"Thirdly, he asks us to trust Him explicitly. Even the slightest doubt eats away at trust. With all of our future at stake, to distrust God places us at risk of eternal loss. He certainly has earned that trust, first by the constant provision of His grace manifested in our protection and provision for our daily needs, and most eminently, on Calvary where He gave himself in order to assure our salvation and restoration.

"God also wants us to recognize at all times the sacred and exalted nature of His person. His attributes and character are embedded in His name. Thus, He expects from us the utmost reverence and respect for His name. It is by His name that we have an identity as Children of God.

Today you see that name lightly used by many in casual conversation, which has nothing to do with His person, and grossly used by many others in cursing and profanity. For those of us who choose to enter into a covenant relationship with Him, He shares His name with us, and it must be protected and reverenced and His character represented in our thoughts, word, and actions.

"And our fifth response, of course, is perhaps the most difficult one–the one we struggle with the most–and that is obedience. Every government on earth that wants to survive for some time must have laws that regulate behaviour and relationships, if it hopes to continue in power. Law and order are natural elements of social structures. And God is the original Author of all the laws in the universe that make everything work, from the orbit of the electron around the nucleus of the atom to the orbit of the galaxies around each other. Evolutionists and atheists cannot and will not be able to account for the infinite order in the universe except if they are willing to accept its design and its Designer."

"Wow! You've said a mouthful." Gerry seemed impressed. "But you started out to tell us about this mysterious covenant greeting. Seems like you got a little sidetracked!"

"Oh, but I didn't get sidetracked. I was laying the background for this special greeting. You see, if you let the fingers of your right hand represent God's five provisions and you let the fingers of the left hand represent our five responses, when we interlock our fingers in this way we are symbolically bringing together the covenant agreement. You see if we understand and can identify God's five provisions and our five responses, but they never come together, there's no covenant. We can believe that God provides us with love, life, liberty, his identity, and his law, but if we stay apart from him, not responding in love, loyalty, trust, reverence, and obedience, there's no agreement, no commitment to a relationship–in essence, no covenant."

"Well, so what? What if you don't care about all this? What if you just want to live your life the way you want, doing your own thing, without worrying about this covenant, what then?" Ben had to test the strength of Guillermo's thesis.

"Well, Ben, it will break God's heart. Millions of people have rejected the offer of the covenant throughout human history. One of the outstanding examples of this rejection is found in the story of the flood. In Genesis, chapter six and verses five and six it tells us that, 'Then the Lord saw that the wickedness of man was great in the earth, and that every intent of the thoughts of his heart was only evil continually. And the Lord was sorry that He had made man, and He was grieved in His heart.'

"And as you continue reading that story you find that God decided to destroy every living thing on the earth. But He finds that Noah was a Keeper of the Covenant, and so God spares him and his family from the coming disaster. He tells him how to build a boat to save himself, his family, and two of every species of animals. But He goes even further in His love and mercy toward the impenitent wicked: He gives them life for another 120 years, and asks Noah to preach to them, to try to convince them to return to the covenant relation with Him.

God does not destroy without first trying desperately to save. So it will be with every one of us. God calls us into covenant relationship with Him. Those who respond appropriately will find themselves covered by His hand when the awful storm makes landfall, the crisis of the end of the world. Those who do not respond will enjoy His protection and grace for a while as He strives to convince them and save them from the wrath to come. But there will come a time when His grace will be exhausted and the consequences of rejection will come with terrible power and anguish."

There was a dead silence for a good while. Guillermo chose to honor that silence, knowing that he had filled their thoughts to overflowing. All this new knowledge had filled the young people with somber thoughts.

What if what Guillermo has said is true? Gerry pondered.

Does the Bible really teach this stuff? Ben found all this a little strange.

If all this is true, how should I respond to God's covenant? Gerry thought with concern.

What will the others do? What will they say, or how will they act toward me if I'm the only one to believe in and accept this covenant thing? each one asked in the privacy of their minds.

The silence was suddenly broken by the clanging of the grandfather clock and at the same time by the quick footsteps of an excited Ahmed running up the steps with three nice, plump trout strung in front of him.

"Lunch is here! Take out your best spices, Guillermo! It's my turn to show you my delectable, culinary talents. What I can't do with a flask and spatula, I can do with a frying pan and oregano. And I learned it all from a Puerto Rican army chef!" Everyone snapped from their pensive state and soon was absorbed in Ahmed's account of stealth and strategy in the watery kingdom.

After a wonderful meal of *trucha en escabeche with papas al mojo de ajo,* (trout in sautéed onions and potatoes in olive oil and garlic) they all had to find a spot for a relaxing siesta. Ahmed and Ben announced dibs on the hammocks hanging on the back porch and overlooking the beautiful scenery with the river below. The girls unrolled their sleeping bags and sprawled out on the living room floor. Gerry was too full of thoughts to sleep. So he sat on a rocker on the front porch and chatted softly with Guillermo so as not to awaken the others.

"You know, Guillermo, what you shared with us today could shake up our lifestyle quite a bit. Sure, we all had some religious training and our parents did the best they could for us. But times have changed. Our generation thinks quite differently than yours. We're not ready to give up all our fun for an ascetic life of prayer and bible study. If what you say is true, then God is asking a lot from us."

"I'll try to ignore the reference to my ascetic life," Guillermo answered with a smile. "In fact, I socialize quite a bit. I go into Sandpoint, and Coeur d'Alene, and Spokane, and even all the way to Seattle to visit friends, and go fishing and sailing and have a lot of fun. I think I have a wonderful lifestyle. God doesn't ask you to stop living life and loving people, Gerry. Having a covenant relationship infinitely enhances other relations because your friendships are more genuine, less selfish, more sincere, and lasting. When we love God and realize how immense is His love for us, that's when we really learn to love and enjoy each other."

"You're really something else, Guillermo," Gerry grinned, "You're so smooth with words and ideas. I could be convinced about this covenant thing."

"First of all, quit calling this the 'covenant thing.' It seems to trivialize it," Guillermo chided gently. "Call it God's covenant or the covenant. You know, people have wrestled with acceptance of the covenant throughout all of history, the majority of them turning down the invitation. Cain, the people of the flood, Pharaoh and the Egyptians, King Saul, and on to the New Testament– the Jews of Christ's day, Pilate, Herod. But there have always been others who have entered into a covenant relationship with Christ, many of them at the cost of their very lives. They stood tall before persecution by the Romans, the Inquisition, and some were even persecuted and killed by Christians who differed from them in belief and commitment."

"Seriously, Guillermo, is it worth dying for this? Would you die for this covenant?"

"You obviously have no idea of what is awaiting those who are true to God and express it by entering into the covenant. Here, take my Bible and read the last two chapters of the last book, Revelation. I'm going inside for a short nap," Guillermo said kindly as he rose from the rocker and headed inside.

 # RITA'S TRAGEDY

The screen door slammed gently, and everyone stirred from slumber.
"Hey, what time is it?" Joyce wondered out loud as she rubbed the sleep from her eyes.

"It's 4:15, and you've all wasted a great afternoon. Just look out there! We came out here to enjoy the outdoors, and what do you all do? Sleep! Well, I'm going for a refreshing dip in the best water hole down there. Anyone going with me?" Gerry extended the invitation. There was a buzz of excited activity as they dug out their swimsuits and towels. That is, all except Rita. She just sat quietly in a rocker and let all the activity pass her by.

"C'mon, Rita, aren't you going with us?" Joyce asked as she headed for the restroom to change.

"No, thanks. I think I'll dig into that book I've been trying to finish for a month now."

"Aw, c'mon. It'll do you a lot of good to cool off with the rest of us. Did you bring your swimsuit?" Joyce wouldn't give up on her.

"Uh…no, I forgot to pack one." Rita seemed rather hesitant as she answered.

"C'mon, I have an extra bikini that will look great on you. We're practically the same size."

Suddenly Rita was aware that the buzz had stopped and everyone had turned toward her awaiting an answer. She felt an uncomfortable warmth as her face blushed.

"Okay, I'll go with you, but I don't want to swim. I… I'll take my book… that'll be enjoyable enough for me."

Down at the river, everyone was having a great time, dunking each other, racing across and back, and diving for objects. After a while, Joyce came up on the bank where Rita sat, and spread her towel on the grass beside her.

"I don't get it, Rita. You were one of the best swimmers when we were kids. You never passed up an opportunity to show off your speed and skill in the water. What happened during those years you moved to Denver?"

"Oh, I just don't look good in a bikini anymore." Rita tried to brush off the subject. But she betrayed an uneasiness that made Joyce even more curious.

"Rita, is something wrong?" She asked almost in a whisper.

At this, the tears began to well up in Rita's eyes. "Joyce, I'm going to tell you something that I hope you will keep to yourself. I'm only telling you this because you've been a good friend all these years, and I feel I have to share this with someone who cares." She raised her eyes toward the river to make sure the others weren't looking their way, and then raised her skirt above her thighs.

"Look at these legs, Joyce! Do you think I want to get into a bikini looking like this?" Rita was now choking back the tears in her voice.

Joyce gasped as she looked upon the long, unattractive scars on Rita's legs. She kept silent as her own emotions responded to her friend's pain. She finally found her voice.

"How did this ever happen to you, Rita?"

Rita had to wait a while until her emotions subsided enough for her to talk. "You remember Ricky, the guy I wrote to you about from Denver?"

"Yeah, I remember. The last time you wrote, you two were getting married, or something. I thought you were a little crazy, talking about marriage just out of high school. We had always planned to go to college and all that. You never wrote again, and I never knew what happened. When you came back, I asked you about it, but you've always avoided the subject, like it was too painful to talk about."

"It's still very painful. I'm sorry, I should have told you before. Oh, Joyce, we were so much in love. He was the type of guy you dream about all your adolescent life. He was handsome, sweet, courteous, and he was…my knight in shining armor. He felt the same toward me. We lost our heads and got married, with plans, of course, of going on to college. He was going to be an engineer, and I was going to be a chemistry teacher."

"What do you mean by was… what changed your plans?" Joyce began to sense the tragedy.

Rita had to pause for what seemed an eternity. "One night, we went out to a movie. We didn't go out very often, since our budget was so tight, what with working and going to school and all. Afterward, we stopped at McDonald's to get a snack and then headed for home. We had had a real good time together. Then…as we crossed an intersection, a drunk came speeding through and crashed into our car…" Rita could hardly talk now, "Ricky died within minutes from head injuries, and I was trapped with my legs broken and bleeding. I miss him so, Joyce… I wish it would have been me that died that night."

Joyce put her arms around her friend as she sobbed uncontrollably. They both wept for a long while. "Joyce, do you think good people like Ricky go to heaven when they die? If I was sure, it would be of some comfort to me…to know that he is all right, not suffering, or anything."

"You know, Rita, I am not a very religious person, but my parents taught me that way when I was younger. I suppose they must have known–they studied the Bible, you know. Hey, why don't you ask Guillermo tonight? He seems to know everything in the Bible. I bet he could give you a better answer!"

Slowly Rita calmed down and tried to be cheerful. "You know, I think I will go down for that swim. I'm going in skirt and all, even if the boys make fun of me!" She was smiling now, as though the long cry had been exactly the therapy she needed.

It was almost dark when they arrived at the cabin, weary from all the exercise and roughhousing at the river. As they entered, they were met with a cheerful smile from Guillermo and the appetizing smell of warm bread, cream of celery soup, and roasted vegetables with chopped roasted almond slices. Putting down their gear, they rushed to the table and began to chant as they laughed, "We want food! We want food!"

Soon they were enjoying deliriously the stuff that Elizabeth had prepared, while they talked excitedly of the great time they had had that afternoon at the river. Even Rita was excited as she shared how she almost lost her skirt to a sudden current. Joyce glanced at her, glad that she had been there when her friend needed her most.

Attempting to show their gratitude, the guys cleared the table and the girls washed the dishes. Meanwhile, Guillermo turned on the T.V. and surfed directly to CNN. Bad news dominated the airwaves, in those days. More unemployment, more labor strikes, increase in crime as people took matters into their own hands. The Democrats blamed the Republicans and vice versa.

The Religious Right, which now made up the majority of Congress and the Supreme Court, were pressing the president into signing a bill forbidding work on Sunday and closing all commercial establishments on that day. In assessing the cause of so many calamities, they had finally concluded that the absence of temporal prosperity was due to the ever-growing iniquity in the general population and the consequent judgements of God on the nation and on the world. If everyone would faithfully go to church on Sunday and pray, perhaps God would change matters.

Soon they started dozing off as the day's activities had worn them out, and the heavy supper also had its effect. So Guillermo thought it prudent to turn off the T.V. and allow them to find their places on the living room floor. Rita, however, was wide awake and awaiting some privacy in order to talk with Guillermo on a subject that was heavy on her mind.

"Guillermo," she half whispered, "I have a question on my mind. Would you join me on the porch?"

"Why yes, of course!" he smiled and opened the door as he hit a light switch for the front porch. Rita snuggled into a ceiling hammock as Guillermo settled into a comfortable rocker. "What's on your mind, Rita? I noticed that you were somewhat quiet during supper, like you were chewing on something other than food."

"Well, I shared something with Joyce this afternoon that started me on a new line of thought." She was glad to have talked about it with Joyce earlier. This time she was calm and in control of her emotions. "When I was eighteen, I married Ricky right out of high school. We had a great marriage for about a year, and then tragedy struck. I lost Ricky in a car accident and almost lost my own life."

"Oh, I'm so sorry, Rita. Losing someone you love is the most painful thing you can go through in this life. Please accept my heartfelt sympathy."

"Thank you, Guillermo. It's been very hard for me to get over it. That's one of the reasons I decided to go to college this last year. Besides, I have to make a future for myself. As a bonus, I've met these wonderful friends though I've known Joyce since childhood."

"They do seem to be a great bunch. I'm glad you found them."

"Ever since Ricky died, Guillermo, I have prayed for his soul every night that he might have rest and not be suffering somewhere. I find some comfort in knowing that he was good person in life. He cared about others; he was involved in things like the food bank and the soup kitchen. Although we didn't belong to a church, there was a respect in his heart for God, and a compassion that he expressed whenever he saw injustice or suffering.

"But there's this nagging doubt in my mind as to where he is and if he's all right. Perhaps my biggest question is if I'll ever see him again…" She couldn't avoid a little quiver in her voice and mist in her eyes that eventually condensed into a few tears.

Guillermo allowed a few moments of silence. He had to say the right thing. Something that would bring comfort and assurance. "Rita, I understand your doubts and concerns. Let me give you some great good news first, because you must know this in order to have peace and to be able to absorb the rest of what I'm going to say. My good news is based only on what the Bible says about death and the dead. These are not my ideas. If you believe that the Bible is the word of God, and have faith in the God who spoke it, then this news will make all the difference in your life and will bring you hope and joy."

"What is it, Guillermo? What is this good news?" Rita's eyes were suddenly wide open and expectant.

"First of all, Rita, the Bible assures you that Ricky is safe, and not suffering the least bit, and, yes, you will see Ricky again!"

"Are you sure, Guillermo? Does the Bible really say that? C'mon, show me, I want to see that for myself?" Rita was intense and excited.

"Whoa, there! One thing at a time! First of all, we need to understand what death is. It is the cessation of life. If life is thinking and breathing and moving and feeling and a sense of existence, then death is just the opposite: that is, no thinking, no breathing, no moving, no feeling, and no sense of existence. Let's look at what the Bible says about death.

"First of all, there's no thinking. In the book of Ecclesiastes, which God directed King Solomon to write, we find a lot of information about death. It says in chapter nine, verses five and six, 'For the living know that they will die: but the dead know nothing and they have no more reward, for the memory of them is forgotten. Also their love, their hatred, and their envy have now perished; nevermore will they have a share in anything done under the sun.'

"So you see, Rita, Ricky is not alive or existing in some other form somewhere conscious of anything. This verse says that he is not a conscious entity. In verse ten of the same chapter, Solomon goes on to say that there is no movement in death, 'Whatever your hand finds to do, do it with your might; for there is no work or device or knowledge or wisdom in the grave where you are going.'

"Furthermore, Rita, there is nothing breathing in death. In chapter twelve, verse seven he goes on to state what happens to your body and your breath when you die. Here, you read it."

"Then the dust will return to the earth as it was, and the spirit will return to God who gave it. I don't get it. What's this about dust? What dust? And besides, it talks about the spirit returning to God who gave it.' Isn't that the spirit that people say continues to live outside the body? I'm a little confused!"

"Easy, easy, Rita. Let's go back to the beginning. Let's open the Bible in the first book, the book of Genesis, and let's look at chapter two and verse seven, 'And the Lord God formed man of the dust of the ground, and breathed into his nostrils the breath of life; and man became a living soul.'

"Now, Rita, Follow the sequence of events in the creation of mankind. First, God formed our first parents from the elements in the ground, basically a dirt dummy. Through his miraculous creative power, he converts the basic elements into tissue, bone, vessels, organs, blood, etc. Then, he blows through the nose of this lifeless dummy his own, powerful, life-giving breath and it comes to life. The heart begins to beat, the lungs begin to breathe, the blood begins to circulate, the brain awakens and begins to think and analyse its surroundings.

"Once the breath of God connected with the lifeless dummy, the first man and, subsequently, the first woman became living souls. If you follow the sequence carefully, you can only conclude that the soul is the product of body and breath. Thus, when the breath leaves the body and returns to God, there is death or cessation of life. The body in the grave eventually disintegrates and the elements of tissue, bone, vessels, organs, blood, and brain go back to dust. Since these two elements have parted, the soul has ceased to exist. The soul only exists while the person is alive."

"You mean to tell me that Ricky isn't alive in a soul state somewhere, either heaven or hell, as most people believe?"

"I didn't tell you that, Rita, the Bible did. You just read it for yourself, and that is one of the wonderful comforts about death–that you don't have to worry about whether your loved one is in heaven or hell, or purgatory, or limbo, or anywhere else but in the grave where he was laid to rest. You see, when one dies, the soul ceases to exist until Jesus returns at His second coming. At death, the body goes back to dust and the breath returns to God. It is at His return, through the miracle of the resurrection, that Jesus will bring the soul back to life, by uniting a newly formed body with his powerful breath of life. Until then, there's no 'soul entity' left to suffer or enjoy anything."

"Wow! I've got to think on that one for a while. You've just overturned my cartful of ideas about death. But, why do the majority of people seem to think that death is the continuation of life in a soul form or even in a reincarnated form? I don't get it! Even the majority of Christians believe in the soul life. Don't they read the Bible? I mean, it seems to be pretty clear!"

"That, dear Rita, is another very long subject. Perhaps at another time we can all sit around the Bible to discover why there is so much confusion and erroneous teaching in the world. Right now I would like to talk about the second great news I mentioned earlier."

"Oh, do, Guillermo! I want to know where the Bible says that I will see Ricky again. Man, if what you say is true, I will have everything to live for! Go on, I'm ready!"

"Okay, now as a preamble to God's promise of seeing our loved ones again, I want you to see another aspect of death that many people don't seem to understand, even after reading it in the Bible. And that is the concept of death as a state of sleep."

"A state of sleep? Now how can a person be dead and asleep at the same time?"

"Believe it or not, we have it from the highest authority that this is so. Let's open the Bible to the Gospel of John, chapter eleven, and verse three to fourteen. In this story, Jesus introduces, the concept of 'death–sleep.' He has just received the news that His friend Lazarus is very sick. But instead of going right away to heal him, Jesus stays in another town for a couple of more days. Then He says to His disciples in verses seven, and eleven through fourteen, 'Let us go to Judea again… Our friend Lazarus sleeps; but I go, that I may wake him up.' Then his disciples said, 'Lord, if he sleeps, he will get well.' However, Jesus spoke of his death, but they thought that He was speaking about taking of rest in sleep. Then Jesus said to them plainly, 'Lazarus is dead.'"

"Well, I can see how they were confused! Why did Jesus mix the two things like that?"

"Let me give you something else to wonder at. In verses twenty–five and twenty–six of the same chapter, Jesus said to Martha, Lazarus' sister, 'I am the Resurrection and the Life. He who believes in me, though he may die, he shall live. And whoever lives and believes in Me shall never die.'"

"Now, wait a minute. Even the most religious people in the world, the big promoters of Christianity, have eventually died. This doesn't make any sense to me!" Rita was perplexed.

"So now we need to put the pieces together into a picture that makes sense, don't we? We've already covered what happens at death. You die, decompose, and return to the dust of the ground. But Jesus, as our Creator, has a different understanding of death than most humans. To Jesus, when you die, it is the same as going to sleep, because–now listen carefully–He has promised to awaken us from sleep (death) in the future, on the day of the resurrection when He returns to this earth. It is within this context that He boldly asserts that 'he that believes in Me'– that is, he that believes in Me as the Lord of life, capable of the resurrection of the dead– 'though he may die, he shall live.' That means that on the day of the resurrection, Jesus will bring the soul back to life by uniting the dust of the ground with His powerful breath of life. The real, final, definitive death is reserved for the wicked at the end of the judgement, according to Revelation 20:9–10."

"Incredible! I never even suspected that the Bible taught that!" Rita was awestruck.

"Well, the Lord's apostles believed it and taught it. Look at what Paul says about that wonderful event. Open to the book of 1 Thessalonians, chapter four, verses thirteen to eighteen. Go ahead. I want you to read it for yourself." "But I do not want you to be ignorant, brethren, concerning those who have fallen asleep, lest you sorrow as others who have no hope. For if we believe that Jesus died and rose again, even so God will bring with Him those who sleep in Jesus. For this we say to you by the word of the Lord, that we who are alive and remain until the coming of the Lord will by no means precede those who are asleep. For the Lord Himself will descend from heaven with a shout, with the voice of an archangel, and with the trumpet of God. And the dead in Christ will rise first. Then we who are alive and remain shall be caught up together with them in the clouds to meet the Lord in the air. And thus we shall always be with the Lord."

"Oh, Guillermo, if this is true, it is absolutely, overwhelmingly wonderful!"

"What you just read is the fulfilment of Christ's promise in John 14:1–3, which says, 'Let not your heart be troubled; you believe in God, believe also in me. In My Father's house are many mansions; if it were not so, I would have told you. I go to prepare a place for you, and if I go and prepare a place for you, I will come again and receive you to Myself, that where I am there you may be also,'

"Until Jesus returns, we have the assurance that every human who has ever died is still in the grave and will come back to life at the creative command of Christ himself.

"Let me give you one more reference so that you can have more evidence. Jesus Himself, talking about the resurrection of the dead, declared that everyone is going to be resurrected: the sleeping who trusted in Jesus will be raised to eternal life of joy and the sleeping wicked will be raised to face their judgement and eternal destruction. Don't take my word for it. Read it in John, chapter five and verses twenty–eight and twenty–nine."

"Do not marvel at this; for the hour is coming in which all who are in the graves will hear His voice and come forth–those who have done good, to the resurrection of life, and those who have done evil, to the resurrection of condemnation.'

"Well that seems pretty clear. But there's just one thing I don't understand about all this: if the dead have decomposed and are just a residue of old bones, what is there left for God to resurrect?"

"Good question, Rita, absolutely good. Now, Let's go back to where we started: the part where God originally creates man from the dust of the ground The dead have turned to dust, but don't you think that if God did it originally, that he can do it again? I believe from these verses of Scripture that God has the original DNA code of every individual that has ever lived, and that all he has to do is to order each particular code into action and instantly have every individual formed again. He can blow the breath of life simultaneously into everyone and, Presto! They're alive again!"

"C'mon, Guillermo. Nobody knew about DNA until the last century or so!"

"Of course, humans didn't know. But DNA is not man's invention…it is man's discovery! It is simply the marvellous work of God when He created us so that we could pass on life to ongoing generations. Look at what God says in Isaiah 49:16, 'Behold, I have graven thee upon the palms of My hands; thy walls are ever before me.' God even knows the number of hairs on our heads. I know this is a lot for you to digest at one time, so I think I'll stop here and let you get some rest."

"Thanks so much, Guillermo. You have given me a lot of hope and comfort. I still have to work this out, but I feel a lot better about Ricky. I'll tell you what; tomorrow morning we girls will make breakfast. Do you have any corn tortillas here?"

"In fact I do! I bought them hoping to try some of the recipes in my Libro de Cocina Mexicana."

"How do you feel *about huevos rancheros, frijoles refritos, and quesadillas?*"

"That sounds scrumptious. I'm looking forward to your cooking. Thanks!"

Sunday morning came with the sounds and smells of Mexican cooking. Quesadillas sizzled on the grill, refried beans were tossed from side to side, and eggs cooked sunny side up on fried corn tortillas. Eyes were smarting from the diced Serrano chilies, as stomachs were gurgling with great anticipation. The girls had been up for an hour, while the guys were goofing off as they threw socks and shoes at each other while pretending to be asleep. One by one they finally rose, washed up, and took a place at the table.

Guillermo turned the TV on to the morning news. The bad news continued. Due to the failure of the European Union to approve a constitution acceptable to all the member nations, the union had come apart, and now there was a massive problem as nationals from one country living in another struggled to get equal treatment in the distribution of dwindling goods and services. The Great Shepherd, a person of worldwide influence in the political and religious arena, made an urgent appeal for fairness and compassion, and some of the European leaders began to listen and to respond by setting up organized distribution points managed by the local churches.

In America, the Great Shepherd's voice was also highly respected, and the conservative religious establishments, having gained control of the political process in Canada, the United States, and most of the Latin–American countries, were following his guidance, not just on religious issues, but even in areas of economics, social issues, and politics. He appeared frequently on T.V. with different world leaders and chief clerics of a wide array of religions. Planet Earth was definitely in deep trouble, and it seemed like the Great Shepherd's solution was the most likely indicated: (1) cessation of all hostilities between the nations, (2) proportionate distribution of food supplies for all, (3) a common pool of medical resources to fight the ravaging diseases, especially in Africa, and (4) a united show of spiritual faith through prayer to the god of all the religions of the world. The idea of a common god for Jew, Christian, Moslem, and Animist was strongly proposed, with Sunday as the most convenient day for all to worship together in unity.

"So! It's finally here!" Guillermo's brow was clouded for a moment, as he muttered under this breath.

"What's the matter, Guillermo? What's going on?" Gerry caught his expression and halfway heard his muffled expression.

"Something is taking off which was predicted in Bible prophecy as one of the most decisive events of the end of time. It is going to affect every single person on the planet, and most people are not even aware of the consequences of their choices."

Oh, no! Here we go again! Ahmed thought as he rolled his eyes. *I've got to think of some way of escaping another two or three hours of religious lecture.*

"Say, guys, I've already satisfied my appetite for fishing, and it doesn't look like we're going to do any camping, seeing a Guillermo here has been spoiling us to no end." He gave Guillermo a half-friendly smile. "So, I have decided to return a little early and visit some friends in Coeur d'Alene on my way back. Gerry, if you'll just give me a ride back to old ninety-five, I can thumb my way back before evening."

"Aw, c'mon, Ahmed, don't be a party pooper. Ben and I didn't get to fish, and I promised Mom I'd return with some nice, fat trout. Besides, we'll all go back this afternoon in time for you to visit with your friends."

"It's no use arguing, Gerry. I've made up my mind."

"But Ahmed, it's about ninety miles to Coeur d'Alene, and its plenty hot out there!"

"Look, Gerry, if you don't want to take me, that's okay. I'll catch a ride with the first wheels going down this country road."

"Okay, okay!" Gerry replied, as he turned to the others. "I'll be back in about an hour."

They drove down the country road for about fifteen minutes without saying anything. Each was absorbed in his own thoughts about the happenings of that weekend.

Gerry finally broke the silence. "I take it you don't really like this guy Guillermo."

"Well, he's all right. I mean he's friendly, hospitable, and generous with his stuff. But he's too religious. He keeps bringing up all this prophecy stuff and I can't find it in my brain to believe him."

They talked on for a while longer and soon arrived at highway ninety-five. Ahmed said goodbye, and Gerry grinned and said, "God bless you," just to see Ahmed roll his eyes.

Meanwhile, the group had been busy finishing their breakfast, cleaning up the kitchen, and packing their sleeping bags for the day. Rita had risen with an unusual sparkle in her eyes that morning, and could hardly wait to share the reason for her sunny disposition.

"Hey, everybody, come sit for a while. I want to share something with you." She was excited as she told the others her personal story about Ricky and her new hope of seeing him again when Jesus returns.

"Guillermo, would you share with the others what you told me last night? I don't know where to find all those Bible verses, and, besides, you have the right verbosity!" She laughed as she exaggerated her college-acquired idioms.

"I'd be happy to, Rita. But, you know, I'd like to wait until Gerry gets here. I want him to share your joy and to get this information too. Otherwise, I'll have to repeat the whole thing all over again."

Soon Gerry was with the group, and Guillermo gave all of them an explanation about death as they had never heard before. There were many questions and a very animated discussion. Even Ben couldn't argue with the Bible evidence presented and Gerry noticed his friend in deep thought and rapt attention as Guillermo presented the subject in a very organized, point-by-point manner. As Guillermo finished the last point, and there was a long silence, Ben finally spoke up,

"This has been quite a lot of stuff to chew on, Guillermo. But I think I'd better do it with a fishing pole in my hand. What do you say, Gerry, ladies, and you too, Guillermo– let's get some sunshine on our face and a fat fish on a string!"

Guillermo knew that he had almost overloaded them with a lot of new ideas and that this was a good point at which to stop. So he headed for the closet, grabbed his hat, and headed out the door with a book, trailed by his happy, tail–wagging companion.

THE ENCOUNTER

Meanwhile, Ahmed stood by the southbound side of old ninety-five, wiping the sweat off his face with one hand and holding his thumb out with the other. One desperate hour had passed by and still no ride. With gas at $5.29 a gallon and bio-fuel at only fifty cents cheaper, few people were on the road. And with the increasing levels of crime and violence in the cities, even less were willing to pick up an unknown hitchhiker.

After what seemed an eternity, an old car came around the bend, and Ahmed hoped against hope that this one would have mercy on him. The driver looked him over as he passed and went on. Ahmed vented his frustration with a few chosen words. Then, to his surprise, the car pulled over about a quarter mile from him and started to back up. His heart began to beat faster. *I hope he didn't hear me. Oh, please, please give me a ride,* he pleaded inside.

"Where are you heading, you man?" the face across the seat was warm, friendly, and kind. Ahmed was thankful, not just for the ride, but for having such a pleasant person to travel with.

"Just going down to Coeur d'Alene to visit friends," he answered eagerly.

"Well, I'll be going by there, so this is your lucky day. Hop in and make yourself comfortable." The driver stretched out his hand, "Jebosh is the name!"

Ahmed took the stranger's hand, "Ahmed is mine, and thanks so much for stopping for me. My heart sank when you passed me by. I've been more than an hour under that unbearable sun! Look at me! Drenched in sweat! I'm sorry if I wet your upholstery,"

"Don't give it another thought. There's a fresh towel on the back seat. Feel free to use it. The air conditioner will do the rest."

It was twelve thirty in the afternoon, and Ahmed's delicious Mexican breakfast had done its duty and was now gone. His stomach gurgled loud enough for Jebosh to hear, which caused Ahmed a little embarrassment.

"Whoa! Sounds like you're ready for some lunch. I've had mine, but I have plenty of supplies. Do you like strawberries?" Jebosh asked, as he reached behind his seat.

"Why, yes…yes I do," Ahmed replied, but his eye almost burst out their sockets when Jebosh brought out the largest, most beautiful strawberry he had ever imagined existed.

He slowly took it in both hands, and calculated in his mind that is must weigh at least one pound. He was speechless for a full minute, while Jebosh turned and gave him the biggest grin ever. He finally found his voice, and turning to Jebosh, asked him, "Pardon my surprise, but where did you get a strawberry like this? In all my visits at county fairs, I have never seen anything even close to this!"

Jebosh was obviously having a good time observing Ahmed's reaction to his gift. "Go ahead, bite into it. See if you like it."

Ahmed hated to break up its beauty, but his appetite drove him on, and he dug his teeth into the luscious strawberry, and slowly relished its sweetness while the juice ran down both sided of his chin.

"Where in the world do they grow fruit like this?"

"Oh, back home this would be considered a small one," Jebosh replied, still enjoying Ahmed's astonishment.

"And where is back home? Where do you come from?"

"My home is in Sector 35X," Jebosh stated casually.

"Uh, is that all your address? No city, no state, no country?" Ahmed's curiosity seemed to grow as he made the strawberry disappear.

"Most people are not familiar with that address. But someday soon, it will be the best-known address to all humanity. There's a city there, a city so fabulous, it's beyond description in human terms. The King is the kindest, most generous and loving person! And his son, Prince Emmanuel, well, I'm sure you've heard of Him. If you haven't, just listen to Guillermo… he knows the Prince, for He is the leader of all the Keepers of the Covenant."

At this, Ahmed began to sweat again, even though the air conditioner was keeping the temperature in the car below seventy degrees. His mind was racing faster than the wheels he was riding on. *What is this? This guy knows Guillermo! He seems to know that I know Guillermo and that he has been telling me religious things! This is really weird! He seems so nice, and yet kinda…out of this world. What if he knows about me? What if he knows that I really don't care about Guillermo's religion or his ideas? This guy scares me! What have I gotten myself into?*

Ahmed was silent for a long time. Jebosh understood and observed the same silence. They were approaching Sandpoint, and Ahmed thought this would be a great place to get out of this car and get another ride with someone normal.

"Uh, you…you can…you can drop me off here in Sandpoint. I'd kinda like to…to do a little shopping here…

before I go on to Coeur d'Alene. And… thank you for the ride and for the fruit. It was really good."

But Jebosh had no intention of stopping. Instead, he turned to Ahmed and tried to reassure him and get him to listen to the message he had brought for him that day.

"Don't be afraid, Ahmed. I know you have never met anyone like me before, but I have some very important information to share with you–information that is vital for your survival in the coming days. Just as Guillermo mentioned to you at his house, about the present crisis and the worsening days ahead, I have been sent to confirm to you that all of that is true, and that the Bible is the most reliable guide for a time like this."

Ahmed's head was swimming. *Could it be? Is it possible that this is an extraterrestrial, one of those the Christians call angels?*

"Yes, Ahmed, that is who I am," Jebosh suddenly spoke Ahmed's thoughts. It shocked him so hard that he began to shake in his seat. Jebosh reached across and touched his shoulder, and the shaking stopped, and Ahmed felt a certain calm come over him. As they entered Sandpoint, they found the traffic backed up throughout the whole town. Nobody could get through, and traffic was being diverted through other country roads that would result in a longer driving time. As they waited, Ahmed rolled down the window to ask a policeman directing traffic what the problem was. It seemed that a truck driver pulled into a gas station to load up on diesel, and found to his distress that there was none left. Supplies were scarce and other trucks passing through had sucked out the storage tanks He was so angry that he went berserk and set his truck on fire. A couple of nearby buildings were now burning, and there was danger that the gasoline storage tanks would also explode.

As they pulled onto a side road, Ahmed happened to glance at the gas gauge on Jebosh's car, and his heart sank as he saw the needle down to empty.

"Uh, don't you think you'd better get some gas? I can help with a few bucks. We'll never get much past Sandpoint on what's left, unless that gauge isn't working right."

"The gauge is working perfectly, but don't worry, I'll take care of it," Jebosh responded with a reassuring smile.

Once down the road, Ahmed finally began to converse with great interest, asking Jebosh to tell him more about himself, his country, his work, and the wonderful future he had referred to.

"At this time," Jebosh began, "it isn't as important for you to know about me and my home or the Great City. The wonders you will eventually find there will keep your mind keyed up for eternity. What is most important for you to know now, Ahmed, is about the Prince and His covenant, because your future depends entirely upon your acceptance or rejection of both."

"I'm ready to listen, now, Jebosh. Tell me all about this Prince and of the covenant I've been trying to avoid."

"Since before your planet was created, time has been measured in eternity. That is because the Monarch of the Universe, the Prince, and the Holy Spirit always existed. There has never been a beginning, and there will never be an end for them. Don't bother trying to figure that out, because humans can't. Ever since the fall of your race, time has been measured for you, and at this time your average lifespan is about eighty years, so you cannot understand eternity.

"The universe is in perfect order, and that brings everyone great joy and peace as we relate to our King and to each other. There are laws, and everyone lived within the laws until recently, say…about six thousand years ago. At that time, a great tragedy took place.

"One of our own, the most beautiful and most privileged of the King's host, rebelled, because he became proud of his beauty and status. He spread nasty rumors about the King and the Prince to my brothers, and tragically, many came to believe him, and joined him in this rebellion. Lucifer was his name. Oh, you should have seen him, Ahmed! What a fabulous sight he was! But his rebellion caused a breach between him and his deceived group and those of us who remained loyal. The King in His mercy and infinite kindness offered to forgive him if he would submit to him and His orderly kingdom. But Lucifer would not give in, and so it became necessary to execute justice. So he was thrown out of the kingly dominions and cast on you planet.

"Is that the person known to most religions as Satan?"

"Yes, Ahmed. He is also known by other vile names like the Devil, the Old Serpent, the Dragon, and the Accuser of the Brethren. All for good reason, his character became so degraded by his pride and selfishness, that he has made it his mission to destroy, to lie, to cheat, to bring reproach upon the King, to cause other beings to hate and despise the Prince whose position and power he covets."

"So why did that King allow him to come here? It seems unfair that our race had to be exposed to this devil."

"Some of these things are hard for humans to understand, but I'll try to explain them as best as I can. You see, when Lucifer, now Satan, was cast to the earth, it had recently been created and was an awesomely beautiful place. The most attractive part was the Garden of Eden, where the King had placed the first couple of humans and made it their home. Back at the kingdom, Satan had made some very severe accusations against the King as to his character: he had said that the King was selfish, arbitrary in his affections, and a master manipulator of all his created beings. He made these accusations because he coveted the positions of the Prince and wanted to have the same status and power. He would not take into account that the Prince is an eternal, all-powerful person, and not a created being like him. There is no way that a creature can be equal with his creator. Many of us tried to reason with him, but his pride just kept increasingly daily, until he was beyond help."

"You know, Jebosh, it is difficult for me to understand the nature of eternal persons, but I can sure see the difference you're pointing out."

"I'm glad you're capturing these concepts, Ahmed. Unless you do, there are other things that you will never understand. Well, now that Satan was on earth, he decided on another strategy to convince his former brothers in the kingdom that his accusations were true. By causing the new people on the planet to disobey the King's commands, he would show them that His demands on His creatures are arbitrary and impossible to obey.

"Now, that King had provided your first parents with everything imaginable to beautify their surroundings and enrich their lives. But He placed a very small restriction on them to test their loyalty before the rest of the universe, and thus lay Satan's accusations to rest. He asked them to abstain from eating the fruit of a certain tree in the garden. He also told them the consequences of disobedience: the cessation of their existence, for that is what death is."

"Now, what was so hard about that? Just one little old tree! Just one of those strawberries you gave me would have kept me in line!" Ahmed was really into the story now.

"You're absolutely right. The King was not asking for something difficult or impossible. But Satan was a very bright, very intelligent individual, and he thought and thought about a way to cause your parents to sin, because that is what disobedience is…sin.

"*Ah!* he thought. *If I can make them eat of the forbidden tree, then all of my brothers, not just the one third of them that are with me, will know that I am right about the King.*"

"And so he used one strategy that the King would never use: the lie, deception. He disguised himself as a serpent–he had a number of incredible abilities–and climbing on the forbidden tree he attracted the woman to it by talking and eating one of the fruits. The woman approached, full of curiosity. She knew all of the creatures in the Garden and had never even imagined that any of them could ever talk. And no creature had ever gone that close to the forbidden tree. The story is found in the book of Genesis, chapter three, but let me paraphrase it in my own words for you. 'So didn't the King say that you could eat of all the fruit of the Garden?' the serpent began the conversation. Mother Eve was greatly fascinated by this creature talking and decided to respond.

"Well, we can eat of all the trees except this one, for the day we eat of it we will cease to exist," she replied.

"Naw, that's not true. The King told you that because He doesn't want you to progress up to the level of the gods. He doesn't want you to be like Him and have His powers. Look at me! Before I ate this fruit, why, I was just a simple dumb serpent. But look at me now! I have the gift of speech and have already progressed to be like you. Imagine if you eat of it! Why, you will be just like the King with all His wisdom and power! Go ahead, here, take just one bite and you'll notice the difference instantly."

"Mother Eve was dumbfounded. *Why, it's true!* she thought. *How else could a serpent talk and intelligently, too!* So she reached out her hand, took of the fruit, and ate of it.

"I remember that day, Ahmed, like it was just yesterday. Everybody in the kingdom was intently and apprehensively following every movement and every word of that encounter. Would she resist the bewitching trap, or would she fall into it?

Your limited mortal mind cannot yet grasp the deep anguish and pain Mother Eve caused to that hearts of the King, the Prince, the Holy Spirit, all of my brethren, and all of the created beings in the universe."

"Everybody was watching? I find that inconceivable! How is it possible to see across the vastness of outer space all the way here?"

"As I told you before, Ahmed, there are elements of science which are secrets kept from the human race. You are not expected to understand it all, just to believe it all by faith and trust in the King."

"Well, to continue, your first parents were exiled from the Garden of Eden, especially because there was another very special tree there to which they had had access, the Tree of Life. The fruit of that tree has the power to prolong life forever. If the King had permitted them to stay, then they and all the subsequent generations of sinners would have lived eternally; as it was, the fact that they had had access to that tree allowed them to live an average of nine hundred years for the first nine generations."

"Nine hundred years! Man that's an awful long time! But wait one minute! If the penalty for disobedience was to die, how come they didn't die right away?"

"Here's another facet of the King's character of love and justice. If Satan and my former brethren would have been destroyed right away, then the questions he had raised as accusations might have never been answered and the King would have come under suspicion. In His wisdom, he chose to let Satan and his followers live and allow them time to show their true character of pride, envy, jealousy, selfishness, and deceitfulness. As time has passed, Satan had proven before the whole universe that he is the one at fault, and not the King."

"But, what about Adam and Eve? Why didn't they die right away?"

"I'm getting to that. Adam and Eve did not disobey out of rebellion, pride, envy, or other defects. They were craftily deceived, and Satan preyed on their innocence. Yet, they failed to turn to the King and submit to His instruction. So, they were guilty of disobedience, but the King offered them an opportunity for repentance and they gladly took it. Satan, as I mentioned before, was offered the same, but he rejected repentance. Because of his great love for all his creatures, the King offered a way in which they could be forgiven and restored to their original state of perfection and happiness."

"Hey, something like that happened to me once. I was speeding on highway ninety coming in to Spokane. A cop spotted me and gave chase. When he finally caught up with me, he was upset, and I knew he was going to throw the book at me. When he came to my window, I was scared. I humbly recognized my fault and told him that even if he gave me a well–deserved ticket, I was sorry for having broken the law. Man, I was shocked with joy when he just sighed and then told me, 'Okay, I'll give you a break this time, but keep in mind the lives you put in danger when you speed on the road. Take it easy.'"

"Ahmed, you had it really easy. You have no idea yet what it cost to forgive Adam and Eve and all the subsequent generations of sinners who sought forgiveness. I wish it could have been as easy as your cop forgiving you. But you know, Ahmed, when a violation of the law goes unpunished, it weakens the law, it trivializes it. One can think, *who cares if I break the law? All I have to do is ask for forgiveness and carry on. No penalty, no suffering, no honor to the law.* But the King's law is so special, so exalted, and so holy, that the penalty has to be paid, if not by the forgiven sinner, than by somebody else.

"Hold on, a moment! Why should the penalty be paid by somebody who didn't commit the violation in the first place? That would be unfair!" Ahmed seemed indignant at the thought.

"You're absolutely right, Ahmed! And this is where the story becomes the most exciting and yet the most humbling. It causes the heart to beat with extreme joy and at the same time experience the deepest sorrow. It causes such admiration for the King and for the Prince that one cannot but fall on one's knees in gratitude and praise. You see, the King could not pass on Adam and Eve's guilt on to an innocent person. That would have been, as you have so keenly observed, cruelly unfair. What was there to do? How could the King allow creatures He loved so much and who were sincerely sorry for what they had done, to die?

"It is sublimely interesting to note that the King, the Prince, and the Holy Spirit had a plan which had been defined before any of us creatures were ever created. You see, in their infinite wisdom, they knew that in creating us and granting us absolute freedom of choice, that there would always be a possibility for disobedience and rebellion. It is the dark side of freedom for which provision had to be made. The plan was that if any creature broke the law or went into rebellion, an offer of forgiveness would be made and repentance would be accepted for reconciliation. However, the penalty had to be paid, or the law would have no force or value, putting the Kingdom at risk of disarray and chaos. Now, since it would be unfair to place the penalty on any other innocent creature, They decided that they would take upon themselves the responsibility for disobedience and pay the penalty, which of course would be cessation of life, meaning death. The King was just as involved in this process as was the Prince. The apostle Paul wrote, 'God was in Christ, reconciling the world to himself…'"

"That is awesome! I never understood these Christian teachings about Christ and the cross and all that. I considered about Christ and the cross and all that religious gibberish. But now it makes sense. How else could man be forgiven and get away with it?"

"I'm glad to hear you pronounce the Prince's earthly name, Ahmed. The Christ, you know, means the Anointed One, the Designated One, designated, that is, to carry the burden of the guilt of all who confess their guilt, repent, and ask for forgiveness. He then becomes the payment for their sins, and such persons are cleansed from guilt. In fact, let me tell you that before all the powers and persons in the whole universe, a forgiven human appears as clean as if he had never disobeyed or rebelled. Everything in his past is wiped out and he can live the rest of his life on earth filled with peace, joy, and hope."

"Is that it? That's all there is to being, as Christians express it, 'saved'? Nothing more to do but wait for the final return of Christ, as Guillermo was telling us the other day?"

"No, that's not all, Ahmed. That's only the beginning. That is only step one, the part called justification, which takes place the moment you go through the process of forgiveness. From there on you begin a new life in communion with the King and the Prince and facilitated by the Holy Spirit. From there on you begin to work on the areas in your life that are offensive to the law of the King as well as to your fellow men and women. You begin to avoid bad language, you stop hating your enemies, you allow only clean thoughts to enter your mind, and avoid anything that is immoral. You start developing love and courtesy and patience and tolerance toward others. It's a process that takes the rest of your life. This process is called sanctification, and though it is a big word, it simply means that you start to imitate the life of Christ, until your thinking and behaviour becomes just like

His sanctified life. Both steps are necessary for restoration of your relationship with the King, and Jesus Christ, the Prince."

"Whoa! God is asking a whole lot! I don't think I can do it, Jebosh. I have some pretty bad habits, and my language sometimes surprise even me. I'm glad you didn't hear me after you passed me by on the road!"

Jebosh just grinned and suddenly Ahmed understood and blushed. "I'm really sorry, Jebosh. I didn't know or understand then what I know now." A mist started to form in his eyes, but Jebosh put his hand on Ahmed's shoulder, and the mist rapidly cleared.

"I forgive you, Ahmed," he said gently. "But it is the Prince who does the final forgiveness, don't ever forget to turn to Him with all the sorrow for your sins. He is not only eager to hear, but also to forgive."

"What about the King, does He forgive also?"

"You have no idea yet how much the King loves you. In fact, one of the most beautiful things that the Prince said while He was here among you is found is your Bible, recorded by the disciple John, in his gospel, chapter three, and verses sixteen and seventeen. Since you don't have a Bible, I'm going to give you this one, and I hope you will become very familiar with its contents," he said as he reached behind Ahmed's seat and brought out a beautiful Bible with gold borders. As he handed it to Ahmed, it fell open on John 3:16. "Go ahead, Ahmed. I'd rather hear you read it."

"For God so loved the world, that He gave His only begotten Son, that whosoever believes in Him, should not perish, but have everlasting life…'" Ahmed paused. A lump was forming in his throat and he found it hard to go on. "'For God sent not His son into the world to condemn the world, but that the world through Him might be saved.'" The last words were almost a whisper, as the tears began to flow down his cheeks. He could say no more, His throat was so tight it hurt.

Jebosh understood the silence. This time he did not put his hand on Ahmed's shoulder. He needed to let those tears flow, for they were washing away the past indifference and recklessness of his life. They were soothing the pain of a lifetime of separation from the Prince of life.

After a long while, Ahmed found his voice again. "I did it, Jebosh. I asked the King and the Prince to forgive me and to give me another opportunity to live according to their plan for my life. Oh, how good it feels to be forgiven! I know it's going to be hard to make such drastic changes in my life, but I'm counting on the Holy Spirit to see me through."

"And He will see you through, Ahmed. Just trust Him fully and do not neglect to read the Bible and pray every day. That's your source of strength and the nutrition for your spiritual life."

They were entering Coeur d'Alene, now, and suddenly Ahmed remembered and looked at the gas gage. He couldn't believe his eyes or his ears, for the engine was not even running, yet they were moving at forty–five miles per hour.

"Jebosh!" he almost yelled with amazement, "we forgot to get gas, and we've travelled almost one hundred miles through all those side roads."

Jebosh just smiled as he stated, "There are secrets of the King's science that…"

"I know, I know," Ahmed interrupted, "but promise me that someday you'll show me how."

"Well, we're almost at your friend's house," This time Ahmed didn't ask him how he knew where to go, since Ahmed had not given him the address. He just smiled, delighted to have travelled with such a special individual.

"I'll probably visit with you some time again. But the most important thing is for you to be at the Gathering."

"What gathering are you talking about, Jebosh?"

"Oh, that's going to be some gathering! When the Prince returns to this earth, there will be millions of Keepers of the Covenant ready to receive him. It's going to be the most wonderful day this world has ever seen. You just watch. This present crisis is going to get much worse, but if you stay in touch with the Prince and his forces, you will live to see it and rejoice in it."

"I'm looking forward to it already!" Ahmed opened his door as Jebosh stepped out on the driver's side.

"So, where are you going from here?"

"I'm going home, Ahmed." Jebosh smiled with incredible contentment. "I have a very important report to give."

"Where exactly is this home of yours?" Ahmed's curiosity wouldn't hold.

Jebosh approached Ahmed, and putting his arm around his shoulders, gave him a firm squeeze as he pointed up at a beautiful, starlit sky. "Can you find the constellation of Orion?"

"Yeah, it's the one with the four star rectangle and the three stars in the middle."

"Well, of those three, I live on the star in the middle."

Ahmed stared into the sky until his eyes watered from the strain. He turned to say something, but Jebosh and his jalopy had silently disappeared. He stood there at his friend's door. The events of that day were just too much to absorb all at once. He would be thinking about them for a long, long time.

DARK PLOTS

"You what? You've lost Ahmed? Just what do you mean by that, Vesuvius?" the gravelly voice of an incensed Prince of Darkness boomed from the ivory throne.

"Please, my lord Lucifer! I did all I could to dissuade him! I worked extra hard on him at Guillermo's house! And he was responding beautifully. I had him practically stomp out of their indoctrination sessions! He finally left the house to escape another brainwash! But that cursed Jebosh picked him up on the highway and worked on him the whole day as he took him to Coeur d'Alene."

"You're a bumbling idiot, Vesuvius! I give you a simple assignment, and you mess it up from the start! I suppose the troops under you command are just a bumbling as you! How are they doing with the rest of that group of simpletons: Gerry, Ben, Lisa, Joyce, and Rita? Are we at risk of losing those too?"

"They haven't made any decisions yet, my lord! My troops are working very hard, though! But we're no match for the power of the Holy Spirit. Guillermo interceded on their behalf, and now the Spirit keeps interrupting our work with His pleadings. Besides, these people are looking at that hated book a lot! Truth is very persuasive! That combination is practically impossible to overcome!"

"You imbecile! I don't want your lame excuses! I have a mind to send you and your troops to the pit!"

"No, my lord! Please, please, not the pit! I implore you to give me another opportunity! I believe I can still persuade them! All is not lost,"

"All right, you have one more chance! See that you use your time wisely. If you fail, General Beelzebub will be eager to tear off your wings and cast you into inner darkness."

"At once, my exalted lord Lucifer! And thank you for another opportunity to prove myself," Vesuvius trembled at the mention of Beelzebub. Of all the generals, he was the cruellest and most cold-blooded.

A NEW LIFE

It was already three o'clock, and Gerry knew they had to get going back to Spokane. His mother would be expecting him, and he didn't want her to worry. Everything had been packed into the two vehicles, and they began to say their good-byes.

"We had a really wonderful time, Guillermo and Elizabeth. You guys are the best hosts and wonderful Christians. Thanks for all you've shared with us. We'll be thinking about it and perhaps we'll come back for some more."

"It was out pleasure to have you, and we wish all of you a safe journey home. We'll be praying for you, that you may find jobs and that the Lord will lead your lives. Be sure and give our best regards to your mom... better still, tell her to come up next time you come this way."

"I'll do that, thanks," Gerry replied as he climbed into his Jeep. The rest of the group yelled out their farewells and waved from the windows.

Gerry and Lisa led out and Ben followed with Joyce and Rita. The two girls had grown closer in their friendship during the weekend, and they chattered the time away while Ben just listened, smirked, laughed, or teased all the way home.

Lisa, on the other hand, had a lot of serious thoughts on her mind. Her parents were in a bind with their debts, and she needed to find a job right away. But things were getting bad, really bad. American industry now belonged largely to foreign investors, and jobs were opened and closed according to their whims and needs. China, for example, had purchased Sears, but brought their own management personnel and took many of the jobs home, where masses of Chinese were vigorously competing for work.

Gerry, however, was trying to put together the events of the weekend with some projection for the future. Guillermo had really opened his mind concerning what was taking place and the biblical predictions about the end of time. He was going back to Spokane still with some hope of finding a job. But he could see how difficult things had become. Yet, he needed to make some fast decisions. There was talk of classes being cut back due to lack of federal funds, and if he couldn't take the necessary courses to finish that year, what would he do? He was already twenty–three years old, and he wanted to finish his career, get, married, have children–the things that most young men and women think of as a normal life projection.

And speaking of marriage… he glanced at Lisa… *this girl might be the one. She was pretty, intelligent, family oriented, and had a good attitude toward life in general.* But he had to proceed slowly. He didn't want to blow his chances by being to bold or too rushed.

They finally arrived in town. Ben turned off at one exit to deliver Joyce and Rita to their apartments, and Gerry went on to Lisa's place. Once there, Gerry helped Lisa carry her stuff to the porch.

"I hope you had as wonderful a time as I did, Lisa. I'm glad we took the time to get away and get to know each other better. I think you're a great person… and…" he was a little nervous as Lisa looked up into his eyes with an expectant smile. He gave her a quick peck on the right cheek as he said a rapid, "Bye. I'll call you tomorrow," and returned quickly to his car.

Lisa just stood there, with a slight look of disappointment on her face. *The lips… the lips, you fool! Not my cheek, I wanted a real kiss! Oh, well, catch ya next time!* She smiled as she waved good–bye.

The weeks passed slowly and the friends met every so often to share their joys and disappointments. Every now and then, someone would ask about Ahmed.

"It's strange how Ahmed just dropped out of sight without saying anything to us. Has anyone heard from him yet?" Joyce seemed concerned.

"You all know that he seemed rather upset every time Guillermo would start talking about the covenant. Maybe he felt somewhat left out as he noticed that we were interested," Ben observed.

"I have this feeling that he's going to walk in on us when we least expect it," Gerry pitched in as he put his arm around Lisa and drew her closer to him. Their relationship had grown a lot during those tense weeks, and he smiled as he observed how Ben and Joyce were also rather drawn to each other.

As for Rita, she had her own hopes. Guillermo had shown her something to hold on to, and she learned to pray differently than she ever had before. As she watched her friends in their blooming relationship, she thought in her heart, *Dear Lord, Bless my friends, and help us all to figure out your plan for our lives. Be with Ahmed, and guide him to you, that he too may find peace in your promises. Please keep me faithful, that I may be reunited with my Ricky when you return.*

Going back to Ahmed after Jebosh's departure, he knocked on his friend's door. The evening was unexpectedly cool in Coeur d'Alene after a rather hot day, and the starry sky had a shine to it he had never noticed before. He stared again at Orion as he waited for his friend's delayed response.

"Ahmed, it's good to see you," Ron exclaimed enthusiastically as he grasped his friend's hand. "Welcome!"

"Come on in! Are you hungry? I bought an extra Whopper and fries thinking you'd be starved after your trip."

Ahmed was glad to see his friend. They had had a lot of good times together–football games, fraternity parties, and fishing trips. So they conversed for a while about their past exploits, but Ron sensed that Ahmed wasn't his old self. He was subdued, as if there were other things on his mind.

"So, what are you going to do with what's left of this summer?"

"I don't know yet, Ron. The last two weeks I've spent a lot of time looking for a job, but times are really bad, as you know. I need to make some money for the next school year. My current scholarship is in danger of being wiped out by government cuts. Do you know of anything available?" Ahmed looked at his friend expectantly.

"As a matter of fact, I do," Ron's eyes lit up. "I'm currently working with the US Forest Service, and my supervisor told me that they're hiring ten more guys as Forest Service Guards."

"Forest Service Guards? What in the world is that? What do they do?"

"Well, you know, there is a critical shortage of fuel oil, and people are afraid they're not going to have heat for the winter. So they're buying up all the firewood they can get a hold of. That, in turn, has created a huge black market for lumber, and the crooks are getting into the National forest at night and stealing any log they can find on the ground."

"Isn't that kinda risky? The guys in black market dealings are tough criminals. They're a mafia. You don't want to tangle with them!"

"Yeah, it's risky. But the pay is great and the benefits are okay. If you want to save money for school, this might be a good option. Besides, they provide you with room and board at their camp. Don't worry. The government is behind you and the guys protect each other. If you want it, you have a job tomorrow morning."

Ahmed knew this was a great opportunity, so he didn't have to think too long on it. "I'm in! Can you take me to my apartment so that I can get my stuff and turn in the keys?"

In a little while they were driving into Spokane and shortly were at Ahmed's apartment loading up all his worldly belongings. It was late, and he had to get the landlord out of bed to turn in the keys. The old man grumbled why Ahmed couldn't wait until the morning and that Ahmed would not get his deposit back.

I'd sure like to stop off at Gerry's to say good-bye. But it's so late, and his mom might get upset. Oh, well, I'll just have to take some time to come back once I'm settled in the new job.

The supervisor was kind but firm. "I don't know about hiring a student. I need people who are going to stick around for a while. This crisis isn't about to go away, and I can't afford to have a lot of turnover. I need people who are going to get experience and then stick it out with us."

"Well, sir, I'm not sure if I will be able to return to school this semester. I've heard they're cutting back on all programs, and I might not be able to finish this year. I really need the job, sir, and you will find me an honest worker." Ahmed was earnest, afraid that the supervisor might turn him down.

"Okay, I guess we'll give you a chance," He said with a smile.

"Thank you, sir. You won't regret it!" Ahmed was relieved, and he turned to Ron, who gave him a smile of approval.

Two weeks passed, and then it came. Congress had played with the idea for a while, and now it would put it into effect. There had been a lot of debate over the constitutionality of the government taking over all food supplies and setting up a system of rationing. But the food shortages, the black market abuses, the trucking strikes, and the hoarding by many at the expense of other's hunger, made this a practical issue.

The conservative religious establishment, strongly influenced by the moral leadership of the Great Shepherd, was in the heart of the fray, pushing for a morally defensible distribution of food to all good citizens who were willing to support the government's efforts to create order out of chaos.

Being a good citizen was defined rather simply: go to church on Sunday, don't get involved in anything deemed illegal by the government, and report misbehaviour or non–compliance with government directives. Everyone who verifiably complied with these conditions would qualify for a ration card.

Ahmed had no problem getting his. He attended the Christian church nearest the base camp, unless he was required to work on Sunday. Government employees had special privileges in order to provide public safety 24/7. Since he had free board at the Forest Service camp, he saved his ration cards for future emergencies.

He had been working for two months, when one day he was sent to Spokane to pick up supplies for the camp. The heat had let up for the last couple of days, so he drove with the windows down and the fresh mountain air rustled through his hair. He'd only driven about five miles when he saw a man standing by the road hitching a ride.

Now why would a man be walking around this forest in a white suit and a wide-brimmed hat? Well, I have plenty of time on my hands, so I think I'll pull over and give him a ride.

"Hi, there! Can I take you somewhere?" Ahmed felt good about helping someone out.

The man lifted his face and smiled as he winked one eye. Ahmed was caught totally by surprise.

"Jebosh! I can't believe my eyes! How are you, my friend? Hop right in… it's so good to see you!"

Jebosh climbed into the cab and grabbed Ahmed's outstretched hand in both of his. Ahmed felt the unusual strength and gentleness of his extraterrestrial friend.

"I won't ask how you are… I know. I have been watching you since we parted. I am very pleased to see that you are interested in following the Prince."

"The Prince means everything to me. I am glad to go to church every Sunday, and I am sharing what I know with my friend Ron. He's not very receptive yet, but then, I was very indifferent when I first heard Guillermo. But now the Ten Commandments are the rule of my life. I love the Prince, Jebosh, and I want to please him in what I do."

"It's interesting that you should mention the Ten Commandments. Are you sure you are keeping God's holy law?"

"Of course, Jebosh! Why do you ask me that way?" Ahmed suddenly felt unsure about his statement.

"Let's look at little closer at the fourth commandment. Do you still have the Bible I gave you?"

"You bet! I always keep it close by," Ahmed replied as he reached behind his seat.

"Let me drive, Ahmed. I'd like for you to re-examine this commandment very carefully," Jebosh suggested, and Ahmed brought the truck to a stop.

Ahmed didn't have very much practice finding Bible verses, but Jebosh made it easy for him. As he opened that Bible, it fell open on the book of Exodus, chapter twenty, the chapter where the Ten Commandments first appear together as God wrote them on two tables of stone. Ahmed read out loud verses eight to eleven:

"Remember the Sabbath day to keep it holy. Six days you shall labor and do all your work, but the seventh day is the Sabbath of the Lord your God. In it you shall do no work: you, nor your son, nor your daughter, nor your male servant, nor your female servant, nor your cattle, nor your stranger that is within your gates. For in six days the Lord made the heavens and the earth, the sea and all that is in them, and rested the seventh day. Therefore, the Lord blessed the Sabbath day and hallowed it."

"Well, I think I'm doing this right. I work six days per week and go to church on Sunday. Is there anything wrong with that? Or am I doing okay?"

"I think your heart is in the right place, Ahmed, but you need to understand exactly what it is that God is asking of you in His commandment so that you can respond appropriately. Let me see if I can help you.

"First of all, the commandment begins with the word 'remember.' When someone asks you to remember something, what do you understand by that?"

"Well, I think it means to bring to mind something I have heard or seen before. Otherwise, it wouldn't make sense to ask me to remember something I've never known."

"Exactly! So to begin with, God is making reference in His commandment to a Sabbath day that He had established sometime before. Now, seeing that the Bible contains God's communication with mankind, where in the Bible do you find where God established the Sabbath day before it appeared in Exodus twenty?"

"You know, I remember reading that in the story of creation found in the first book, the book of Genesis."

"Okay. Let's go there." Jebosh was patiently leading. Ahmed read the whole first chapter, noting the order of the literal days of creation and what God had created during each one. Then he started reading the second chapter, which says:

"Thus the heavens and the earth, and all the host of them were finished. And on the seventh day, God ended the work he had done, and He rested on the seventh day from all the work He had done. Then God blessed the seventh day, and sanctified it, because in it He rested from all the work God created and made.

"I sense that I'm doing something wrong here, but I don't understand what it is, Jebosh."

"It has to do with the right day, Ahmed. Do you have a small calendar with you?"

"Why, yes, as a matter of fact, I do," Ahmed fumbled through his wallet.

"Now, tell me, what day is the seventh day on your calendar?"

"Well, the seventh day from left to right falls on Saturday…wait a minute! Are you suggesting that Saturday is the right day to rest on?" Ahmed was suddenly struck with a new reality.

"I'm not suggesting anything, Ahmed… the Bible just told you in the fourth commandment that the… seventh day is the Sabbath of the Lord your God…'"

"But all Christians rest on Sunday, and Moslems keep Friday holy. How did they get away from what the Bible is saying here?"

"It is a long story, but I'll tell you the short version. God had set aside the seventh day as the Sabbath from the beginning and established it as the sign of the covenant between Himself and all His creation. The enemy of God, the fallen angel Lucifer, now known as Satan, in his rebellion, decided to attack the very day that brought man and God together. His purpose was to alienate man from God and obtain the worship due to God to himself. So he established his own religion, known today as paganism. He inspired mankind to worship the sun and attribute to this star the power of life.

"Now, it is true that the sun, through its rays, maintains the proper temperature for life, and contributes to the maintenance of life on earth by stimulating photosynthesis in plants, the plants becoming food for man, and maintaining life on earth. But Satan obscured the fact that God was the creator of the sun and that it was He who set up this system of maintenance for the existence of man and animals.

"So much emphasis was placed on the beauty, power, and functions of the sun, that the mind of man was turned away from worshipping the Creator to worshipping what He created. Thus, sun worship is the oldest, most widespread form of paganism that exists today. This form of religion has coexisted with the worship of the true God through the centuries, and we see the struggle between the two throughout the whole Bible.

"Satan's efforts, however, would not stop there. He wasn't content with this coexistence between the true and the false systems of worship. His ultimate end was to destroy all faith in the true God and to subvert all his followers. In the days of Noah, he almost accomplished his goal, except for Noah and his family. That's when the world was destroyed by a flood, and God began through Noah a new line of true worshippers. But human nature, being basically corrupt, was drawn away again by Satan and his cohorts, and paganism began to flourish again and the struggle between false worship and the Keepers of the Covenant resurfaced.

"Finally, only one family was left that still believed in the true God: Abraham and Sarah. So God called them from their pagan surroundings and led them to what today is known as Palestine where they could develop into the new line of Covenant Keepers. The descendants of Abraham, today known as the Jews, now became the objects of Satan's attacks, and we find the same struggle in their history, with events of pagan worship, and periods of outright desertion from the true God. We see in the Bible their triumphs and their losses, their repentance and restoration and then falling again.

"As the result of their great departure from God's covenant they were taken into captivity by King Nebuchadnezzar of Babylon (now in Iraq) who also destroyed the city of Jerusalem. It was during this period of captivity that God gave the prophet Daniel a vision of the final apostasy (or great departure from God's covenant), which would take place and last until the end of time.

"In Daniel, chapter seven, God outlined to Daniel, using the figure of beasts, the progression of kingdoms on the earth, and how a kingdom would arise that would attempt to 'change times and the law' and would thus desecrate the true Sabbath and establish a different day of worship. Satan, of course was behind all of this, moving on people's minds to establish paganism as the official religion of the world.

"By the time the Prince came to earth to fulfil the promise of redemption of mankind, the true Sabbath was observed only by the Jews. But, because of their bitter experiences in captivity by other nations, they went overboard in their strictness of Sabbath keeping, loading the day with so many detailed rules, that it became a burden rather than a joy to keep the Sabbath holy.

"Thus, the Prince spent a lot of time on the subject of true Sabbath keeping, showing His people that it is a day to be kept joyfully, abstaining from the cares and routine work of the week, and seeking contented fellowship with God and with their brothers and sisters of like faith. He showed the world that 'the Son of man is Lord even of the Sabbath'" (Matthew 12:8).

Ahmed listened intently, without even the slightest interruption, captivated by such a story as he had never heard before. He didn't even mind that Jebosh had driven past his original destination and was doing circles throughout Spokane as he told the story.

"The disciples of Prince Jesus learned to appreciate the Sabbath just as he taught them, and after the Prince returned home, they practiced and taught the same happy principles to the new generation of Covenant Keepers wherever they went. The New Testament in your Bible is the story of how the Christian church was born and how the doctrines were taught and practiced by all believers in the New Covenant.

"However, don't forget that Satan had not ceased to exist. He and his wicked angels had made the Prince's life painful with temptations and attacks, even to the point of leading their wicked followers to kill the Prince of Life. Now they turned their fury upon the followers of the Prince, and they were sorely persecuted and killed. Satan went on further and inspired some of the more careless believers to modify and change teachings so that the original faith was distorted over time.

"He used men in power, both in the government as well as in the church itself, to set up the kind of worship which would lead Christians to follow his original deception in worshipping the sun, while pretending to be worshipping and King and the Prince. Through subtle deception, and using the influence of men in political power and others in religious leadership, they placed upon the first day of the week the importance and sanctity of the original seventh-day Sabbath.

"They reasoned that because the Jews were responsible for the death of the Prince, and because the Jews had become so hated by the Romans, they didn't want to be mistakenly identified with them through Sabbath keeping. So they sought out an argument that seemed plausible to them; that since the Prince had risen from the dead on the first day of the week, his resurrection would now be the new basis for their religious observance of a day of rest. The change was not sudden, but rather took a long time before it became the official Christian day for worship. Thus, Daniel's prophecy was fulfilled to the letter. Satan had induced the leadership of the church to change the 'times and the law' against God's will."

"That's incredible! And the deception was quite successful, too!" Ahmed was amazed by the discovery. "The whole Christian world believes that Sunday is the Sabbath. I don't know of anybody who keeps Saturday as the Sabbath, do you?"

"Yes, Ahmed, I do. In fact, would you be surprised if I told you that there are more than four hundred different groups around the world who worship on Saturday?"

"Four hundred? I can't believe it! How come nobody knows about them? I've never heard of a church that worships on Saturday!"

"Well, most of these groups are very small, and they vary quite a bit in their doctrinal beliefs. The largest, however, has a membership of about fifteen million people, spread out all over the world. They have churches in every city and in almost every town in the United States, and they are present in every country in the world except Nepal. They are the closest to being the last Keepers of the Covenant."

"You mean…you mean…Guillermo and Elizabeth? They're Sabbath Keepers?"

"Yes, Ahmed, they are loyal to the Prince. In fact, they are responsible for our meeting on the road and our friendship," Jebosh commented with a smile.

"How can that be? They weren't present to introduce us!"

"Well, it works this way. When you were visiting at their house that weekend, Guillermo noticed your lack of interest in spiritual matters. He was concerned about you, and wished that you would want to get to know the Prince and his plan for your life. When you departed so abruptly from his house, he went to his bedroom, got down on his knees, and with a burdened heart, asked the Prince to give you a special opportunity to get to know him and his covenant. The Prince was deeply touched by Guillermo's love and concern for you, so he called me to the temple and assigned me the task of leading you through the Bible so you could understand this plan of you."

"Guillermo did that? For me? Man, I must have seemed like a real fool. I'm really sorry, Jebosh. I'll make it up to him. I will also pray to the Prince for his protection, and the moment I can get back there, I want to thank him personally!"

"That's great, Ahmed. Well, now you know more about the Sabbath. What are you going to do about it?"

"Well, of course, I'm going to find one of those churches who keep the Sabbath and the Covenant. Surely, you know where they're at Jebosh. Why don't you just point one out to me?"

"I'm sorry, Ahmed, but I can't. I have been instructed to let you make some personal effort to serve God. But you will find them. Just make sure that they are keeping the complete Covenant and not just merely worshipping on Saturday."

Just then, Ahmed realized that the truck had stopped in front of the warehouse where he was to pick up the supplies. He turned to Jebosh…but he was gone. A police car was right behind the truck with its rainbow of lights flashing away. An officer stepped out and walked toward the driver's side of the truck, rather apprehensively. Ahmed was still sitting in the passenger side, when the officer stuck his face through the windom.

"Where's the driver of this vehicle?" he inquired with a look of disbelief.

"He…ahhh…stepped out, officer. Is anything wrong?" Ahmed was at a loss for words.

"Well…no… its just that I couldn't make out anybody behind the wheel for several blocks… just this bright light shining through the rear window. I could see you where you're at, but I couldn't see him."

"Well, I've got to pick up some supplies here. If it's all the same to you, I better get going," Ahmed replied rather nervously. The officer noticed his Forest Service uniform so he didn't see a need to detain him any further and walked back to his car mumbling to himself.

When Ahmed got back to the camp in Idaho, the supervisor was waiting for him.

"Ahmed, I have some orders here for you to report to another camp near Bend, Oregon. I already have a bus ticket and about a dozen ration cards to put you through 'til you're completely settled. Good luck. I hope you like your new assignment."

A look of disappointment crossed Ahmed's face when he heard the news. He had hoped to visit Guillermo the following weekend. Besides, he was sharing his new experience with Ron and needed more time to explain the covenant to him.

"What's the matter, Ahmed, you don't think you'll like Oregon?"

"No, sir, that's not it. You know, you make friends, you have a familiar routine, you like what you're doing… new places mean starting over from scratch."

"I'm not worried about you, Ahmed. You seem to have a knack for starting new things. I think you'll be fine!"

CONFRONTATION

The gang was gathered around the table at Lisa's house. It had ceased to be, for the present, the happy little group it had been before the crisis broke out. They had returned to Spokane after their weekend with Guillermo, full of new ideas and expectations of the future. Yet, with jobs very scarce, they soon began to experience some serious financial woes. Ben, Joyce, and Rita had moved in with Lisa and her parents, as they had had to vacate their own apartments for lack of rent money. Gerry had wanted to bring them home, but Sonia had refused to take them in.

"I know they're good kids, Gerry, but I can't afford to keep them here. We are able to survive, ourselves, only because of my position with the government. But if they find out I have a herd of unemployed youngsters with strange new ideas that don't contribute to the advancement of family life, I could lose my job, and then where would we be? You certainly couldn't expect me to join Guillermo's little idyllic group, could you?"

"What's happened to you, Mom? You seemed to believe in the Covenant and would tell me all those exciting stories when I was a kid… stories of how different people in the Bible lived, and loved, and even died to defend it. Look around you, Mom! Look at what's happening in the world–

the diseases breaking out, the natural disasters, the famines, the environmental chaos, the failing economies, and even, yes, the religious turmoil that's causing people to abandon their faiths to join in a desperate coalition to save the world! Don't you see the fulfilment of the prophecies in the Bible? You did at one time."

Sonia listened in silence as her son reminded her of how she used to be and how far she had come around to the thinking of her mixed up world. But she could no longer hold her silence, and burst out, her face red with anger. "Gerry, you can't talk to me that way! I forbid you to pass judgment on me, and if you want to believe all that stuff, then pack your things and get out! Go join your little fantasy in the wilderness. I have a responsibility to carry out on behalf of this city!"

Gerry was stunned. He never would have believed he would hear what he just heard. With a grieving heart, he slowly turned and headed for his bedroom and began packing his clothes and his most cherished belongings–pants, shirts, underwear and socks, and on top, his Bible and a framed picture of his mother. He closed his suitcase, grabbed his camping gear, and headed for the door. But Sonia was blocking the way. Her eyes and cheeks flooded with tears, she grabbed Gerry's arm as he approached.

"I'm so sorry, Gerry. I never should have said that. Please forgive me! Please, Gerry, please don't go. This whole thing will eventually blow over, and we'll have a good life. You'll finish college and find a good girl to marry, perhaps… even Lisa…"

"I'm sorry too, Mom. But I have to go…" There was a lump in his throat so hard it was painful for him to talk. "Perhaps…I'll come back… but for now you need to think this one out alone… I love you, Mom." He couldn't go on. He just grabbed her small frame and gave her a long hug and quickly walked out the door before she could see the tears in his eyes.

Gerry had a lot to think about as he headed out to Lisa's house. He couldn't abandon his mother, yet she had to make some choices of her own. Although he loved her dearly, he had also come to love the Prince and wanted to keep His covenant. Life with Mom would be very difficult if she was going to oppose his new beliefs and experience.

He had just enough money in his pockets to make it out to Guillermo's place. But he couldn't go without visiting his friends one more time and see how they were doing. Lisa's heart leaped when she saw him through the living room window. She ran out the door without even telling anyone what she had seen. Gerry saw a vision in blue jeans and pink sweater running toward him, and this time he couldn't contain his feelings. He met her in his arms and kissed her as they embraced for a few minutes. When they finally came up for air, he tenderly looked into her eyes and softly said the words which had taken so much time in coming, "I love you, Lisa Griggs. I love you with all my heart and being. I would like one day soon for you to be my wife."

The tears of happiness flowed freely down her cheeks as she tried to speak her own heart.

"I've loved you for a long time, Gerry. I have dreamed of this moment for a long, long time. Now that I know how to pray to the Prince, I have asked Him day and night to take care of you and to make it possible for the two of us to face this final crisis together. I am so happy and so grateful to Him for answering my prayers." They held each other's hands as they headed toward the front porch, where their friends stood waiting with smiles on their faces. Gerry and Lisa did not have to explain anything. They had seen and understood it all, and all they could do was whoop and clap.

That evening, as they sat around the table enjoying the simple fare that Mrs. Griggs had prepared, they recounted their recent experiences, thanking and praising God for His goodness and protection in so many difficult situations.

"Well, I might as well tell you what happened today at my house," Gerry sadly began. "My mom and I had a serious confrontation over the Covenant and the lifestyle it engenders. I told her that I had chosen to follow the Prince and His teachings in the Bible and invited her to do the same. I think I touched a raw nerve when I reminded her that she used to believe like me, and had somehow lost her way. She was totally defensive, to the point of asking me to live my new life somewhere else. Well, it hurt a lot, but I felt she needed time by herself to think these things through. I'll be praying for her, that she may choose to follow the Prince and accept the Covenant in which she once rejoiced. I also ask for your prayers on her behalf."

Lisa seemed to feel his pain, and squeezed his hand gently as she and the others expressed their support and willingness to pray for Sonia.

"Let's do it right now," Ben suggested, and they all knelt as he began, somewhat awkwardly.

"Dear Lord, I'm sorry I don't have experience talking to You. So, I'll just tell You that we are happy to know You, to know what You did for us on Calvary, to know the promise of Your forgiveness, and to know that You are soon coming back to take us home. But please, Lord, do not let Gerry's mom be left behind. Speak to her heart and help her to understand Your great love and to go back to the Covenant she once knew and loved. We thank you for giving us salvation, and we ask this in Your wonderful name, Amen!"

"That was a wonderful prayer, Ben. Thanks so much." Gerry was deeply moved both, by Ben's prayer and by his friend's new commitment. "Well, I've decided to go visit

Guillermo once more. I have so much more to learn from the Bible, but I have some difficulty understanding some things on my own. If any of you want to join me, you're welcome to come along." Gerry surveyed their faces for a positive answer. He preferred to have company rather than going alone.

"Are you kidding?" Ben's face brightened. "We'd all love to go. We were talking about it before you came in. We could all use some more knowledge."

"C'mon, Ben, tell the truth! You loved Elizabeth's cooking," Joyce kidded as she pushed his shoulder.

"It's settled, then. Get your stuff together. If we hurry, we can make it there before dark."

Gerry's car was packed to the hilt. It was a little crowded for five people and a lot of baggage, but this group had become closer than family; and they enjoyed the closeness and the fun interaction along the way. They looked forward to seeing Guillermo and Elizabeth, remembering what a good time they had had the first time they visited, the great food, and the cherished teachings they had heard, which had changed the course of their lives.

It must have been the extra weight of passengers and luggage that caused the car to use up more gas than anticipated. Gerry watched the needle nervously as it moved closer and closer to empty. Eventually the engine began to gasp, and then sighed its last stroke as Gerry coasted the car to the right and finally stopped. A gloom settled among the formerly happy group.

"I'm sorry, guys. I miscalculated the distance we could go on this tank." Gerry felt helpless.

"Why be so glum, people? Don't we have a friend to turn to? C'mon, let's pray to the Prince so that He will send help," Rita cheered the group. As they bowed their heads, Rita reached out in prayer to her new friend and comforter.

"Dear Jesus, please help us. We need gas, and we are stuck in the middle of nowhere. We trust in your promises and will wait for assistance with patience. Thank you for hearing us. Amen."

After about ten minutes, a dignified older gentleman pulled up in front of them, driving a vintage MG with the top down and the wind streaming through his white hair. He stepped out and came to Gerry's window.

"Hi, my name is Don. Are you folks having car trouble?"

"Thanks so much for stopping, Don. I'm Gerry, and yes, we ran out of gas. Do you know if there's a gas station anywhere near?"

"I'll tell you what… we're about five miles from my house in Bonner's Ferry, and I happen to have a large tank for my vehicles. Why don't you ride with me and we'll bring back a five gallon can full of gas?"

Gerry's worried expression broadened into a big smile. *What a great guy!* he thought. *And what a wonderful friend, who sent this angel of a man to help them in their hour of need!*

Riding in the MG was a lot of fun, and Don was not only friendly but also a very interesting character to converse with. Once they had returned and poured the gas in the tank, Don remarked that they were welcome to come by the house and have something to eat before they continued their journey.

"We don't know how to thank you, Don. But we know that God sent you in time to help us. However, we have to get going in order to get to our destination before it gets too dark. We'll gladly take you up on your offer when we come this way again."

"See that you do!" he answered and hunkered his six-foot frame into the little car, speeding off like a teenager with his first set of wheels.

The sun had set and it was growing dark as they made their way through the hills to Guillermo's house. As they pulled up in front of the rambling ranch house, the dog seemed to recognize Gerry's vehicle and its occupants, since he barked a little and wagged a lot, running back and forth between the car and the front porch as if welcoming the group back. Guillermo came out to see what the commotion was all about, and was thrilled to see his young friends returning for more fellowship.

"Welcome home, my friends. How are you Gerry?" Guillermo embraced him and shook hands warmly with the ladies. Ben just grinned as he interlocked his hands and held them out before him. Guillermo's eyes opened big as he smiled with surprise.

"Tell me it's true, Ben! Tell me that you have become a Keeper of the Covenant!" he exclaimed, as he locked both his hands and contacted Ben's.

"We owe you a great debt of gratitude, Guillermo. When you shared the story of Christ with us and taught us about the covenant of redemption, God's great love, his forgiveness, and his promise to come back for us, you gave a totally new meaning to our lives. We had to come back to see you, and to thank you and Elizabeth for your great kindness."

Guillermo had to embrace him too and then wipe the mist from his eyes. "Well, come on in. What are y'all standing out here for? Elizabeth, come out here and see who's come to visit!"

"Well, praise the Lord! It's so good to see all of you! Come in, come in! She said as she wiped her hands on her apron and greeted each one with a warm hug. "We weren't expecting you, so you'll have to give me a few minutes to throw more water in the soup and cut up some more vegetables." She added with a grin.

"How have you all been?" Guillermo asked as they stowed their sleeping bags and light backpacks in a corner of the living room. "I've heard nothing about you since you left, and with all the civil and political agitation in the cities, we have been a little worried about all of you."

"Oh, Guillermo, we've had our share of troubles. Very few jobs available, and of those, preference is given to people who have proof of community involvement and church attendance on Sunday. Of course, since you pointed out the difference between worship on the first day of the week and worship on the seventh day of the week, we have studied the Bible and we are convinced that the true Sabbath falls on Saturday. We have not dared to confront the employers on this issue. We've just stayed away and did whatever odd jobs we can find on weekdays without actually becoming employees."

"But the Lord has never failed us!" Lisa felt that she needed to make that clear. "We have not been without food so far, and He has even provided gasoline when most needed." She grinned as she remembered Don and his little speed monster.

They spent the next hour recounting the significant events of their lives. Smiling at times, and at others controlling the emotions that come when sad news must be shared. Gerry told Guillermo and Elizabeth about his mom and her confusion over the Covenant and its provisions.

"You know, Gerry, you've got to give God time to work in people's hearts. Some have bigger barriers than others. The Lord is not going to give up on Sonia until she makes her final decision. We must continue to pray for her."

"You know, even though the calendar says that today is Friday, the Sabbath really begins when the sun sets on Friday and lasts for twenty-four hours until the sun sets again on Saturday evening. So we have already spent the first three hours of the Sabbath together. Before we sack out I'd like for us to welcome the Sabbath with a few songs and the reading of a good, encouraging passage from the Bible, and then we'll have prayer for Sonia and for all who are still struggling with acceptance of Christ and his Covenant. What do you say?"

"That sounds great, Guillermo, except I don't know any Christian songs, and I sound like a soprano frog when I try to sing." Joyce had to get a laugh out of the group.

"How about a simple little chorus to begin with? There's one that the Apostle Paul wrote and it goes like this," Guillermo responded as he began to strum his guitar.

"Rejoice in the Lord always and again I say, Rejoice!" his booming baritone voice invigorated the room. Soon, all were repeating the chorus with enthusiasm and gladness at being together and worshipping God with grateful hearts.

Suddenly Guillermo stopped strumming. It hit him that someone was missing in the group.

"Gerry, what happened to Ahmed? I just realized that he didn't come up with you."

"You know, Guillermo, we haven't seen or heard from Ahmed since he left here in a huff. I think he felt uncomfortable with your presentation of the Covenant, so he chose to go back early. He said he was going to visit some friends in Coeur d'Alene. But since we returned to Spokane, I've tried to find him without any luck. His landlord said he moved out late one night and didn't even come back for his deposit."

"That's too bad," Guillermo replied sadly. "I've been praying for him that the Holy Spirit will reach his heart. He seemed like a fine young man. I hope you're able to find him, and if you do, try to get him to visit here again."

"We've been praying for him too," Ben chipped in. "He's not a religious person, but he has a good heart and he really cares for people. I hope the Prince is able to reach him."

"Speaking of the Prince," Joyce opened up slowly, "I've been wondering about what he does all day. I don't mean to be disrespectful, but when I pray, I try to imagine what he looks like, where he is, and what he's doing. I try to focus on him as a person so that my prayers may seem real; you know what I mean? I mean… I want to feel that I am really talking with a person, and I imagine him to look like the pictures I've seen in books and in museums."

"I think we all go through that experience, Joyce. And no, I don't believe you are being disrespectful at all. Nobody that I know of today knows exactly what Prince Jesus looks like, but the Bible teaches us that he has a human appearance, that is, he looks and appears to be a just like us. Pull out your Bibles, and let's look at a few verses that can help us see this more clearly." Guillermo paused, as they rustled through their knapsacks for their Bibles.

"To begin with, we see that in the beginning we humans were created in the image of God himself. We read this in the book of Genesis, chapter one, verse twenty–six. Please read the first sentence for us, Rita."

"And God said, 'Lets us make man in Our image, according to Our likeness.'"

"Now, even though we carry that image, we must understand that there is an infinite difference between our nature and His. He is the almighty God, the Creator and sustainer of all life. We are creatures, totally dependent on His power and sustaining grace for our existence. In fact, all that exists in this world and in the universe came from His hands.

"Along with God the Father, and God the Holy Spirit, the Prince has always existed and has no beginning and no end. He made that clear to the Jews when in John 8:58, he declared himself to be the I AM. That's why the Jews immediately took up rocks to stone him to death– because

He had applied to Himself the term that defines the Eternal God. To them He was committing blasphemy, but we know now how accurate He was in His identity.

"We all know from the Bible that the Prince, who had taken upon Himself the responsibility for our sins and rebellion, took on a human nature so that He could experience what we experience, and feel what we feel, and go through the same trials and temptations as we do. This was necessary, so that, by identifying Himself with us, he could take our place on the cross of Calvary. He had to die as a man, so that we could be redeemed, and be restored to our original sinless state. Paul puts it so poignantly and yet so beautifully in 2 Corinthians 5:21, 'For He made him who knew no sin to be sin for us, that we might become the righteousness of God in Him.'

"So since the Prince identified Himself with us, we can imagine Him in our prayers as a beautiful human being, but never forgetting that He is also the Everlasting God, and is to be treated with all reverence and adoration."

"That's awesome, Guillermo!" Rita expressed her wonder at the Prince's great love and humility.

"The other thing I asked you about, Guillermo, is if you know where the Prince is and what has He been doing these last two thousand years since He left. Does the Bible say anything about that?" Joyce was full of curiosity that evening.

"Yes, Joyce. In fact, the Bible clearly teaches that when Prince Jesus returned to heaven, He went into the Heavenly Sanctuary, the main place of worship in heaven where the throne of God the Father is set. There He ministers on our behalf, obtaining forgiveness for us every time we pray and confess our sins, and presenting His sacrifice on our behalf as the atonement for our sins. Let's look at the book of Hebrews, chapter nine, and verse twenty–four. Would you please read it, Ben?"

"For Christ is not entered into the holy places made with hands, which are copies of the true, but into heaven itself, now to appear in the presence of God for us."

"Wait a minute, Guillermo. Please explain this–about holy places and a sanctuary. This is somewhat mysterious to me." Ben interrupted.

"I understand, Ben. I'll try to make it as simple as possible. After the Jews had been freed from slavery and led out of Egypt, God appeared to Moses on Mount Sinai and gave him the Ten Commandments written by God himself on two stone slabs. These were the main conditions of the Covenant that God was renewing with the descendants of Abraham. At that time, God also gave Moses other instructions, statutes, and ordinances for the establishment of a government in Israel.

"Among these, were the statutes and ordinances that had to do with their religious life, their worship style, and detailed instructions for the system of animal sacrifices. If you review the book of Genesis, starting with chapter four, you will find that neither the Ten Commandments nor the religious statutes and ordinances were anything new for the fledgling nation of Israel. The Ten Commandments have always existed, and in fact, it was the breaking of the commandments that caused Adam and Eve to be sinners and be denied direct access to the presence of God. And once out of the Garden, God ordained the system of animal sacrifices as a symbol of the future death of the Prince for the forgiveness of sins and eventual restoration to eternal life. And that's why Abel sacrificed a lamb, and why Cain, in his rebellion against God, killed his brother.

"Now, the people of Israel were about to enter a new land, and God, in establishing law and order in their government, reminded them of the Ten Commandments and renewed the system of animal sacrifices as part of his Covenant with them. In order for all of this to be done in such a way that it would represent God's plan to save mankind, He gave Moses a vision of the temple in heaven, where the angels and other created beings gather to worship God and where the actual and final forgiveness of sins and the granting of righteousness to repentant sinners takes place. After Moses had seen the temple in heaven, God instructed him to make a scaled–down model of it as a sanctuary, with replicas of the furniture, departments, and functions. Let's look at what the Bible says concerning this in Exodus 25:8, 9, and 40. Please read it, Lisa."

"'And let them make Me a sanctuary; that I may dwell among them. According to all that I show you, that is, the pattern of the tabernacle, and the pattern of all its furnishings, just so you shall make it…And see to it that you make them according to the pattern which was shown you on the mountain.'"

"Thanks, Lisa. Moses had been on Mount Sinai for forty days. Why do you suppose God kept him up there so long? Well, God had a lot of instruction and planning to review with Moses. He gave him civil laws, health and dietary statutes, regulation for social interactions and business transactions, building designs, furniture design, establishment of holidays, and regulations and procedures for the whole system of ritual sacrifices. The books of Exodus and Leviticus, particularly, contain all of these instructions, and became the books of the law along with Genesis, Numbers, and Deuteronomy.

"The point I'm trying to make with all of this history is that the Sanctuary which Moses built at the foot of Mt. Sinai, and the subsequent temples built by Solomon and rebuilt by the Jews when they returned from their captivity in the kingdom of Persia, were all patterned after the Sanctuary or temple in heaven. The Apostle Paul supports this truth in the book of Hebrews, chapter eight and verses one and two. Your turn to read, Gerry."

"Now this is the main point of the things we are saying: we have such a High Priest, who is seated at the right hand of the throne of the Majesty in the heavens, a Minister of the Sanctuary which the Lord erected, and not man.'"

"What this is saying," Guillermo continued, "is that there is a sanctuary or temple in heaven which was built by the hand of God and not by man, and that there is a High Priest or Minister there who sits next to God. Let's identify that High Priest by looking at chapter four and verse fourteen. How about you, Elizabeth, will you read for us?"

"'Seeing then that we have a great High Priest, who has passed through the heavens, Jesus, the Son of God, let us hold fast our confession.'"

"Isn't that exciting? Jesus is up there, in the Heavenly Sanctuary, right by the throne of God the Father, representing our case and interceding in our behalf by presenting His own sacrifice as His atonement for our sins. By this, I mean to say that although the sacrifice took place on the cross of Calvary, the symbolism of that sacrifice is presented before God, every time someone confesses his sins, as the atonement for sin. This is what the word grace means–granting us the favour of forgiveness and atonement totally undeserved by us! Praise the Lord! I am overcome with joy and emotion every time I think about this."

The room was silent for a few moments, while the group drank in the enormous significance of such a wonderful gift.

"It's that simple, that easy?" Gerry asked in wonderment.

"It's that simple for us," Guillermo answered with a slight tremor in his voice. "But it wasn't easy for Prince Jesus. We will never fully understand the terror and the struggle He went through in Gethsemane while deciding to go through with the sacrifice. And what He went through on the cross of Calvary, the shame, the rejection, the seeming separation from His own Father, and the ingratitude of so many—Oh, I can't imagine it!"

Again, silence… moist eyes, even some tears, as the enormity of Prince Jesus' passion passed through their imagination.

"So, if the Prince did it all on Calvary, why does he still have to work on our behalf in the Heavenly Sanctuary?" Ben finally found his voice.

"Well, the full plan was not finished at Calvary. That part was just the beginning. Now the Prince was to deal with our part on a daily basis. He made the final sacrifice, but we humans have to make the final decision—acceptance or rejection of the Covenant which was sealed with His blood.

"Every day the invitation goes out to humanity to accept God's offer of forgiveness and of eternal life. First through the disciples themselves, then through their inspired writings, through every minister and missionary year after year, century after century until the time appointed by God for the end of the invitation and the end of the Prince's intercession for us. That moment is fast approaching… we are living very close to the end of time."

"How can one tell if he has received the invitation?" Joyce asked.

"First, let's finish the last two verses of chapter four. It's very encouraging to anyone, no matter what he or she has done, no matter how low he has sunk, no matter how evil his or her life has been, listen to what the Apostle Paul says. Go ahead, Rita."

"'For we do not have a High Priest who cannot sympathize with our weaknesses, but was in all points tempted as we are, yet without sin. Let us therefore come boldly to the throne of grace, that we may obtain mercy to help in time of need.'"

"Let's turn now to Isaiah 1:18 and see just how good the Lord is toward us. Please, Joyce."

"'Come, now, and let us reason together, says the Lord, though your sins are like scarlet, they shall be as white as snow; though they are red like crimson, they shall be as wool.'"

"One more, this one by the Prince directly. Ben, please look up Matthew 11:28–30."

"'Come to Me, all you who labor and are heavy laden, and I will give you rest. Take My yoke upon you and learn from Me, for I am gentle and lowly in heart, and you will find rest for your souls. For My yoke is easy and My burden is light'"

"How can you go wrong with these offers?" Gerry exclaimed with deep emotion. "God is so good!"

"Amen! Gerry," Guillermo responded. "There's a little song that expresses just that, and I would like to teach it to you," he continued as he grabbed his guitar and began to strum.

> God is so good
> God is so good,
> God is so good,
> He's so good to me!
> God answers prayer,
> God answers prayer,
> God answers prayer,
> He's so good to me!
> He's coming soon,
> He's coming soon,
> He's coming soon,
> Coming soon for me!

"Oh, that was wonderful! I hope that I can always be as hopeful and as I happy as I feel right now, Guillermo." Lisa said, expressing the joy they all felt in knowing Prince Jesus.

"I'm so happy to hear you say that, Lisa. This is indeed a good moment to express our joy and gratitude to the Prince of the Universe, for today is the Sabbath of His creation, and it is the day He set apart for worship, communion with Him, and for rejoicing in His great salvation. We're not the only ones who keep this day holy, you know. Many millions around the whole world are meeting to welcome the Sabbath as the sun goes down within their time zone."

"Well, what do you do on this day to make it so special, Guillermo?" Ben asked.

"We begin just as we did today–with songs of praise, with prayers, with the reading of Psalms and other scriptures, and with sharing experiences of God's grace in our lives. Tomorrow morning we have a more formal worship service, with a preacher presenting a special topic, followed by a fellowship luncheon. In the afternoon, we go for nature hikes or go down to the river with our guitars and sing to fishermen, tourists, or anyone who wants to listen. On special occasions, we have baptism for people who want to be Keepers of the Covenant, accepting the provisions of salvation by the Prince, and making a commitment to follow His plan for our lives."

HEAVY DECISIONS

"Baptism! I've wondered about that," Gerry spoke up. "I know it's done in most Christian churches, but why is it so important?"

"Well, Gerry, this is a ceremony that was begun by John the Baptist under instructions by God Himself. It is a symbol of being totally cleansed from sin and its awful stains on our lives. When it is done in the name of Father, the Son, and the Holy Spirit, it becomes the threshold through which we cross into a new life with Christ, overcoming sin from then on through His power and grace.

"Jesus, the Prince of Life, went through that ceremony Himself, not because He had any sin in his life, but because He wanted to encourage His followers to follow His example. We read in the gospel of Matthew, how when Jesus came to John to be baptized, John was astonished, because he knew baptism was for sinners, and he knew that Jesus had no sin. Let's read that story in Matthew 3:13–17. Since you asked, Gerry, you get to read," Guillermo said with a wink.

"Then Jesus came from Galilee to John to be baptized by him. And John tried to prevent Him, saying, 'I need to be baptized by You, and You are coming to me?' But Jesus answered and said to him, 'Permit it to be so now, for thus it is fitting for us to fulfill all righteousness.' Then he allowed Him. When He had been baptized, Jesus came up immediately from the water, and behold, the heavens were opened to Him, and He saw the Spirit of God descending like a dove and alighting upon Him. And suddenly a voice came from heaven, saying, 'This is My beloved Son, in whom I am well pleased.'"

"Thank you, Gerry. We see here, my friends, that baptism is so important that Jesus himself set the example, even though He didn't need it. In fact, He considered it so important that in His final few words to his disciples before returning to heaven, He instructed them to impart baptism to all who confessed Him as their personal Savior and became disciples until the end. We find this at the end of the same gospel of Matthew, chapter twenty–eight and verses nineteen and twenty. Please read, Rita."

"'Go ye, therefore, and make disciples of all the nations, baptizing them in the name of the Father, and of the Son, and of the Holy Spirit, teaching them to observe all things that I have command you: and, lo, I am with you always, even to the end of the age.'"

"Well, if that is so important, then I want to be baptized," Gerry said excitedly.

"Me too!" Lisa exclaimed, with the others following almost in a chorus.

"How soon can we do it, Guillermo? Can you do the honors?" Ben asked earnestly.

"We'll do it tomorrow!" Guillermo could not contain his happiness. "It is our custom to have a minister, a person trained in the preaching of the gospel and especially ordained to minister the special services of teaching, baptism, marriage, and other services. You all came at an auspicious moment,' cause tomorrow we have as our visiting preacher, Pastor Fred, a retired minister from Creston, B.C. as our guest preacher. The river is ready and waiting!"

Marriage! Did he say marriage? Gerry's mind began to sort Guillermo's statement while his heart raced. *This is it! This is the moment! I don't know if we'll have another chance!* He looked intently at Lisa, who apparently had not caught on and was wondering what was behind the excitement in his eyes. About that moment, everyone began to stir from their places, moving furniture so as to spread their sleeping bags. Gerry signalled Lisa to meet him on the front porch, and they slipped out almost without being noticed.

"What is it, Gerry?" Lisa asked, wondering what the excitement was about.

"Listen carefully, Lisa. You know that I love you more than anything else on earth. I have already told you that I want to marry you some day. This is our great opportunity–a preacher is going to be here this weekend. With all of this crisis going on, I don't know if and when we will have another chance. Now, I'm going to formally ask you to marry me. Will you, Lisa? Will you marry me and spend the rest of your life and eternity by my side?" Gerry asked, hardly able to contain his emotions.

"Oh, Gerry," she answered half crying, half laughing. "You don't even have to ask… but since you did, the answer is yes! Yes! A thousand times, yes!" and she threw her arms around his neck and just held on for a little while. The rest heard all the commotion and rushed to the porch to see what it was all about. They found them still in an embrace, so they shyly let go, though their friends figured out what was going on.

"Okay, okay, I might as well tell you the grand news. I've just asked Lisa to marry me, and she has said yes, which of course you all probably heard." A flurry of hugs and congratulations followed as their friends expressed their joy at such an outcome of friendship.

"So, when's the day?" Ben asked, "And do I get to be best man?"

"Well, what do you guys think about this? We're going to have a minister here this weekend. It's perfect timing. We don't know if we'll get another chance, given the nearness of the end of time. We can always get the license later from the County Clerk in Spokane."

"What do you think, Guillermo? Do you think he'll do it?" Ben turned to their host.

"I'm sure he'll be happy to do that, if your commitment to the Lord is sincere and your vows are true," he turned to Gerry and Lisa directly. "We can have the baptism tomorrow and the wedding on Sunday afternoon. That will give us enough time to prepare for a nice celebration."

When they finally bedded down for the night, they were a very excited bunch and could hardly find sleep until late that night: Gerry and Lisa because their dreams were being realized; Guillermo and Elizabeth because they had come to really love these young people, and Rita because she was looking forward to seeing Ricky again and introducing him to her dear friends.

But it was Ben who had the most trouble finding sleep. He hadn't realized how much he was in love with Joyce until his friend had disclosed his sudden engagement and imminent marriage. He too wanted to be married to a lovely Christian girl such as Joyce. Of course, he had not courted Joyce directly but had given her some indications of his affection for her. But the questions nagged on his mind. *Will we have another opportunity later on? What if we don't get to see a preacher again? Can I stay with the group, seeing Gerry and Lisa's happiness without enjoying my own?* Suddenly he felt very lonely. He reached over and gently took Joyce's hand who eagerly responded by squeezing his.

"Joyce," he finally whispered, "we need to talk sometime tomorrow." Joyce was now fully awake, and in her great anticipation, found it difficult to go back to sleep.

Sabbath morning came and everyone was up early. They had to straighten out the house quickly because there would be lots of company that day. Guillermo's large living room had become the meeting place for a number of Covenant Keepers in the area, so around nine in the morning people began to arrive. Guillermo and Elizabeth welcomed everyone, did all the proper introductions, and made everyone feel at home and comfortable.

"Pastor Fred, I'd like for you to meet our new friends from Spokane. This is Gerry and his fiancée Lisa, and their classmates Ben, Joyce, and Rita."

"I'm so pleased to meet you all. It's always so invigorating for us oldies to be surrounded by youth," Pastor Fred told them as he shook hands with everyone.

"The pleasure is all ours, Reverend," Gerry answered on behalf of the group.

"Please, not Reverend…just Pastor," Pastor Fred replied with a smile.

"Yes, sir…if you'd rather. I just assumed all ministers should be addressed as Reverend since that is the custom among Christians."

"We'll I'll be glad to explain why a little later, Gerry. Right now I'm getting ready for today's program," Pastor Fred said kindly.

Before the singing began, Guillermo pulled Pastor Fred aside and informed him that his services would be required for a baptism and a marriage ceremony, to which he very gladly agreed.

Ben hurried through the morning chores, helping to set up for the fellowship meeting, which would start promptly at 9:30. But once everything was done, he gently took Joyce by the hand and escorted her out the door and toward the country road.

"C'mon, Joyce, I need to talk with you," he said rather nervously.

"Well, this sounds rather mysterious, but I'm game," she answered with a warm grin. They walked until they were out of earshot of the others.

"Joyce," he began softly, "we've known each other now for two years. We've had some good times and a few bad times, but we've always managed to help and encourage each other. I think part of the reason is that…" he paused, searching for the proper words to say, "…that you have become a very special person to me. What I'm really trying to say is that I… I'm convinced that I'm in love with you." He had to stop there and catch his breath, which gave Joyce a chance to get over her blushing and slow down her quivering lips.

"I…I didn't know how long it would be before I'd hear you say that to me, Ben. You see… I feel the same way about you…ohh, let me say it right…I love you, Ben Woodhouse!"

Ben didn't give her a chance to continue. He put his arm around her small waist and drew her to him and gave her a kiss that left them both exhilarated.

"Joyce," Ben said now, more excited than ever. "I had planned to tell you how I felt a little later down the road. The main reason I'm telling you now is that we have a fabulous opportunity to get married tomorrow, alongside of Gerry and Lisa! Oh, Joyce, I know this is really sudden, but we don't know about the future. Things are so uncertain in our present day, and we are convinced that we are living in the time of the end. When the Prince returns, I'd like for us to go already united for eternity. I think I can bear whatever is coming if I have you as my lovely wife by my side!"

"Oh, Ben, my dearest Ben! The answer is yes before you even ask!" she exclaimed as she threw her arms around his neck and kissed every inch of his cheeks, laughing and crying at the same time.

"Hey, we'd better get back. They're probably wondering where we disappeared to." Ben grabbed Joyce's hand as they ran back laughing and short to breath.

They snuck in quietly, as the group had started to sing a song of praise. The service was the first one the group had attended on a Saturday. It felt a little strange and at the same time exciting. To be meeting on the day the Lord had created and reserved for fellowship with His creation was very special to all present.

Pastor Fred preached a very encouraging sermon, assuring the presence and protection of Prince Jesus

during the difficult months ahead. He closed with a short message about the importance of baptism, and how it is a symbol of cleansing from sin and the beginning of a new life. Then he announced that there would be nine persons sealing their acceptance of God's Covenant through baptism. He had only planned for four, but to his delight, Guillermo had informed him that five young people had made their decision the night before.

As they sang a song, they all walked down to one of the deeper and clearer pools at the river. Although it was still summer, the water was deliciously cool and refreshing. One by one, Pastor Fred took the hands of each candidate in his left hand for support, while he raised his right hand toward heaven, invoking a blessing in the names of the Father, the Son, and the Holy Spirit. Then he would place his right hand behind the neck and lower the candidate totally under the water, as John and Jesus taught their disciples to do.

After Ben was baptized, he waited for Joyce to be done, and then gave her a big hug. Then something unexpected happened. Ben raised his hand and asked to speak. Everyone was silent, not knowing what Ben was going to say.

"I'd like to say something to my friends here and to all our new brothers and sisters present. This has been a touching and wonderful experience, one that brings a lot of joy and hope to my heart. I am looking forward to a very long and exciting friendship with all of you and with all Covenant Keepers of all the ages and throughout the whole world. I also have some other exciting news to share with you. "He took a very deep breath through a very big smile.

"Tomorrow, our dear friends Gerry and Lisa will join their lives forever through a marriage ceremony. You all know that because it was announced this morning. What you don't know yet is that…" he looked at Joyce who was smiling and blushing at the same time, "…is that someone I have come to love very deeply and who loves me just as much, has agreed to share my life through marriage… and that we will be married tomorrow, if Pastor Fred doesn't mind doing two for the price of one."

"I would be truly delighted to do so," he replied, as a pandemonium of cheers and hugs took place in the very river. Lisa and Rita were so excited that as they hugged Joyce, that they lost their footing and ended up under the water again. They came up laughing and coughing up the water they weren't able to keep out. Gerry got to Ben as quickly as his legs could move through water and gave him a tight embrace, and Guillermo didn't worry about getting his clothes wet as he went in to do the same. It was a very fitting end to a beautiful baptismal event.

It was a beautiful Sabbath day, garnished with a great potluck lunch in the midst of natural surroundings. After a brief rest, Pastor Fred talked to the group about heaven and of the glorious description of the Holy City, the New Jerusalem, as described in the book of Revelation, chapters twenty-one and twenty-two. The new members of the

Covenant community were filled with amazement at the love of God who provided such a fabulous city and existence for His people.

But such amazement was surpassed by the story of what it cost to provide all of this for us. That the Son of God, being God himself, should put aside the immeasurable glory which was His from eternity and the worship and admiration of all the angels and heavenly beings, to come to this sin-sick world to suffer rejection, violence, and pain and to finally lay down his life before a furious mob of his own countrymen, that is beyond the human mind to comprehend. Every heart was deeply moved that afternoon, and songs of praise and gratitude could be heard down the river for quite a distance.

Evening came, and once the other guests had left, a flurry of activity broke out in Guillermo and Elizabeth's house. Everyone was so excited about the weddings that creativity was well mixed with laughter and a happiness that could be hardly contained. Lisa and Joyce had not come prepared for a wedding, so they had to borrow skirts and blouses from Elizabeth and the guys borrowed white shirts and ties from Guillermo.

In all the flurry, Joyce paused to look at Rita and, seeing her eyes wet, took her by the hand and led her out to the porch.

"Rita" she said, "I feel so excited about my wedding tomorrow… that I can't help but feel guilty at having so much joy… because it seems but we have left you out. This must bring some sadness to your heart…I mean, you know… having had this happiness at one time and now being alone without Ricky. I'm so sorry, Rita. I so wish that he was here to hold your hand and rejoice with us."

"Oh, you misunderstood my tears, my dear friend," Joyce replied with the broadest smile her face could muster. "I'm not the least bit sad. I weep for joy that you and Ben and

Gerry and Lisa have found each other and that now you all will enjoy that special fellowship that God intended all men and women to enjoy. As for me, I treasure the thought every day that soon the Prince will return, and on that day, He will deliver my Ricky back to me. Oh, won't it be wonderful, Joyce, you and Ben, Gerry and Lisa, Guillermo and Elizabeth, and Ricky and me, all together…living in that beautiful city as neighbors and friends forever?"

"I should have known that a friend like you could only be rejoicing with me! You are really something, you know? That's why you're so special to all of us. Thank you, Rita.

"Thank you for being just who you are." Joyce regained her smile as she hugged her friend tightly for a few seconds.

As everyone prepared for bed, Gerry approached Pastor Fred with some curiosity about their exchange over the title of Reverend.

"You seemed rather determined not to be called Reverend, Pastor. I'm curious to know why it makes any difference to you."

"Right, Gerry. I did intend to give you an explanation. You see, the title Reverend cannot be used to address any human being. It is a sacred title that belongs only to God. Suppose you open that Bible to Psalms one hundred eleven and verse nine and read it to me," he said pointing to Guillermo's Bible on the corner table.

Gerry found the verse and read, "He has sent redemption to His people; He has commanded His covenant forever: Holy and Reverend is His name."

"Did you catch the meaning, Gerry? Reverend is the description or definition of God's sacred name. It's blasphemy for any human being to use that title for himself or to allow others to address him that way. The title of Reverend appears only one time in the Bible and it only describes God Himself."

"Whoa! I never knew that! I don't think other Christians know that, either. I guess you never know these things until you study the Bible very carefully," Gerry responded thoughtfully.

"But there's more. I have heard people use the title "Holy Father" to address another human being. That title is extremely sacred, and it also appears only one time in the whole Bible. In the Gospel of John, chapter seventeen, Jesus is in private conversation with God the Father. In one of the most fervent prayers recorded in the Bible, Jesus, in verse eleven is asking His Father to keep His disciples safe from the fury of Satan and of the world. No other Bible writer has recorded that title, much less allowed it to be used for the glory of any human being. Go ahead and read it."

"'…Holy Father, keep through Your name those whom You have given Me, that they may be one, as We are.'"

"How's it possible for so many Christians to have overlooked this? It appears to be very clear. Thank you, Pastor. I'm so glad that you explained this to me. I will be very careful with God's names from now on."

"I'm glad you understand, Gerry. And now, we better get some sleep. We have a very exciting day ahead of us tomorrow."

NO WAY!

"I can't believe it! I saw the whole thing! You all stood around like a bunch of quivering idiots, while that odiferous Guillermo and his puppet minister completely snatched that group of simpletons right out of your hands! Tell me, Vesuvious, how would you like your wings plucked off–one good wrenching tear or little by little as a Beelzebub enjoys doing?" the gravelly voice seared through Vesuvious as if the torture had already begun.

"Please, my lord Lucifer. I left Petrocious in charge, since he's our specialist at twisting the truth about the Sabbath. I trusted this task to him, since he has been foremost among us in convincing the Christian world that the Sabbath was changed by direction of your enemy Himself. He failed! He's responsible! Let his wings be torn off!" Vesuvious was shaking badly and his voice quivered as he addressed his dreaded master.

"Petrocious! Front and center!" the voice that conveyed terror boomed across the enormous cave. Petrocious, simmering in fear half stumbled toward the marble stage.

"You are one of my most talented fiends. You have served me well in the past, and I still have a lot of important tasks for you. So, I will not give you the punishment you deserve. But you failed me badly, here. And I need to remind you of where your allegiance lies. Beelzebub! Spend the next half hour retraining Petrocious. Just be sure he can still fly when you get done with him!"

The shrieks of pain and terror coming from the torture chamber were soon drowned out by the angry barking of a gravelly voice.

"The Sabbath! Ha! It's going to be just like the wretched white woman said! I will work at cross–purposes with God. I will empower my delegate, the man of sin, to take down God's memorial, the seventh–day Sabbath. Thus, will I show the world that the day sanctified and blessed by God has been changed. That day shall not live in the minds of the people. I will obliterate the memory of it. I will place in its stead a day bearing not the credentials of heaven, a day that cannot be a sign between God and His people.

"I will lead the people who accept this day to place upon it the sanctity that God placed upon the seventh day. Through my vice–regent, I will exalt myself. The first day shall be extolled, and the Protestant world shall receive this spurious Sabbath as genuine. Through the nonobservance of the Sabbath God instituted, I will bring His law into contempt. The words 'a sign between Me and you throughout your generations' I will make to serve on the side of my Sabbath. Thus, the world will become mine. I will be ruler of the earth, king of the world. I will so control the minds under my power that God's Sabbath shall be an object of contempt!"

NEW BEGINNINGS

That night, it was very difficult for anyone to fall asleep. The air was still charged with the excitement of the evening and the anticipation of the morning. Still, everyone managed a few hours of rest, but once the sun began to light the morning sky, nobody overslept.

Elizabeth was already up, and soon the sound of hash browns sizzling on the grill and the aroma of hot, whole-wheat pancakes permeated the whole house. Pastor Fred had been up an hour earlier, studying the Word and communing with his Heavenly Father. Soon everyone was up, clearing the living room before a short morning praise session followed by a great breakfast.

The wedding was to take place outdoors with the altar set up between two large pines, already witnesses of God's creative power and his ability to nurture and maintain that which he had ordained. The organ had been moved to the porch where, at 10:00 a.m. sharp, Elizabeth made it sing with full treble and bass resounding among the surrounding hills.

All the Covenant Keepers from the day before had arrived, most of them carrying useful and precious gifts in grocery bags for the favoured couples: beautiful homemade quilts, a lovingly crocheted shawl, a finely polished set of silverware handed down for several generations…just beautiful, fine gifts that made the heart almost burst at such sacrifice and generosity.

Pastor Fred spoke beautifully about marriage, one of two cherished practices instituted by God at the time of creation, the other being the Sabbath rest. Both were intended to last through eternity, and for those who cherish them, it will be so. Wedding vows were exchanged, and a fervent prayer sent to heaven for the blessing and protection of the new homes being formed. Guillermo's rich baritone could be heard for quite a distance as he sang The Lord's Prayer. And then the moment came that always causes smiles and cheers: Ben and Gerry took their brides into their arms and kissed them until they blushed.

During the dinner celebration, Pastor Fred approached the two grooms and began some casual conversation.

"Well, what do you boys propose to do next? Where do you go from here?"

"I suppose we'll be heading back to Spokane to continue hunting for jobs. The prospects are dismal, but we need those jobs more than ever now, being husbands and all!" Gerry winkled at Ben as he emphasized the husband part.

"No, it doesn't look too good in Spokane," Pastor Fred agreed. "Tell you what, though, my nephew Joseph mentioned to me that a new government program–to help prepare the poor for a seemingly disastrous winter–is hiring people to chop and bind firewood for the folks in Oregon and to export to other states. They just announced it two days ago, so there might still be a chance for you boys."

"Say, Gerry, maybe we should go down and see." Ben was ready for any opportunity. "Pastor, did your nephew say where one can go to apply?"

"Why, yes, Ben. I believe he said that there's an office in Bend," the pastor replied.

"Now, wait a minute, Ben! How're we going to get there? Gas is more than $5.00 a gallon. We don't even have enough to get back to Spokane!" Suddenly Gerry was feeling down. Fortunately for them, Guillermo had listened in on the conversation and came to the rescue.

"Hey, guys, don't fret about the gas. Elizabeth and I are giving you your wedding presents in green paper. Here's and envelope for you and Lisa, Gerry, and one for you and Joyce, Ben."

They called Lisa and Joyce over and eagerly opened the envelopes, to find two beautifully hand–painted wedding wishes, and three crisp one–hundred dollar bills for each couple. Suddenly they were mute with emotion and amazement. Ben found his voice first.

"Guillermo, you can't do this! This is a lot of money! I mean… how can you afford to give this much money?"

"No, Ben, it's not too much money. We have been blessed greatly throughout the years, and now we must bless others. Besides, we don't have a lot of time left to use it, and we don't want to leave it behind when we leave. You kids have brought a lot of joy to our home, and now we want to give you a little start on you new life. Here's an envelope for you too, Rita. It will help you get some things you might need."

It seems like tears of joy and gratitude had become a frequent response to life in the last few days. God was so good to them through the love and generosity of others! After all the hugs and thanks, they settled around the living room to watch the latest news from around the world.

NATURE GONE BERSERK

The events around the world had continued to deteriorate. Millions were dying every month from starvation in Africa, India, the Middle East, and the Far East, while severe shortages and even hunger were threatening the Americas, and all Northern and Southern Europe. The American desert had spread to almost half the continent due to so many fires and extended drought. The fruitful valleys of California and Washington now produced about one fourth of previous crops, and much of it was in black market hands.

The President of the United States was in continued consultation with religious leaders, trying to determine if there was anything that could be done to appease the wrath of God for the nation's former indifference toward religion and its descent into violence and immorality.

The Religious Right, now practically ruling the country, kept pushing the President toward the establishment of a religious state, for only that way could the people be forced to mend their ways and regain God's favor. The President had been resisting because of the Constitutional ban on the establishment of religion by the state. But things were getting pretty desperate.

Congress, on the other hand, was ready to amend the Constitution, doing away with the despised establishment clause and "returning America to its religious roots." The debate was hot, but the balance was going in favour of the religious amendment. After all, wasn't the government already encouraging church attendance on Sunday by handing out government food coupons at services?

The United States was not the only country going that route. Under the urging and leadership of the Great Shepherd, at his headquarters in Babilovia (a small city–state in Europe), the idea of uniting to seek God's favour was spreading rapidly. Previously Europe had been almost totally disinterested in Christianity, Northern Europe, and China had been strongly influenced by either communism or some form of humanism, while the Middle East, parts of Africa, and India were immersed in Islam and Asia in various forms of paganism. Now, everyone seemed eager to compromise their belief systems for the sake of safety, security, and basic survival needs.

It was a really critical time for the senior population in America, as elsewhere. In the USA, Medicare was a thing of the past, Social Security had gone bankrupt several years before, and medicines were out of reach for even the middle class. Hospitals were full of people dying for lack of equipment, materials, and attention. Tuberculosis was now rampant, and leprosy had escaped the boundaries of the leprosarium, as its patients sought food and medicines where there was none. HIV was no longer a medical priority, and more people were contracting AIDS. At this point, Guillermo turned off the T.V.

"I don't think I can take any more bad news tonight, how about you all?"

"You're absolutely right, Guillermo," Pastor Fred responded, and everyone else agreed. "It's going to get a lot uglier before the whole thing is over. But we need to focus on God's promises if we're going to keep our sanity. After all, we do have such great and precious promises in God's word that we don't have to get depressed over what's happening in the world. We just have to be sure that we are on God's side, committed to keeping the covenant, so that we may be sheltered when the storm comes in its full blast."

That evening, there was some devotional time dedicated to songs of praise and a short reading of the word of God. Pastor Fred focused on God's promises of care and protection during the end time.

"Psalm twenty-seven is one of my favorites," he said. "Please read it, Rita,"

"'The Lord is my light and my salvation; whom shall I fear? The lord is the strength of my life; of whom shall I be afraid? When the wicked came against me to eat up my flesh, my enemies and foes, they stumbled and fell. Though an army may encamp against me, my heart shall not fear; though war may rise against me, in this I will be confident.'"

"Thank you for asking me to read that, Pastor," Rita continued. "I needed that so much. Sometimes I feel so alone in the world, but God in his loving mercy has given me these wonderful friends who have become my family. So thank you all. You too, Guillermo and Elizabeth!"

Joyce put her arm around her friend, squeezing her shoulders. No words were needed. That was how everyone felt about each other. The pastor offered a fervent prayer to God, especially asking for protection for the little group, as they would travel in the morning.

They all went to bed confident and somewhat excited to know just what God would have for them next.

Dawn found everyone still asleep, except for Elizabeth. She had risen to prepare, not only an abundant breakfast, but also an ice chest full of bread, fresh and dried fruit, nuts, some cheese, and some vegetables and plastic dinnerware. But the smell of hot pancakes, simmering oatmeal in cinnamon, and scrambled eggs can break the spell of dreamland, and soon there was an excited bunch of campers huddled around the table.

Suddenly, Pastor Fred came rushing from his bedroom and headed for the T.V. set.

"I was just listening to the morning news on my podcast. Something serious has happened in Texas, and I think we all need to listen to this." He turned on the T.V. and all the Channels seemed to be talking about the same thing.

"Three oil refineries and four bio–fuel plants were the targets of terrorism early this morning. It appears that bombs were set off almost simultaneously and the inferno had destroyed other buildings and dwellings nearby and killed about 275 people living near the refineries. The fires are beyond control and will probably destroy most of the refineries before they go out. The President was notified immediately, and it is expected that he will be making a statement within the hour."

This was stunning news, and suddenly nobody was very interested in food. There was a long silence as each one took in the meaning of this feared event.

"C'mon, everybody! I poured my heart out into making this breakfast, and I don't plan to eat it by myself," Elizabeth broke the silence and tried to be cheerful. "C'mon, do I have to read Psalm twenty–seven again? Do I have to remind you that God is in control, and that He is watching out for us? He has a plan, young people, and the first part, I believe, is a good breakfast to get our brains started on some creative thinking!"

"You're absolutely right, honey," Guillermo worked up a smile, and led the group back to the table. They seemed to recover their appetite, even as they discussed the possible repercussions of that morning's news. They left the T.V. on low volume so as to catch the president when he came on. Within a half hour, they heard the familiar, "Ladies and gentlemen, the President of the United States."

"Good morning, my fellow Americans. During the last couple of years, this country has been facing one crisis after another. Yet our resilience and commitment to supporting our democratic institutions has pulled us through. I expect that this new attack will again prove the mettle of our people. During the last five years, we have seen the price of gasoline go up due to the war in the Middle East and to the destruction of oilrigs in the gulf by violent hurricanes. Now we face the bombing of these refineries as a cowardly act by our enemies, who shall not go unpunished. We will do everything in our power, and use all of our police resources to pursue these bandits and bring them to justice.

"Meanwhile, there are some measures that must be taken in order to deal with the emergency. The first measure has to do with fuel conservation. Gasoline and bio–fuel supplies are going to be severely restricted. So I have made a decision that I know will be very unpopular but is absolutely essential. I have directed all fuel companies and distributors to restrict the sale of gasoline to government and emergency vehicles, public transportation such as buses, and the sector of the trucking industry transporting food supplies. Local bus schedules are being posted on local T.V. channels and on the internet at emergencyschedule.gov. This measure shall be in effect for the next six months and has the force of a national law. Anyone not falling into the above–mentioned categories who is caught buying or selling gasoline shall be prosecuted to the full extent of the law.

"The second measure to be implemented, beginning this weekend, is the closure of all business and sports facilities on Sundays. All good citizens are expected to be at the church of their choice. The reasons for this measure are threefold: first, we want to promote family unity, and give opportunity for parents to spend time with their children talking to them about drug use, unsafe sex practices, underage smoking and alcohol use, and loyalty to their country. Second, we need, as a nation, to seek God's favour on behalf of all the suffering this country is going through with all the natural disasters occurring around us. Ever since Hurricane Katrina destroyed much of the South in 2005, Mother Nature has grown increasingly vicious, producing more hurricanes, tornadoes, and floods in one sector of the country, while drought is eating away the formerly productive sections of our land. Earthquakes on the west coast and central plains have destroyed many roads and structures, making travel difficult and leaving many dead and homeless. It is expected that all Americans of good will and of patriotic hearts will respond to this measure, which will also have the force of law.

"Thirdly, this measure is intended to flush out the enemy responsible for the terrorist attacks against our infrastructure and institutions at one end of the spectrum, and those who, to a lesser extent are disloyal to our American ideals and unsupportive of our laws. If anyone is not at church on Sunday, we want to know why. It is not essential to be a believer in order to be a supporter. Therefore, let us all unite in rebuilding our crumbling country, revitalizing our institutions, and bringing back our national pride and the glory that was once America. God bless America, and God bless you all."

The mood in the living room was somber, as the President finished his speech. The newlyweds were especially downhearted as they contemplated the future. Gerry was most always the leader of his little company, yet this time words were hard to find.

Finally, he said with almost forced cheer, "The only way to respond to this blatant attack on our religious freedom is to remember who we are and where we are going. Until we met Guillermo, we were spiritual drifters with no godly direction to our lives. Now we know that the only true God in heaven is in charge and in control of His universe. Whatever presidents and legislators want to do or say must not weaken our determination to be faithful to God's truth."

"Well said, Gerry," Guillermo responded, "and you are all welcome to stay here and ride out the storm. We can work together to survive and spend time spreading the good news to the people around us. I believe there are people who have not heard the biblical truth as Jesus taught it and that many will also become Keepers of the Covenant."

"Thank you for your always wonderful generosity, Guillermo. But I'm afraid we won't be able to stay. We have Lisa's parents to think about. We must go back and make sure they are out of danger and taken care of. I also want to see my mom and try to reason with her. Perhaps the latest events will persuade her to quit that organization and join us." Then, as an afterthought, "And if we're lucky, we might even find Ahmed."

"Very well, Gerry. Let me at least take all of you down to Sandpoint. I know the buses stop there for sure." Turning to the whole group, he said, "Ya'll better pack your stuff. The earlier you leave, the better your chances of getting a seat on the bus."

Once everything was packed and loaded in Guillermo's double–cab pickup, they gathered in the living room, forming a circle. Holding their tears back, they bowed before the Prince of Peace as Pastor Fred led in a fervent prayer for their safety, asking that God would lead them until the Great Gathering when the Prince would return as King of Kings and Lord of Lords.

They gave Elizabeth and Pastor Fred hugs of gratitude and then boarded the pickup for the trip down to Sandpoint. Conversation was light, focusing on what steps they would take once they had taken care of Lisa's parents. It had been decided by Gerry and Ben to go on down to Bend, Oregon, and see about those jobs Pastor Fred had told them about. Rita decided to go with them, for she had nothing waiting for her in Spokane.

AN UNCERTAIN FUTURE

The bus ride was long and tiresome. Like the proverbial milk run, the bus stopped in every town and along the road wherever anyone flagged it down. It was now the main source of transportation for travellers. Once in Spokane, they walked the twenty blocks to Joyce's house, backpacks flopping with every tired step.

"Oh, kids, we're so glad to see you!" Mr. Griggs expressed with a deep sigh of relief as the young people walked through the door. "You have no idea what we have gone through this weekend."

"Dad, are you all right?" Lisa said anxiously. "Is Mom okay?"

"Yes, honey, we're okay. It's just that the marshal came Sunday morning, just before we were going to church, with an eviction notice. The house has been foreclosed on, and they want it right away because there is someone ready to buy it and move right in. We didn't know what to do and were hoping you'd get here as soon as possible."

Lisa reached out to hold and comfort her mom who was crying with her apron over her eyes. "Don't cry, Mom. Everything is going to work out. I know how much you love this place. I myself have a lot of wonderful memories growing up here. But now we have to be brave as we go through this time of trouble. It's going to be tough for everybody in this world until the final storm passes. But we must not hold on to anything here. We have such a great treasure of peace, joy, and everlasting life waiting for us...oh, Mom, wait till I tell you about everything that happened this weekend!"

Mrs. Griggs gave one last wipe of the apron over her eyes, and with a slight smile of curiosity awaited Lisa's account. Everyone in the group was suddenly smiling with anticipation in sharing the good news.

"Well, to begin with," Lisa had to take deep breath because of her excitement, "we had a wonderful time with Guillermo and Elizabeth. They are the greatest people, friendly and generous to a T. There was a gentleman staying with them who is a minister by the name of Pastor Fred. He preached a most wonderful sermon on baptism and its meaning. So guess what? All of us were baptized this weekend!"

"That's wonderful!" Mr. Griggs exclaimed. "Was it by immersion, the way your mom and I were baptized many years ago in the Baptist church?"

"Yes, Dad. And it was so cool, 'cause we were baptized in a river, just like Jesus was baptized by John the Baptist. But that's not all! Sit down, Mom. You might not be ready for this…" Lisa had to stop and take a really deep breath. "Gerry and Ben got up the courage to propose to us, and we…we accepted. We got married yesterday, Mom, Dad! What do you think?" The Griggs' surprised faces turned to big smiles as they rushed to their daughter to hug and kiss her. They hugged Joyce too, and Ben and Gerry.

Then came the question: "But why so rushed? You didn't have time to plan a nice wedding! We would have enjoyed being present!" Mrs. Griggs asked, a bit disappointed.

"Oh, Mom, I'm truly sorry, but it was a very difficult decision. You see, with the crisis in which we find ourselves and with being Covenant Keepers, it would have been very difficult to plan a wedding on a Sunday and even to get a minister to do it. Since Pastor Fred was present and happy to perform the ceremony, it seemed logical to go ahead with it. We just didn't know if we would have another opportunity like this again. And we love each other so much, Mom and Dad… we want to be together till the end," she finished as she held tightly to Gerry's arm.

"Oh, it's okay," Mom said with a smile. "I'm so glad that you young people found each other. May the Lord bless your homes and take you to the one He's prepared for you in His kingdom." Then she looked at Rita. The beautiful young Hispanic had been their daughter's friend since high school. The older couple considered her almost as their own child. They felt sad for her as they saw the happiness in the other's faces.

"What about you, Rita? Is there a young man waiting somewhere for you?"

"Oh, yes, Mrs. Griggs! There definitely is!" Rita answered with a wide, bright smile. "The Prince of Life has Ricky's life in the palm of His hand, ready to give him back to me!" she said triumphantly.

"For the Lord Himself will descend from heaven with a shout, with the voice of an Archangel, and with the trumpet of God. And the dead in Christ will rise first. Then we who are alive and remain shall be caught up together with them in the clouds to meet the Lord in the air. And thus we shall always be with the Lord."

1 Thessalonians 4:16–17

"That was precious, Rita!" her friend put her arms around her, as everyone was touched by such an expression of faith and hope.

"Well, now that you are here, we should plan what to do," Mr. Griggs opened the more immediate subject.

"We have been thinking of going down to Bend, Oregon. Pastor Fred said that the government was hiring people in some energy conservation project. We've had no luck here, so we might as well go and try. Since you no longer have a home, Mr. Griggs, perhaps you and Mrs. Griggs would like to go with us. That way we could all look after each other."

"It's very kind of you to think of us that way, Gerry. We certainly can't stay here. I've asked our neighbors, the Larsens,' if we could store our furniture temporarily in their barn, and they were kind enough to say yes. If you young men can help me move everything tomorrow, we can leave the next day."

It was all agreed; the next day they would spend the day emptying the house and preparing for the journey. But Gerry still had one more thing to do–visit his mom. He borrowed Mr. Griggs' old bicycle and pedalled over to his mother's house. Sonia was still up, working on some forms from the office. Gerry didn't knock. He gently put in his key and opened the door. He stood there, taking in the scene. *Mom was always a diligent worker. That's why she always got ahead in life,* he thought.

"Hi, Mom," he said softly yet loud enough to startle her.

"Gerry! It's good to see you, my son," she sprang out of her chair and almost ran toward him, grabbing him in and embrace. "Oh, Gerry, I'm so sorry for the things I said before you left. I could never mean anything like that. I'm so glad you're home! Have you eaten? I have some spaghetti left with a delicious sauce, just like you like it."

"Thanks, Mom, but I had a good dinner at Lisa's house. I just wanted to drop by to see how you were doing."

"I'm glad you came, son. I'm just fine. I'm getting some statistics together for Senator Collins, who will be addressing the Family Life Coalition on Wednesday. He's running in the primaries for president, you know, and I am in a favourable position to be in his campaign committee. Working in these local family life organizations has opened a lot of doors for me. But what about you? How was your weekend out in the country with the hoot owls?" She couldn't avoid a sarcastic smirk.

"Well, get ready for all this,' cause it was a very exciting weekend. I picked up the gang at Lisa's house and we went to visit Guillermo and Elizabeth."

"And how are my old friends, Guillermo and Elizabeth?" she asked somberly.

"They are just the greatest people, Mom, and they sent a warm hello and their sincere wishes to see you again."

Sonia said nothing, but Gerry could see that she had little interest in her former friends.

"Now, this may come as a shocker to you, but I…I was baptized by immersion this weekend along with the rest of my friends." He kind of blurted it out and then held his breath for a response.

"You what? You were baptized? How did that come along? I didn't realize you were that much into religion, much less one that is not legitimately recognized by this country!" Sonia was now visibly upset.

"Mom," Gerry now went bravely on, "I am now a Covenant Keeper. We are a people destined to tell the world the truth about the origin and destiny if this world and to help prepare the people for the soon return of Christ to this earth."

"Well, go tell somebody else, Gerry. I don't want to hear your version of it. I always had doubts about Guillermo's influence, and now that I have been working with the true religious leaders in this country, I am convinced that he is wrong. We've got to focus on the positive things, Gerry, on what we can do for the suffering and for society in general," her tone shifted for a moment as if pleading with him. "All this talk about doom and judgment only scares people; it doesn't help them at all. Please, Gerry, forget all this nonsense! I can get you a good position in the coalition–a good salary, good benefits, food ration cards, even a government vehicle for you to get around and maybe even find a level headed girl and settled down."

"Uh…that's another thing I need to tell you about, Mom. You know that I have known Lisa now for two years, and we've grown very fond of each other. Well…" Beads of perspiration were forming on his forehead. "Well, we got married this Sunday, by one of our preachers who was visiting at Guillermo's."

Sonia was speechless for a few moments. She regained her composure, for she didn't want to say the wrong thing this time. "Okay, Gerry," she said deliberately. "I am not going to make the mistake again of turning you out of the house. But I will tell you this, if you bring Lisa to live here, life will be very difficult for all of us. There will be an obvious uneasiness between us. And besides, if you two are not going to get with the government's programs because of your religious beliefs, that's going to put my position at risk, and I cannot tolerate that. So you have some decisions to make, and you'd better make them soon."

"Thank you for letting me decide, Mom. I already have, and tomorrow we will be leaving for Bend, Oregon, where we believe we'll find jobs." He paused, long enough to swallow hard as he prepared his farewell. "Good-bye, Mom. I'll try to keep in touch."

He bent over and gave her a quick kiss on her left cheek before she could resist, but Sonia made no effort to return the gesture. He turned quickly and made his way out the door, with great pain in his heart and tears in his eyes. He knew not how long before or if he would ever see his mother again.

The next morning was spent on loading and unloading Mr. Griggs' wagon, pulled by a tractor, from their house to the Larsens.' Mrs. Griggs packed an ice chest full of non-perishable food items for the long journey. They notified the bank that the house was being vacated and the keys would be left on the kitchen table.

With backpacks harnessed on and taking turns carrying the food chest, they walked the twenty blocks back to the bus depot. Soon they were on their way toward Bend. Though they tried to be cheerful, deep inside they all had some misgivings about those jobs and some anxiety as to whether they'd find food and lodging for the seven of them.

Once they arrived in Bend, they sought out a park area in the outskirts of town and set up their tents for the night. Since camping had been one of their favourite activities in the past, they were cheerful about their accommodations. They next morning they left everything inside their tents, took only the necessary documents, and headed into town to the employment office for government jobs. After several inquiries of strangers and even the police, they arrived at the right place–an old two–story building which had functioned at one time as the local heating oil company.

Gerry felt personally responsible for representing the group, so he went up to the information window and addressed the heavy–set lady behind the desk. "Good morning. I am inquiring about government jobs which had been announced about a week ago, something about preparation of alternative fuels."

"Honey, it ain't nothing but just plain wood chopping and trying into bundles. No fancy names here." The lady was kind, but went straight to the point. "There's been so many people come for those few jobs, and I feel bad to have to tell you what I've already told so many–those jobs are gone. They've been filled. I'm so sorry. Did you come from far?"

Gerry's face fell with disappointment. "Yes, ma'am. We came from Spokane. Is there anything else available? We are three married couples, and we're strong and willing to do anything." He was almost pleading.

"I'll tell you what, come back tomorrow. Something new appears every so often. Perhaps your luck will be better then." The lady was sympathetic but had nothing to offer them.

Gerry returned to the group, and as he approached, they could read the frustration on his face. He informed them of the conversation, and expressed his regret for having led them there.

"I'm sorry, guys. I just don't have a whole lot of alternatives to offer you."

"Oh don't feel bad, Gerry. We are all in this together. The Lord is in charge, and we must submit to His will and His plan. You watch! Things will start happening very soon," Ben tried to cheer up the group.

For four days, the little group went to the employment office only to return to their tents with no hope for jobs. The food had run out on that fifth morning, and they were returning to their tents not knowing where they would get their next meal. As they waited at an intersection of the signal light to change, a truck approached at a fast pace, trying to beat the red light as he maneuvered a right turn. The little group had to step back to avoid being hit by the extended mirror on the passenger side. It was a government vehicle, and the driver seemed to be in a real hurry.

He turned briefly to make sure he hadn't hit any of them, and almost lost control as he came to a screeching halt about sixty feet down the street. He stepped out quickly and walked toward the group, smartly dressed in his Forest Service uniform, cap, and dark glasses. The little group suddenly found their heartbeats accelerated, and a sense of anguish in their throats as the officer approached. Gerry immediately stepped forward to meet him and deflect any possible danger to the others.

"Gerry? Is that you?" the officer asked with a creeping grin on his face, as he took off the hat and the dark glasses.

"Ahmed!" he practically shouted and immediately grabbed his friend and embraced him with a very heavy sigh of relief. He immediately turned to the little group who was still recovering from the surprise. "Hey, guys, it's Ahmed!"

The recovery was quick, and they all surrounded the young officer as they took turns hugging and welcoming the former threat.

"What in tarnation are you all doing here? What brought you down from Spokane?" Ahmed's questions were fired one after the other.

"We came here looking for jobs, but is looks like they're all gone up in smoke." Ben spoke with despair in his voice.

"Well, I'll see what I can do for you. Meanwhile, let's have some lunch. I have a lot to tell you and I want to hear all about your latest adventures." Ahmed was so excited to see his friends that he put his current mission aside for a renewal of old times.

"Uh, Ahmed, I'm sorry to tell you that we have no food or money left. This trip has taken everything we had, with the hope that we would soon be able to replenish our funds." Gerry was sad and apologetic.

"I'm sorry, my friends. But don't worry. I have plenty of food ration cards that I've accumulated over the last few months. I get them just for being a government employee, but don't use them 'cause I get all my meals at the camp mess hall. Tell you what, there's a government commissary across the street. Let's go there and get you all supplied for a couple of weeks while we try to find jobs. What do you say?"

"Well, if you're sure this won't cause you any trouble, Ahmed...we sure could use the help!" Gerry's eyes brightened.

"C'mon, then, let's go load up." Ahmed led the relieved group through the commissary doors, and grabbing a couple of grocery carts, they began to gather the more essential items for the preparation of their meals. Once they had their carts full, they headed for the cash register.

"May I see your ration cards, please?" the clerk requested as they put the items on the counter. Lisa handed over the cards and watched nervously as the clerk turned them over and over again. She looked up at Lisa and said rather sternly, "These cards are expired! Why weren't they used when issued? How did you get a hold of these anyways? These are issued to Forest Service personnel!" She turned abruptly and grabbed the telephone by her aside.

"Security to counter number five! Security to number Five."

The men had stood at a little distance talking as the ladies had shopped and now, as they overheard the commotion at the register, they rushed over just as two armed security guards briskly approached the now frightened little group of ladies.

"What seems to be the problem, Miss Applebaum?" one of the guards inquired as he looked suspiciously on the group, now made larger by the presence of the men.

"These people here," she answered disdainfully, "are trying to get rations by using outdated cards not previously issued to them."

"All right, now, let's have some reasonable explanations. First of all, where did you get these card and why are they expired before use? Second of all, which of you is a Forest

Service Officer?" the second question coming with a note of sarcasm.

Sweat broke out on everyone's face as the officers stared them down. Slowly, Ahmed made his way from the back of the group to face the inquiring security guard. It seems they had focused their attention on the trembling ladies and had not taken notice of the young man in full uniform, his hat in his hands, or perhaps they thought he was a curious bystander.

"I am the Forest Service Officer, and those cards were issued to me. Since the base camp serves all my meals, I never use them. I saw these folks in the street and they looked hungry, so I decided to help them out. I'm sorry; I never noticed that they had an expiration date. Please let these people go…it was my mistake." Ahmed was hoping and praying that would put an end to the inquisition.

"Okay, officer. It seems like an honest mistake. No harm done." The security officer replied. "However, it boggles my mind that anyone should be out in the street hungry, when ration cards are available to everybody everywhere. They are being issued through the churches. Haven't any of you requested them at church on Sunday?"

They looked at each other, each one hoping that one of the others would have a good explanation. They especially focused on Gerry, who already had experience as the group spokesman. So he took a deep breath, and facing the officer bravely said, "We don't attend church on Sunday."

"You don't attend church on Sunday?" he asked incredulously. "What do you mean you don't attend church on Sunday? What other day is there to go to church? Everybody goes to church on Sunday! Are you some of those holdout Jews? Or maybe some of those dissident Covenant Keepers?" his voice was getting loud and angry.

Gerry was breathing a fervent prayer to God, asking for valor and strength at this moment of crucial testing. *Please dear God, don't let me falter when you most want my witness. Don't let me shame your name, nor give your enemy the victory. In Jesus name, Amen!*

"Don't just stand there staring like an idiot! Answer me! Are you or are you not a dissident!" The guard was now shouting almost at the top of his voice. Every shopper in the commissary had stopped what they were doing and were crowding around the frightened little group.

Gerry felt Ben's presence by his side as his friend put his hand on his shoulder for support and strength. Yes, sir, we are Keepers of the Covenant, and as such, are committed to observe and keep holy the original Sabbath day established by God in the Old Testament and confirmed by Jesus and His apostles in the New Testament. Furthermore–

"Stop your jabbering! I'm not interested in your perverted doctrines. If I have to listened to religion, I'll put up with it on Sunday. Meanwhile, I have orders to arrest any dissident, so you are all under arrest." He said with relish, as both of the guards pulled their guns. "Any resistance and you will be shot immediately. Willis, you watch them while I go get some more handcuffs."

"You'd better get and extra set!" another voice came from the group, which startled both the little band as well as the guards. A murmur was also heard among the small crowd of shoppers, as they watched Ahmed taking his place next to Ben.

"Officer, what is the meaning of this?" the guard appeared shocked. "And why are you trying to protect these misfits? Go back to your duties, sir. This is none of your affair!"

"I'm afraid it is very much my affair. You see, I too am a Keeper of the Covenant!" Ahmed answered with an almost defiant tone, and then turned and grinned at his dumbfounded friends. Gerry and Ben couldn't contain their almost shocked thoughts. *Ahmed? A Keeper of the Covenant He practically stomped out of Guillermo's house at the mention of the covenant! What has happened to him since we saw him last. How did that miracle take place?*

"I see…" the guard said with a look of concern. "You realize that you're throwing away your career, your freedom, and your self-respect. Are you sure you want to stick with your declaration? I can forget I heard it, if you want me to!"

"You can forget it if you want to. But it will not cease to be true. I will never be anything if not a Keeper of the Covenant and a faithful follower of Jesus, the Prince and soon–coming King of Kings." His voice was now one of humble confidence and bounding courage.

"Very well, be a fool, if you want to. I will bring an extra set," he said as he turned and walked to his office while they waited for his return. Gerry and Ben turned with uncontrolled curiosity to Ahmed, who was obviously expecting their whispered inquiries.

"Ahmed…I can hardly believe it! In fact, I wouldn't believe it if I hadn't heard it directly from your lips! How did it happen?"

"Shhh! We'll have time to talk later. I'll tell you every exciting detail later on."

"But, Ahmed, you could have walked out a free man! Don't be a fool! Tell the guard you're sorry and that you're not really what you said!" Gerry had decided to test Ahmed's veracity.

"The Prince needs fools like me, for the foolishness of God is wiser than men.' Paul said that in 1Corinthians 1:25, now hush! We'll talk later."

He's quoting Paul? He knows the Bible that well? Oh. Dead God! Thank you! Thank you for this miracle of your wonderful grace! Help us all to be strong and faithful till the end, no matter what happens. Please keep us together, for we love each other. Strengthen us to withstand whatever trial is ahead, that you name may be glorified in us and that we may glory in the cross of our Lord and Savior. Gerry was satisfied, and he now held his peace as he turned and gave the others a reassuring smile.

By the time the guard returned, there was a Humvee parked outside the door waiting for them. They were handcuffed and led out amidst boos and derogatory remarks from the shoppers who had witnessed the scene.

"Throw them in jail, and throw away the key!"

"Dissenters aren't deserving!"

"Make them pay the price!"

The humiliation was hard on them, and they eagerly climbed into the Humvee so as to get away as soon as possible. The ladies wept softly but visibly, while the men held back their own tears and comforted the ladies. Following Gerry's directions, they drove by the park, where the soldiers tossed all their belongings on their laps and at their feet, except for the tent, which they wrapped up and dumped in a trashcan.

Soon they arrived at their prison, formerly a high school that had closed due to budget restrictions. But at least this school had not been a prison for very long, and the buildings and facilities were still in a good state of repair. Security bars had been installed at all the windows and doors, and desks had been replaced with army cots and footlockers.

Everyone was taken to the gymnasium for processing and assigning of "barracks." The women were assigned different quarters from the men for practical purposes. This was to be a heart breaking moment for the little group. Upon learning that all of them were married except for Ahmed and Rita, the captain in charge gave them a break.

"All right, you have half an hour to say your good–byes, since you won't be living with each other for quite a while, at least until your trials come up."

Ahmed and Rita stepped to one side to allow the married ones a little more privacy. The others just held one to each other and whispered all the things their broken hearts could bear to say.

"Ahmed, I can't believe that you can be so calm at a time like this! Do you realize what can happen to us?" Rita was quite shaken by the events of that day.

"My dear Rita," Ahmed put his arm around her shoulders, "It will take you some time to understand and absorb what I'm going to tell you. The Apostle Paul went through a time just like this, a time of persecution and imprisonment. But I read something he said that really struck me today as I made my stand for the Prince, 'for if we live, we live to the Lord; and if we die, we die to the Lord. Therefore, whether we live or die, we are the Lord's (Romans 14:8).

"And days before he was to be executed, he wrote to his close friend, Timothy: 'For I am already being poured out as drink offering, and the time of my departure is at hand. I have fought the good fight, I have finished the race, I have kept the faith. Finally, there is laid up for me the crown of righteousness, which the Lord, the righteous Judge, will give to me on that Day, and not to me only but also to all who have loved His appearing' (2 Timothy 4:6–8)."

"Thank you, Ahmed. That was beautiful. I really needed that, and I'm going to share it with the others. Don't worry about me…I'm going to be all right."

Meanwhile, Gerry addressed the couples with words of encouragement and schemes for any possible communication. After a final long hug and kisses, they were separated by the guards and taken to different quarters to begin the long wait until a trial could be set up.

Life in prison was hard at first. The most difficult thing was the separation between husbands and wives and friends. At least, however, they would be able to talk through the fence and touch each other's hands for a brief time each day as they were let out for a little sunshine and exercise.

They were eager to exchange stories about their experience as new Keepers of the Covenant. Ahmed's story was particularly exciting.

"You mean to tell us that you have established a friendship with an angel?" Ben asked with eyes full of wonder.

"Yes, Ben. It was awesome to eat strawberries from heaven and to ride in a car fuelled by a mysterious source of power! I'm telling you, it was the most fantastic experience I could have ever imagined. I guess the Prince must have thought I needed something really dramatic to change the stubborn course of my life and to destroy my resistance to His invitation."

"Wow, that is awesome!" Gerry was also very impressed. "We've got to share this with the ladies tomorrow. This is so great, I'm sure it will boost their spirits and increase their hope for the near future."

Just then, a tall, handsome young soldier opened the door and stepped into their quarters, carrying a metal basket covered with a plaid cloth.

"Good afternoon, gentlemen. My name is Jerrod, and I have been assigned to take care of your needs. I understand that you haven't eaten all day, so I hope you enjoy what I have brought for you. Your ladies have already been fed, according to your custom. Enjoy! I will return for the basket in an hour," and he turned around without another word and walked out, locking the door from the outside.

The little group quickly opened the basket and pounced on fresh hot bread, a large bowl of lentil stew, and a variety of fresh fruit.

"Man, this is great stuff!" Mr. Griggs expressed his delight. "if we get fed like this every day, this prison might not be so bad!"

"If we get fed like this every day, we better do a lot of exercise. Otherwise they will have to roll us out of here, that is, if we can get through the door!" Ahmed quipped with a wink as he served the last of the stew.

Jerrod stepped into the room an hour later to pick up dishes and any possible leftovers. He was to be disappointed over the leftovers…there weren't any. As he was about to leave with his burden, Gerry stepped up and held him by his arm.

"Pardon me, but we'd like to get to know you better. You are the first person to treat us with such kindness since we were arrested. We want to thank you, and let me tell you that meal was really good!"

"Well, I want to make sure you're well taken care of. You see, the officers in this command don't know something I'm going to tell you, and please promise that you won't let this get out: I too am a Keeper of the Covenant. So you and your wives and Rita are in good hands."

Gerry was overcome with emotion and had to turn to the wall while the others felt the same feeling of awe and gratitude to the Prince for this provision. *Oh, dear God, how wonderful you are to us. Thank you for sending Jerrod to take care of us. Please protect him from any harm or discovery of his identification with us. Amen!*

They all recovered quickly from their surprise and stepped up to shake Jerrod's hand and to welcome him into their fellowship.

"Jerrod," Ben began, "we don't get enough time or privacy with the ladies to tell them everything we would like. But we know that they are anxious to hear how Ahmed became a Keeper of the Covenant. If he tells you the story, would you be kind enough to share it with them?"

"I would be very delighted to do so. Go ahead Ahmed. I'm listening." Jerrod said as he sat on the nearest foot locker and the others sat on the nearest bunks. The weeks passed one by one and their trial was not set up. The little group of Covenant Keepers whiled the time away reading a Bible that Jerrod had smuggled into the prison.

They comforted each other with God's promises and with the welcome messages from the ladies' quarters that were carried daily by their faithful friend and keeper. The world outside was suffering greatly due to a lack of food, severe storms, drought, and the lack of sufficient fuel for the most basic needs. Yet somehow, Jerrod managed to keep the little group well fed and their other needs met. He washed their clothes and their bed linens and always managed to find a bar of soap and an occasional razor.

About eight months into their imprisonment, there was a sudden stir of activity at the old high school. Trucks began to arrive and prisoners were transferred somewhere else.

Jerrod had managed to get information as to the movements, since he had access to the daily chatter among the troops. He would pass the information to his incarcerated friends.

"What's happening out there, Jerrod?" Gerry asked him when he brought breakfast in.

"There are orders to move all the prisoners out of here. It seemed that the Three Sisters are about to blow their tops, and the much observed Oregon Bulge near here is bound to make things much worse than what those three volcanoes can do,"

"Whoa, brother! We've been expecting something to blow out of that bulge for a long time. So where are they taking us?" Mr. Griggs inquired.

"The word is that you're going to the former military compound at Hanford. It's been a nuclear waste site for years, but when the stuff got too hot, they got everybody out of there and closed it down. Now they are using it to house all prisoners in the Pacific Northwest, hoping the radiation will do them in and save the country any further expense. There's already a very large group of Covenant Keepers there, though I hear none of them have died from radiation. Somebody sure must be looking after them!" he said with a broad smile and a wink.

At the military commander's office, there was some confusion. The orders to move the prisoners were clear. However, the Central Command for the Pacific Northwest had not made any provision for fuel.

"Captain Darnell," the voice was loud and angry over the phone. "You get those prisoners up to Hanford by tomorrow, do you understand? Those are your orders!"

"Yes sir, Colonel, I do understand the orders. What I don't understand, sir, is how I'm going to execute those orders without any fuel. We have just enough to maybe make it to the Washington border."

"I'll call you back in ten minutes, Captain. I must confer with the Washington headquarters as to what to do. Meanwhile, load them up, you hear?"

"Yes, sir," the frustrated captain replied as he passed the orders on to Lieutenant Carson.

The prisoners were led out of the classrooms and loaded onto three Humvees. The first two held prisoners who had been caught in various crimes–black marketing, looting, murder, etc. For some reason that God seemed to have ordained, the little group of Covenant Keepers were reunited in the last vehicle of the convoy. The wives and husbands, holding on to each other for the first time in eight months needs no description beyond exceeding joy, tears, hugs, and praise to the Prince for at least this much–needed closeness.

The phone rang and the orderly informed the captain that the colonel was on the line again.

"Captain Darnell, here, sir."

"All right, Captain, if you reduce the number of Humvees, can you make it to Hanford?"

"Yes, sir. If we reduce the convoy by one Humvee, and take its fuel in containers, I believe we will barely make it."

"Can you pile all of the prisoners into the other two Humvees?"

"No, sir. We are already filled up to capacity."

"Who do you have in the third Humvee?" the colonel was growing impatient.

"We have a group of misfits, sir, some Covenant Keepers. What do I do with them?"

"Offer them a chance to repent from their stupidity! If they do, let them go and fend for themselves. If they refuse, take them a little into the forest and shoot them. The less of them, the better. Do you understand my orders, Captain? The general will cover for you."

"Yes, sir, loud and clear!" The captain called Lieutenant Carson over out of hearing of the prisoners and gave him his orders. After freeing or shooting the prisoners, he and the sergeant were to walk into town and take one of the last buses to Spokane, where they were to report to the detachment there. The lieutenant assented quietly, and the captain returned to the first Humvee. The lieutenant ordered the last vehicle's gas emptied into military containers that were then attached to the sides of the other two.

What in the world is going on here? Gerry's mind echoed the perplexity of the whole little group as the lieutenant ordered them out of the Humvee. They saw the first two military vehicles disappear into the distance as Lieutenant Carson addressed them in harsh tones.

"All right, you misfits. This is your lucky day. The military command has decided to grant you your last opportunity. I have here a document that requires your signatures stating that you are giving up all of this religious garbage and that you are willing to submit to the requirements of the state and of the state church. Step right up and at least put an X if you can't write," he smirked, as he ended on that humiliating remark.

Nobody moved. They looked at each other, perplexed by this turn of events and alarmed by what the alternative could be.

"Don't just stand there like a bunch of dumbbells! This is your chance to be free! Okay, just nod your heads and I'll enter your names on the document."

Ahmed stepped forward, took the document from the lieutenant's hands, and tore it into pieces as he boldly spoke right into his face, "We are keepers of the Covenant, not cowards! Do what you must, Lieutenant. We know in whom we have believed!"

The lieutenant became infuriated by Ahmed's daring and struck him in the face with such force that his nose and mouth were now bleeding.

"All right, Sergeant, let's go do what we gotta do. You lead, I'll follow behind." Then, pointing at Gerry and Ben, he barked an order. "You two, grab those shovels. Let's go, on the double!"

They started marching toward the edge of the forest, and everyone knew what was about to take place. The women shivered in horror, and the husbands were dumb with fear. Then slowly and at first softly, Ahmed began to sing. "Amazing grace, how sweet the sound…"

Rita joined him on the second line, and by the second verse, they were all singing. A cooling breeze was coming from the forest and seemed to give wind to their spirits, as in their minds they realized that indeed, "whether we live or die, we are the Lord's."

About four-hundred feet from the road he ordered them to stop. "All right, you men will dig a trench four feet wide and ten feet long by four feet deep. Unless, of course, you prefer for your bodies to rot on top of the ground, and for the birds and badgers to eat you up."

A strange calmness possessed the little group of Covenant Keepers as the men toiled for several hours to dig the prescribed trench. At about three in the afternoon, the lieutenant finally said, "That's goods enough. You women go down and join the men, standing in front of them. We figure on saving as much ammunition as possible," he said with a sarcastic laugh. The men helped the ladies into the trench, and each husband held on to his wife, while Ahmed held on to Rita. As the lieutenant and the sergeant took their positions, and loaded their weapons, they whispered their goodbyes to each other, speaking words of faith and hope.

Ahmed looked at the lieutenant, the blood caked dry on his face, and said to him in his kindest tone, "Before I die, I want to ask your forgiveness for my brash disrespect. I should not have done what I did. Please forgive me, sir."

"Forget it, misfit, that won't save you!" was the harsh reply. The two soldiers finally lifted and pointed their weapons. "On three, sergeant: One, two…" A screeching of vehicles coming to a stop on the road interrupted the count. Lieutenant Carson whirled around to see what the commotion was about. He saw a military limousine with a two star flag on each side, followed by a Humvee. The driver of the limo stepped out and walked around the front to open the door to a tall, distinguished looking Major General. The high official walked briskly toward the lieutenant who met him halfway and then stood stiffly at attention with a smart salute.

"As you were, Lieutenant! I understand that you have here a group of dissident Covenant Keepers, is that correct?"

"Yes, sir," the nervous lieutenant responded, looking straight ahead as if penetrating the senior officer.

"Well, I'm taking personal responsibility and custody of these people. I will dispose of them personally. Release them immediately and load them into the Humvee behind my car!"

"Yes sir!" and turning to the sergeant still standing by the trench he ordered, "Bring the prisoners out, Sergeant, and load them on the Humvee."

One by one, they marched single file toward the vehicle. The general, turning his back to the lieutenant, stepped over closer to the trail as if to inspect them carefully. The little group was filled with amazement at their last–second reprieve, but did not dare to look into the face of their liberator, not knowing what he had in store for them. But Ahmed could not resist his curiosity. He looked up directly into the face of the general, and gasped at what he saw.

"Jebosh!" he whispered out loud, but could say no more. The general smiled, winked with one eye, and put his finger to his lips. "Shhhh, not now, Ahmed."

A TIMELY RESCUE

Suddenly his feet were so light, he had to control himself to keep from jumping for joy. The general followed them and, upon nearing the Humvee, said to the driver, "Captain Jerrod! You have your orders. Proceed." Then turning to the lieutenant and the sergeant he said, "You men have fulfilled your mission. Do as Captain Darnell instructed you, and report to the detachment in Spokane." He returned their salute and sped away in his limousine.

Once the Humvee was out of sight, the joyful confusion began.

"Jerrod! It's really you!" Ben was beside himself with excitement. The others also expressed their delight at having their good fellow believer driving them to freedom.

"Wait a minute! Early this morning you were just a corporal. How did you become a captain in a few hours?" Gerry was eager for details.

"I'm sorry! I didn't tell you everything about me. I became a captain as easily as Jebosh became a general. I am also from Sector 35X and have been assigned to assist all of you during this final journey of earth's history."

Meanwhile, Lieutenant Carson reached for his cell phone and called Captain Darnell to report the general's intervention and to ask for any further orders.

"You what? You let the misfits go? Who was the general who gave you those orders?"

"It was Major General Jebosh, sir, I assume he is from Central Command Headquarters. He turned the prisoners over to a Captain Jerrod." Lieutenant Carson was surprised that the captain was not aware of the change in plan.

"Who is General Jebosh? I've never heard of him or of Captain Jerrod! Hold on a minute, Lieutenant…" and turning to his orderly, he barked, "Bring me the Command Staff Roster, quickly! (there was a long pause) Lieutenant! There is no General Jebosh in the roster nor a Captain Jerrod! Either you're lying or you were duped, Lieutenant!"

"All I can tell you, sir, is that everything appeared genuine to me–the vehicles were U.S. Army standard, the uniforms were legitimate, he seemed to know you personally–I had no basis on which to question him, sir."

"All right, Lieutenant," the captain was exasperated, "Which direction did they take? Can you at least tell me that?"

"They seemed to be headed north, sir, perhaps back to Spokane, where they originally came from."

"Return to your detachment, Lieutenant. You and the sergeant will have to make a fully detailed report when you arrive. I'll personally take his case from here."

Lieutenant Carson was now really perplexed. Could this really have been a pair of impersonators with counterfeit vehicles and all? But everything seemed so real! I should have asked for his ID and a copy of the new orders. Now, he probably also had a fake ID and orders. Well, we'll see where this is going to take us!

Captain Darnell conferred immediately with his superiors, informing them of what had taken place.

"Personally, I'm not too concerned about the Covenant Keepers," Colonel Gooding said, seeming to be in deep thought. "Sooner or later they will be caught, since everyone in the country has been warned to keep an eye out for them. Someone will turn them in. What really concerns me is having someone impersonating a high-ranking officer on the loose and interfering with government missions."

"I agree, sir. Do I have your orders to pursue this matter? I may be able to head them off on their way here."

"Yes, Captain. I'm assigning your complete detachment to this mission. Block the main roads coming in from Oregon between Goldendale and Walla Walla, checking especially for any military vehicles on the road. If they are caught, you will bring them directly to this command. Are there any questions?"

"No questions, sir. The orders will go out immediately." Captain Darnell smiled with relish at the chance of catching those who tried to make a monkey out of him. *They will pay dearly for this!* he thought.

The captain mobilized his men immediately, and they left in groups of four toward the different key highways to watch for the little group of Covenant Keepers. He also stationed men on highway ninety going west of Spokane as far as Ritzville and east as far as the Idaho border going into Coeur d'Alene. Jerrod, however, was aware of what was going on, and he smiled as he thought on the foolishness of fighting against the forces of the Prince of heaven. I guess the evil captain has never read what the Prince said through His friend David, *'The angel of the Lord encamps all around those who fear him, and delivers them!'* (Psalms 34:7).

"This is Captain Darnell; let me talk to Sergeant Wilson... Wilson, any news yet?"

"Yes, sir. I'm at a gas station in Biggs, just before the bridge crossing over into Washington. One of the attendants told me that he saw a military limousine and a Humvee about half an hour ago. They didn't cross the bridge into Goldendale. Instead, they took I-84 East toward Hermiston.

We didn't make it here soon enough. I recommend we watch highway 730 before Hermiston, as they might want to catch 395 North through Tri–cities and up toward I–90."

"All right, Sergeant, pursue toward 730. I'm taking a helicopter and I'll have a reception for them at the junction of 730 and 395." The little group of Covenant Keepers were having a joyous ride, singing songs of praise and thanking Prince Jesus for His wonderful care. Jerrod helped pass the time talking about his home in the Beautiful City.

"Everything you've read in the book of Revelation about the New Jerusalem is true, but John ran out of words to describe the beauty of the place. You are just going to love living there! The buildings, the parks, the aquarium–let me tell you about the aquarium. It isn't a tank where the sea life is held captive, no! There is a large lake in the middle of the city, and all the beautiful creatures that live there come into the aquarium area to play with us. The grass is a living green, the flowers truly out of this world, the fruit of the land, well… let Ahmed tell you just about the strawberries, eh, Ahmed?"

"We don't have words to describe the taste. Awesome is the closest I can get," Ahmed smiled broadly.

"Sickness and pain and death are not known there. We have only known about it as we have watched, grief stricken, the tragedy of your land. But your reward includes eternal youth, and vigor, and strength, and a life that will never end. This is the reward of those who have been willing to put it all on the line for the honor of God and 'loved not their lives, even unto death' (Revelation 12:11)."

"Say, Jerrod, I have a question for you. Mankind has this insatiable curiosity about outer space and what is out there. We have walked on the moon, and set up a space station in orbit around the earth, at incredible cost and even human sacrifice. Humans are so fragile that elaborate efforts have to be made to preserve life in space with special suits, and oxygen tanks, and much more. Yet you and Jebosh travel through space as easy as I walk down the street. How do you do it?" Gerry asked, his eyes wide with wonder.

"I am not permitted to share these secrets with you yet. The science of God's universe is so incredible! But, if you are faithful till the end, you will not only learn all of this science, but will rejoice in experiencing it first hand. You will all have the opportunity of traveling through space and visiting, not just that white little orb called your moon, but vast worlds, enormous galaxies and planetary systems, and meet holy beings also created in the image of God, and you will meet them is their original perfection. Oh, it's going to be marvellous, Gerry!"

"Oh, I could go right now, Jerrod," Rita said, her heart bursting with longing and excitement, "how much longer do we have to wait?"

"It won't be long, Rita," Jerrod answered with a smile. Then his expression changed. "Earth must now go through the worst time in its history. The Prince will soon cease His intervention on behalf of mankind and will put aside His robe as High Priest in the temple in heaven. Then the grand ceremony will begin: the crowning of the Prince as King of Kings and Lord of Lords. But during that process, you will witness a time of trouble as has never taken place on the earth. The seven last plagues, talked about in the book of Revelation, will be poured out on the world, and the final separation will take place between those loyal to the Prince of Life, and those loyal to the Prince of Darkness. The enemy of Christ will make his last effort against His people to destroy all of you. But be faithful, for surely he will come back for you."

There was solemn silence for a while as each member of the little group pondered all of this in their hearts and recommitted themselves to the Lord's care.

Captain Darnell had caught up with the military vehicles just as they approached, the fork at I–84 and Highway 730. He had picked up his right–hand man, Lieutenant Carson, and together they were now pursuing the little band led by the general and his captain. As they approached the interchange, the Humvee turned into 730 but the limousine stayed on I–84.

"Look, Captain, they're splitting up! The misfits are heading north! We can block them as they approach the bridge into Washington." The lieutenant was in earnest. "Easy, Carson. We already have a roadblock there. I'm more interested in nabbing that fake general who made a monkey out of you and of the whole army," the captain retorted as he gave instructions to the helicopter pilot. By this time there were additional Humvees on the ground in pursuit of the limousine, as well as state troopers. Because of the gasoline shortage, however, they soon started to drop out of the pursuit as their tanks went dry.

It was dark now, and since Jebosh did not turn on any lights, it was hard to keep track of him or the limousine. He pulled off the road unseen into some dense brush, and abandoned the car as his pursuers continued at high speed down the road.

Shortly thereafter, as Captain Jerrod continued on Highway 730, he noticed someone at the edge of the road waiting for a ride. He knew who it was, so he pulled over, and General Jebosh stepped in. What a thrill it was for Ahmed as he gladly introduced his heavenly friend to the group. Everyone noticed his handsome, manly appearance, and his gentle demeanor. He smiled brightly as they expressed their gratitude for his intervention. Soon they were entering Umattilla and approaching the bridge over to the Washington side of the Columbia River. From a distance one could see all the bright lights of the blockade, with Humvees lined up across all lanes, allowing for only narrow passage as vehicles were checked and allowed to pass. Soldiers armed to the hilt were everywhere, while Captain Darnell, who had given up the chase on the vanished limousine, hovered in his chopper overhead.

"Here they come," an excited Darnell shouted into everybody's radio. "Take your designated places and point your weapons. Do not fire until you hear my orders, is that clear?"

"Yes, sir." Lieutenant Carson, now on the ground responded crisply.

Inside the Humvee, the little group looked at the general. Ahmed, who had the closest relationship with Jebosh, smiled as he asked, "What now, General?"

"Captain Jerrod, wait till they can see the whites of our eyes," he chuckled, "and then make this ship fly!"

Captain Darnell was mystified. This driver had no intention of stopping at the blockade. Instead, his Humvee was gathering speed, and coming at the troops at about, it seemed, 200 miles per hour.

"Open fire! Open fire now!" he shouted with desperation. But nobody responded. Every soldier was awed at the sight. The heavy three–ton Humvee had taken off into the air as gracefully as a Phantom jet on a runway. The helicopter pilot had to jerk the chopper rather abruptly to avoid colliding with the flying Humvee, but not before Captain Darnell caught a good glimpse of General Jebosh, sticking his head out the window and smiling as he waved his hat. Pursuit would be ridiculous, since the Humvee seemed now to be traveling near the speed of light.

The chopper touched down, and a very depressed captain stepped out. Lieutenant Carson was quickly by his side.

"How did that happen, sir? Tell me that you saw what I saw… that I didn't imagine it!"

"There's only one explanation, Carson… witchcraft! Those lousy misfits are heavy into witchcraft! That's why we have to destroy them on sight! They're in league with the devil himself."

Inside the Humvee. There was also awe and silence. There were tears of joy and gratitude, and lumps in throats that were to overcome with emotion to speak. Jebosh stepped over and, with a big grin, touched each one on the shoulder, the lumps disappeared, and the excited little group expressed their wonderment.

"How did you ever do that, Jerrod? That was the most thrilling experience I've ever enjoyed!" Ben exclaimed.

"The law of gravity is one of God's laws. He gives us control over it when it is necessary to take care of his loved ones. Someday, you will also have control over gravity as you wing your way throughout His wonderful universe. Enjoy the ride!"

They landed on Highway 95 near the junction where one enters Bonner's Ferry.

"We have to pick up two more passengers here," Jebosh stated as Jerrod directed the Humvee toward Don's house. As they approached the house, they noticed that soldiers were stationed at the entrance to the driveway and at the front and rear of the house. Don and Deena were under house arrest and waiting to be picked up by military authorities. As they approached, the sentry snapped to attention, having recognized the officers inside the Humvee.

"We're here to pick up the dissenters, Corporal."

"Yes, sir, right this way, sir." The corporal almost tripped over his own feet as he led the Humvee to the house.

I know this place! Gerry thought. *This is the guy who gave us gas when we ran out on our way to Guillermo's place!*

"Hey, guys! Remember the older guy with the hot MG who gave us gas sometime back? This is his place." And turning to Jebosh, he asked, "Are these folks Covenant Keepers?"

"Yes, they are." Jebosh responded with a warm smile. "I'm sorry for Captain Darnell! He'll be sorely disappointed!"

They had no trouble getting them out and into the Humvee, for this contingent of soldiers were under a different command in Idaho and had not heard of the incidents with the general and his captain.

Once on Highway ninety-five again, they headed for Guillermo's place. After all the introductions, Don and Deena sat the rest of the way, thrilling to the stories of God's love expressed through these wonderful, supremely powerful yet gentle beings, who have spent the last six thousand years watching over and caring for God's faithful people.

Before they knew it, they were at Guillermo's. they stepped out in front of the house, and eagerly headed for the porch. Jebosh and Jerrod accompanied them. As they filed in, Guillermo and Elizabeth were overjoyed and relieved to see them come back safety. Then Guillermo was transfixed as he saw the angels still in their military uniforms.

"Jebosh! You've returned, my good friend!" and he rushed to hug the large figure looming in his doorway. "But what's with the military getup? And who's the captain with you?" he asked with a puzzled look on his face.

Jebosh let the little group do all the explaining. They were so excited as they told of the events of the last week that they kept interrupting each other and laughing at their eagerness to talk. Meanwhile, Jebosh and Jerrod removed their military uniform and returned to the living room in gleaming white robes with a silver band around the waist and a multicolored band at the bottom border. It was an awesome sight to behold.

About an hour later, when the conversation began to slow down, it occurred to Guillermo that his friends might be hungry. So he and Elizabeth hunkered down in the kitchen, preparing good fast food: quesadillas, Spanish rice, and frijoles de la olla. It was delightful to watch Jebosh and Jerrod relishing human food. The friends were moved by such condescension on the part of these exalted beings that had become their best friends.

"It's time for us to go," Jebosh began as he and Jerrod rose from the table. "We have other errands to do for the Prince. You must plan to leave here by tomorrow. Captain Darnell's fury has been multiplied a hundred fold, and he will be scouring the country with his troops. He is extremely angry, especially toward me. But since he cannot harm me, he will seek to take out his vengeance on any Covenant Keeper he can find. You can be sure that we will be watching over you, but you must be obedient and not put yourselves at any unnecessary risk.

"Go up into the mountains… you will find shelter, and water and food will be supplied to you. Good–bye, for now. We'll see you soon."

They never heard an engine start, but they stood at the porch and watched the Humvee disappear down the road for the last time.

INTO EXILE

There was lot of preparation to be made. The little band had lost everything except for the clothes they had on. Guillermo distributed his clothes among the men and Elizabeth among the ladies. The men's clothes didn't quite fit, since Guillermo was a little huskier than the others. But they were happy just to have something clean to change into after a good, refreshing shower. Non-perishable food items were placed in backpacks and other portable containers, and some camping gear and utensils were also packed for the journey.

They finally slept their last night in that comfortable country cabin, rising before the sun, to begin the most amazing camping trip of their lives.

Elizabeth went from room to room, looking at the things she had cherished for most of a lifetime, as if saying goodbye to old friends. As she walked out the door, she thought contentedly, *"as much as I loved these things, they are as nothing is comparison with what my Prince has in store for me. Thank you, Lord for easing my departure with your promises!"*

"Let me brief you on out trip before we take off," Guillermo instructed the group. "I know these woods quite well, and there are several good hideouts not known to outsiders. As we travel throughout the day, we must stay in single file, keeping as much as possible under the shade of the trees. That will keep us cooler, and if some surveillance aircraft should pass overhead, it might not detect us. We'll start off by going down to the river and walking through the shallow areas for several miles. That way, if they bring dogs, they will not be able to find the trail right away. If anyone has any other ideas that will help, please don't hesitate to speak up."

"Sounds like a good plan to me, Guillermo," Ben replied. "Lead on; we'll follow."

The little group of Covenant Keepers, aware of the dangers still ahead for them, cheerfully stepped into the water and slogged on for seven or eight miles. They finally came to a spot where the water became a waterfall, so they stepped out and began to climb the mountain, staying close to the water so they could get back in it at the top of the mountain. It felt so good to walk in water on a hot day such as that.

They finally left the water and found a nice spot for lunch and relaxation. Guillermo's dog entertained himself chasing squirrels and birds as they ate. After a good rest, they shouldered their burdens and took off into the thicket under Guillermo's lead. It was a long day, but they finally arrived at a sheltered spot with a wonderful view of the valley below.

"Come see your quarters for the next few weeks or months," Guillermo invited the group behind some large bushes. Pushing them aside, he revealed the mouth of a cave, which was very conveniently hidden from sight. Inside it was cool, but dark. It was a perfect hideout for sleeping and protection from wild animals. Just beyond the clearing, among some large rocks, a spring provided fresh cool water. The little group just couldn't do anything more than to fall on their knees and fervently praise and thank the Lord for the provision of their most basic needs. Then they set up a little shower stall with the vegetation surrounding them, and, filling a special five-gallon plastic bag with water from the stream, each one enjoyed a luxurious shower after a long, hot, dusty day.

Captain Darnell walked into his office the next morning and glumly sat to write out a report of the previous day's events. He didn't know how to start. *How am I going to write a report about a flying Humvee? I'll be laughed out of the Army! Well, no… there were about thirty witnesses there! All the soldiers saw it! Colonel Gooding will have to believe it.*

"Good morning, sir," the orderly interrupted his thoughts.

"We have received a report from Central Command that General Jebosh and his captain struck again last night."

"Where?" the captain was startled to his feet by the announcement.

"In Idaho, sir, at Bonner's Ferry. The Idaho Command had some troops holding a couple of old Covenant Keepers on house arrest until the official orders could come to take them into custody. Last evening, it seems, some Major General arrived in a Humvee, took the prisoners off their hands, and disappeared. They never saw the Humvee again not the direction they took."

"Drat, those stupid troops! Another group of nincompoops who couldn't take the initiative to call headquarters to verify the identity of those fakers nor of their supposed orders!" The captain was overwrought with anger and frustration.

"Colonel Gooding called earlier, sir, and wants you to call him right away. I'll have him on the line in just a moment." The orderly returned to his desk to put the dreaded call through.

"Darnell!" the colonel half screamed his name, and the captain cringed. "I've been informed of what happened last night! And don't you think for a moment that I'm going to believe that cockamamie story about flying Humvees, you hear? I don't know how you blew that mission, but don't you dare write out a report with supernatural excuses... are you listening to me?"

"Yes, sir, I hear you loud and clear."

"Now, listen up, Darnell! I've arranged for you and your Lieutenant Carson to have access to other command areas so that you can pursue this matter. I didn't do this because of your competence, but because you have more knowledge of this case than anyone else. I understand you even saw the impostor face to face, is that right?"

"Yes, sir, I saw his face as he... well, yes, sir, I did!"

"All right. I'm sending over an artist for a composite picture. Give him an accurate description and then get your body over to Idaho. I understand that's his last locus of operation."

"Yes, sir, right away, sir." The captain was now sweating profusely.

"Don't blow it again, Darnell! I'm sticking up for you one last time. After this, you are on you own."

"Yes, sir, thank you, sir!" Captain Darnell's mind was racing and agitated. *I think I hate this colonel almost as much as I hate the fake general! But at least the colonel is on my side. As for this general, if I find him, I don't think I'm going to bring him back alive! The jerk has almost caused me to be court-martialled! I'll get him if it's the last thing I do!*

The breeze was cool as it rustled through the trees around the clearing in the mountains. It was Gerry and Lisa's turn to cook for the little group, but Lisa was feeling sick that morning, so Ben and Joyce stirred up the fire and set the pot to boil for a delectable vegetable stew. They had used most of the time during the last two weeks clearing a small piece of forest and planted a number of vegetable crops using seeds that Guillermo had accumulated over the years. Some were already sprouting, and soon they would be able to eat off the land. They spent time every day studying the Bible, seeking to understand more of God's plan for their lives. Guillermo was a great teacher, but even he prayed earnestly for guidance and a humble attitude as he shared with the others what he had learned.

MEANWHILE, IN THE GREAT TEMPLE

In the Holy City, the New Jerusalem, there was a flurry of activity, as preparations were made for the grand coronation of the Prince of Peace, now to receive His title of King of Kings and Lord of Lords and begin His reign over the universe for the rest of eternity. A few moments before, a most solemn event had taken place. Everything stood still, and all heavenly persons paused and bowed their heads for the defining moment in planet earth's destiny. The Prince stood before the altar in the Great Temple and, putting down the censer, declared with a most solemn tone, "…The time is at hand. He who is unjust, let him be unjust still; and he who is filthy, let him be filthy still; he who is righteous, let him be righteous still; he who is holy, let him be holy still. And behold, I am coming quickly, and My reward is with me, to give every man according to his work. I am the Alpha and the Omega, the Beginning and the End, the First and the Last" (Revelation 22:10–13).

Then Prince Jesus moved on to another apartment of the Great Temple, where He removed His priestly robes and attire and dressed in His kingly robes. From there, He would be led to the coronation, which was to take place before God the Father, who would place the universal crown upon His scarred head, the same precious head that once bore a crown of thorns for an ungrateful race.

Jesus' declaration was also the signal for the Holy Spirit to cease the work He was doing on behalf of mankind. The Spirit had been attempting to reach every human heart, appealing to the conscience and enlightening those who responded to the Prince's sacrifice by yielding their lives to Him. For almost two thousand years, He had represented the Prince on the earth and had successfully persuaded and transformed millions of people into future citizens of the Holy City. But many millions more had rejected the offer. And now it would never again be extended. The Holy Spirit took His place next to God the Father to await the glorious coronation.

Jebosh was among those personally attending the preparations. He caught the eye of the Prince, who called him over and asked with a smile, "How's My little group in the Idaho forest doing?"

Jebosh bowed his head in reverence and then answered with a bright smile of satisfaction, "You saw what happened outside Bend! They would have gladly taken a bullet for You, every one of them!"

"I did see it," the Prince replied, beaming with joy as a holy radiance surrounded His face, "and they thrilled My heart. They're going to make it, Jebosh, and I'm looking forward to bringing them home."

"It is all they live for, my Prince," Jebosh answered, his heart thrilled to its limits for having shared the joy of the soon–to–be King of the Universe. He had put off his crown and left His throne by the heavenly Father in order to take humanity upon Himself, to live a human life, to suffer mankind's deserved punishment, and to redeem them from eternal death. Jesus got this across to a listener as recorded in John 3:16. Upon His return to heaven, He had donned the garb of High Priest in order to complete the atonement. He did this by offering His sacrifice before the Father as humans would confess their sins and ask forgiveness in His name. The Apostle Paul makes this clear in Hebrews 4:14–16. Now, His ministration ended, He will put on His kingly robes once more, and receive the crown which is rightly His, to reign forever. Daniel 7:13-14 foretells this event.

"Now begins the final trial for the world, Jebosh. The seven plagues will begin to fall upon the finally impenitent, and there will be turmoil and suffering such as never before has been on the earth. Stay close to them, My friend. They're very precious to Me, as are all the other Covenant Keepers spread throughout the doomed planet."

"It will be my greatest joy to present them to You on that day, my Lord." He bowed again in deep respect and adoration, as he departed to take care of his responsibilities.

SNATCHED FROM THE WOLVES

After a fine dinner of stewed vegetables and baked bread, Guillermo turned on the portable radio to hear what news he could get from the outside world. He found an NRC affiliate broadcasting from Spokane. Everyone gathered around for the six o'clock news.

"...and here in New York, the flooding continues to worsen as hurricane Patrick continues to pound all five boroughs and New Jersey to the south with winds of 180 miles per hour and twenty inches of rain pouring over an ocean surge of twenty–five feet. In spite of early efforts to evacuate Manhattan, thousands are drowning in their cars due to a severe back up caused when the George Washington Bridge split after being battered by the high winds. The stately Triborough Bridge has lost two spans, and the Brooklyn Bridge is long gone. The Lincoln and Holland tunnels are full of water, and we doubt if there will be any survivors coming out of there. We are operating on generator power, but the NRC building here in Manhattan is swaying badly and we don't know how long we'll be able to broadcast. We have learned from our reports in different cities that the whole eastern seaboard is being severely battered, from Boston down to Washington D.C. This seems to be ten times worse than anything we ever saw when Katrina hit New Orleans years ago. Back to you, George."

"Thanks, Bob. That was Bob Arnold, directly from the NRC News Desk in New York. We'll take a look at a startling development with international implications. A dreadful disease has broken out in Europe and spread like wildfire throughout the continent. It is characterized by painful flesh–eating sores, which leave its victims in extreme anguish, since they can hardly sit or even lie down without great pain. The United States has closed all airports to European traffic, fearing the spread of the disease to this country. We now go to the Centers for Disease Surveillance for a statement by CDS Chief, Dr. Daniel LaRue."

"Good evening. The Centers for Disease Surveillance is very concerned with the outbreak of this new and unidentified disease in Europe. We want to assure the American people that we are doing everything possible to protect everyone here from contagion. The government has put a moratorium on all visas from Europe, and all returning Americans are being carefully screened and a quarantine facility has already been prepared.

"We have some samples of affected tissue and are proceeding to culture them so that we can work to identify the causative organism. We have the finest investigators in the world here working on this project, and we have asked Dr. Rolando Rodriguez, a physician and a leading bacteriologist who has worked with Doctors Without Borders for years in Africa, to head this investigation. Dr. Rodriguez has done outstanding work in the containment of Ebola and other hemorrhagic diseases in Africa, and we are certain that we will soon make headway with this new disease. Dr. Rodriguez, would you like to say a few words?"

"Thank you, Dr. LaRue. Ladies and gentlemen, this is a very dread disease. It would almost seem like a plague has struck that continent. I have seen some of the sufferers in Europe and, believe me; we don't want that in this country. We will do all we can to identify the cause and to take preventive measures. I know that my dad has all his fingers interlaced in prayer for all those who have placed their trust in God."

"That's my Rolando!" Guillermo interrupted the broadcast with glee. "Did you take notice of his closing remark? He mentioned the interlaced fingers! You know what that means, Elizabeth?"

"Yes, Guillermo, I know!" Elizabeth responded with a smile of deep satisfaction. "It means that he is still a Covenant Keeper. But he is in great danger, Guillermo. He is like a sheep among wolves. If those government people discover that he is one of us, that could be the end of him. He needs our prayers badly."

"Then we'd better pray for him right now!" Gerry said as he bowed on his knees and the rest of the group followed him. "Oh, gracious Heavenly Father, we bow before You in recognition of Your glorious person, Your incredible love, and Your magnificent salvation, Unworthy as we are, we come before Your presence in the name of our wonderful Prince Jesus, Your Son, to request Your protection for Rolando. This wonderful young doctor has risked his life to serve the suffering for years, and now faces the daunting challenge of this dread disease while surrounded by enemies who would destroy him if they knew he is a Keeper of Your Covenant. We also want to include in this request, the same protection for all of Thy covenant keeping people spread out in small groups all around the world. Keep us faithful until the very end, when we shall see Your Son's glorious face as He comes in the clouds of glory. 'Now to Him who is able to keep you from stumbling, and to present you faultless before the presence of His glory with exceeding joy, to God our Saviour, who alone is wise, be glory, and majesty, dominion, and power, both now and forever, Amen' (Jude 24–25)."

As Gerry closed with that moving quote from the book of Jude, everyone remained silently kneeling, as if overcome with a mixture of joyous reverence and recognized unworthiness, before such glorious love and condescension by Jesus, their Prince. The weeks turned into months, and the epidemic had by now gone worldwide. As infected travellers returned to their countries they carried the seeds of suffering to everyone they came in contact with. Soon there were so many people infected that governments gave up establishing quarantine camps. The suffering was beyond belief.

Meanwhile, Rolando toiled over cultures, test tubes, and microscope as he and his team tried to follow the infectious cycle of the new plague on rats, pigs, and monkeys. One by one, his personnel had to be replaced as they themselves contracted the disease. Another thing that made the work almost impossible was the lack of pure water for the preparation of reagents and the cleaning of instruments. Weeks before, a strange but catastrophic event had taken place. The water in the oceans had turned to blood, killing all sea life, which in turn had turned the beaches into stinking, putrid sepulchers for immeasurable tons of dead sea life. That, of course meant the end of desalination plants that had been operating to produce some of the water lost to the prolonged drought. He prayed that God would give him wisdom and help him decipher this mystery.

One day, a stranger walked into his lab and asked to talk with him.

"Can we go into your office? What I have to say is very sensitive," the stranger, tall and distinguished in his immaculate white suit, insisted.

"Who are you? I don't have time to talk to anyone right now!" Rolando was kind, but firm, as he led the stranger into his private office.

"My name is Jebosh. I am a messenger of the Prince of Peace to all Keepers of the Covenant. I have been sent in response to a request made by your father and a small group of Covenant Keepers hiding in the mountains of Idaho."

"You… you mean you're… an angel?" Rolando looked at the kind stranger in utter surprise.

"Yes, Rolando, I am. And you are Guillermo and Elizabeth's son."

"How are my parents? Are they safe? I've been worried sick about them ever since this persecution of Covenant Keepers began."

"They are safe. Their guardian angels are always with them. Now, listen, Rolando. You're prayers have been heard by the Prince, but the answer is no. You cannot decipher the puzzle of this plague. It is a judgement of God and not a natural phenomenon. There is nothing more that you can do for the people of this earth. It's time for you to go to a place of safety."

"All right, I'm ready to go. But I also have a family, Jebosh. We need to pick up Melinda and little Willie. I can't leave without them. They're at–"

"I know where they are, Rolando. They're in the car, waiting for us." Jebosh answered patiently.

"But how will we get out of here? This lab is under quarantine, with heavy security all around, twenty–four hours a day!" Rolando looked perplexed.

"You leave that to me. Follow me out to my car," Jebosh smiled confidently.

They walked out of the lab and headed for the gate, where a couple of armed military police watched jealously the coming and going of all personnel. Sophisticated identification procedures included thumbprint and iris readers. As they approached the electronic threshold, the reader did not identify Jebosh. The MPs immediately pointed their high technology weapons at Jebosh and one of them, the staff sergeant in charge, barked out the challenge, "We don't have you ID on record! How did you get in here?"

"Here's my ID," Jebosh replied, as he showed the guard a whited card with his picture on it and some official looking print and seals.

"I haven't seen this one before, but is certainly looks official enough," the MP said as he looked intently at Jebosh's face. *I've seen this face somewhere before, but I can't remember where! Oh, well, it's probably some high official from Eastern Command.*

"And where are you going, Dr. Rodriguez, sir? You are not permitted to leave this compound, sir. All personnel are under quarantine while working with Disease Agent X. You'd better get back to the lab, sir."

"I have been ordered to move Dr. Rodriguez to a more secluded place." Jebosh intervened.

"All right, sir. But you'll have to sign a release form in conformity with CDS orders." The staff sergeant replied, as he reached for a clipboard with an official paper.

Jebosh signed the form, handed it back to the sentry and headed for a Humvee with Rolando following close behind.

Hmmm. A civilian driving a lousy Humvee! I haven't seen that before. You'd think this government could provide such a high–ranking employee with a decent car! Well, things have been going to the dogs with everything that's happening in this country! the MP muttered in his mind as the Humvee disappeared in the distance.

Once inside, Rolando embraced his wife and child.

"Rolando, what's going on?" Melinda was still confused over that afternoon's events. "This man told me you were in danger and that he had to get us out of the area immediately. I was impressed to go with him, but I still don't undetstand what's happening!"

"I'm not quite sure myself, Melinda. But somehow I trust this man." Rolando thought he was in a dream state and could not wake up. *Am I awake or dreaming? Is this for real... an angel of God talking to me and getting me out of that virtual prison like one did for Peter? This is amazing!*

"Yes, Rolando, this is for real and you are awake. I was with your father just a couple of weeks ago. He is leading a small group of Covenant Keepers in a secluded spot in Idaho. The Prince of Peace is giving all His people a short time of respite from the storm in order to prepare them for the last final confrontation with the Prince of Darkness."

"Uhh...where are you taking us?" he asked rather sheepishly. He was startled to find Jebosh reading his thoughts.

"I'm taking you to another sheltered spot where a group of Covenant Keepers are gathered. They're in your state of Tennessee," Jebosh gave Rolando his characteristically assuring smile. "This group will benefit from your knowledge of the Prince and His book. They are new converts, and although they are fervently committed to the Prince, they need information that will boost their faith and hope. You can do that for them while everyone awaits the Great Gathering."

"That will be fine with me, Jebosh. As long as I know that my parents are fine, my mind is at peace. Do you know anything about my sister, Isabella?"

"Why, yes, I do. Isabella and Shawn are prisoners, at the Hanford facility. It used to house a variety of prisoners, criminals of various types. But those have been dying off due to the heavy radiation from leaking waste. There's a large group of Covenant Keepers, though, and they are in pretty good health. You know Isabella and how she loves children.

So she teaches regular school during the week and Sabbath school on the Lord's day. Shawn, of course ministers to the prisoner congregation both with his music and with his preaching. They are fine and are awaiting patiently the Great Gathering."

"Oh, I'm so glad to hear that, Jebosh," Rolando yawned. "I'm so tired, being up late hours working on that bug. Please excuse me while I catch up on some sleep." He placed his head on Melinda's shoulder and was out like a light.

Jebosh only smiled. He always smiled as he thought on the special privilege the Prince had granted him to minister in so many enjoyable ways to his people.

Sergeant Major Rivers got out of his army Ford, and walked toward the guardhouse.

"Sergeant, any new developments this evening?"

"Nothing spectacular, Sergeant Major; just a transfer that came through for Dr. Rodriguez."

"A transfer for Dr. Rodriguez? I thought he was restricted to the lab at CDS's request! Who authorized a transfer? And where was he transferred to?" the sergeant major seemed alarmed.

"There was a high government official here with an official looking ID and orders for his transfer, Sergeant. I had him sign the customary release form," the now nervous staff sergeant handed the form to the sergeant major.

"Jebosh...*hmm*...Jebosh. Wait a minute! Did you get a good look at this guy?" the sergeant major was now really agitated.

"Yes, Sergeant Major. He was tall, curly black hair, very fine features, dressed in a spotless white suit. What's the matter, Sergeant?" The poor staff sergeant was surprised by the sergeant major's reaction.

"What's the matter? What's the matter?" The sergeant major grabbed the startled staff sergeant by the arm and almost dragged him to an adjoining office. "Look at this composite picture, you idiot! Does this look like the guy you just described?"

"Why, yes he does. But I don't understand why you're so stressed out over all this," the staff sergeant was beginning to shake.

"Read it for yourself, you fool! You've just let the most wanted criminal slip out of your hands! You'll be court-martialled for this! You'll be lucky if they just bust you down to buck private. Report to your barracks! I'm suspending you from active duty until the investigation is over!"

The Humvee came to a halt, and Rolando woke from a very refreshing sleep. Jebosh led them through the forest on a well–disguised trail for at least an hour before they entered a clearing with about eight tents arranged in a circle under heavy foliage.

"Come on out, everybody!" Jebosh called out. Folks began to flow out their tents still in their PJs. It was seven in the morning, and there was no reason to rise any earlier. But the sun was shining and the birds had been singing beautifully for an at least an hour.

"Hey, it's Jebosh!" someone shouted, and they all rushed to greet him and to gawk at the new members of the group.

"Folks, this is Dr. Rolando Rodriguez, formerly of the CDS, now of the KOC," Jebosh introduced Rolando and his little family with a grin and a wink of his eye, using the abbreviated form, KOC, used by the enemies of the Keepers of the Covenant. "They will be staying with you until the Great Gathering.

"Meanwhile, he has a wealth of information to share with you from the Bible, and he will help you understand more about the Great Controversy and how it is going to end. Enjoy their fellowship! I've got to go! Farewell!" And with that, he disappeared into the forest.

They looked the handsome young couple over as each one stepped up and, interlocking their fingers, touched the back of their hands to the other's hands and told their names. For the next two months, the new converts matured in the knowledge of the Scriptures, as Rolando led them in Bible study day after day. Soon many of them could recite large portions of scripture by heart. They thrilled to sing songs of praise, especially on the Sabbath, when they rested from their weekly labor to commune with their Prince.

A DESPERATE ENEMY

The Prince of Darkness angrily paced back and forth on the gleaming marble platform under his ivory throne.

"I can't believe it! I just can't believe it! We've lost the whole little group from Spokane to my wretched adversary! First Ahmed and then the rest of them! Why, oh why am I stuck with such incompetence? First, I assign one demon per human to work on them throughout their lives! On top of that, I assign a group captain to make sure my plan is carried out! We have a great organizational structure above them, and yet we cannot persuade a few ignorant, fanatical followers of my enemy! Sure, we've got the vast majority of mankind in our grasp. But we've also lost millions to him during the last six thousand years!"

Then, turning to the trembling demons before him, the gravelly voice boomed out,

"So, what do you have to say for yourselves, nincompoops? Vesuvius! Do you remember what I promised you if you failed to bring in this little harvest of KOCs?"

"Yes…I do, my lord! But please! Relent from your punishment! We did everything we could. We had them humiliated, imprisoned, and even before a firing squad! But they chose to die rather than yield their allegiance to the Prince of Peace!"

"Don't mention that name! Not ever again... you hear me? I hate him! As for all of you, you deserve to go straight to the pit! But, I'm going to be kind..." And a hellish grin painted itself across his evil face. He laughed a grotesque laugh that chilled even the evil angels before him. "Me? Kind? How careless of me!"

"Well, the reality is that I need every agent left that is still active," he said, changing to a more serious subject. "I gather from the chatter among the enemy angels that the time for anyone to change allegiance has passed. My enemy will no longer recruit KOCs, for the time of human probation is past. I also have read the dreaded book and am aware of the order of things, that is, of the final judgements to fall on mankind. But before it is over, I want all KOCs dead you hear me?! Dead!"

"Yes, my lord Lucifer! And thank you for sparing us the punishment we well deserve!" The fiends were shaking less, and their pungent perspiration decreased.

THE PLOT THICKENS

In the New Jerusalem, the coronation of Prince Jesus, making Him King of Kings began. The human mind falls so infinitely short of words to describe the splendour and majesty of the occasion. On a great white throne sat the Father and the Holy Spirit, while the seat in the middle remained empty for the moment. The throne was lifted up, high in the middle of the city. All its grand avenues, paved with glittering gold and lined with lofty columns of the most precious stones, each one holding cascading garlands of ivy with gorgeous flowers, were filled with persons representing all of the inhabited worlds in God's vast universe. Each group wore the characteristic colors of its region, forming a rainbow of colors awesome to behold.

The ceremony went on for weeks, according to earthly time, and one wonderful event followed the other. Musical concerts offering praise to God were presented by beings from different regions of the universe. Gorgeous displays of animals and flowers were paraded down the gilded avenues, enrapturing the senses with praise and gratitude to God for having created them.

To look away from his glorious sight and focus on the tragically chaotic state of the earth is, indeed, a heart breaking switch. The suffering was now increased by the next plague.

The rivers and streams, lakes, ponds, springs, wells–all fresh water sources–were turned into blood. Every faucet in every home put out this red substance normally running only through the arteries of humans and animals. The consternation seemed indescribable! People appeared to be beside themselves, asking, What to do? There was precious little water to begin with! Now this! Emergency meetings were called by every government to decide what measures to take. Suddenly, there was a critical demand for water filters everywhere. These varied in their efficiency, some filtering out the cells better than others, but the plasma left was not any tastier nor more palatable than the whole blood. Nobody wanted to drink the stuff at first. But the longer the put it off, the thirstier they became, until, in their desperation, they began to drink blood.

The religious establishment, in conference with government leaders, sought an explanation for these weird and catastrophic events. Some remembered reading about the last plagues at the end of the world.

"These are the judgements of God! There can be no other explanation! God is punishing the world for being disobedient to His laws," one of the leading theologians of the day expounded forcefully.

"How can you say that, Reverend Fowler? All the nations came to an agreement nine months ago to unite in a universal recognition of a higher power, regardless of personal creed! As far as has been reported, everyone, everywhere, of every religious persuasion is conforming to the universal creed, uniting on a single day of worship, that is on Sunday, to appease God's anger and seek relief from the terrible lashes that are whipping the world!"

"Yes," a deep gravelly voice suddenly arose from among the leading men. "Yes, everyone. With the exception of the hated scum known as the Keepers of the Covenant."

Everyone turned and fastened their eyes on a person of very large stature, with deep-set eyes that seemed to glow with anger and hatred. By the outlines of his face, one could conclude that at some time in his past this person must have been very handsome and strong. But time had taken its toll, and the wrinkles and sagging of tissues told of an old and tired warrior.

"The chair recognizes…uh, what is your name, sir?" the chairman did not remember having seen this delegate before, and he thought he knew everybody in the leading religious establishment.

"Never mind, let's just say that I have been around long enough to know that the rotten apple really does spoil the whole barrel."

"With all due respect for the gentleman, I cannot see how God would punish everyone on earth because of a relative handful of dissident misfits! God is merciful, and if He has to punish, He'll punish the guilty," another delegate put in after obtaining the floor.

'Well, I agree with the gentleman," another preacher spoke up without waiting to be recognized. "I remember reading a story in the Bible about a man named Achan, who stole a piece of gold and some clothes, and how God punished the whole nation, causing them to lose a battle and getting a bunch of them killed, And that was just one man offending God." The meeting then went into an uproar, most of the delegates and government representative siding with the last speakers.

"Mr. Chairman…Mr. Chairman," a representative from the military struggled to obtain the floor. The chairman banged his gavel until it seemed it would break into pieces. Finally, the meeting calmed down.

"The Chair recognizes the newly-promoted General Gooding. Congratulations General!"

"You're very kind, Mr. Chairman, thank you." The general chose not to speak from his seat but took the podium up front.

"Ladies and gentlemen of this most prestigious conference, I am about to share with you some information that just recently has been declassified so that the military can shed some insight into this problem with the Keepers of the Covenant. A couple of highly unusual incidents have led us to believe that these people are getting assistance from supernatural sources.

"As is well known, about a year ago, the military reserve at Hanford, in the state of Washington was converted to a prison for criminals and misfits. The first evidence of supernatural intervention is the fact that in spite of the high level of radiation leaking from the storage of nuclear waste there, not one of the Keepers of the Covenant has gotten sick, even though most of the other prisoners have died–or are dying. The KOCs appear to be in the best of health, even though they are getting sparse rations of low-quality food.

"The second evidence we would like to introduce to you is so unbelievable, that I personally berated a junior officer when I heard about it. However, I later verified that at least forty soldiers were present when this incredible event happened, and every single one of them confirmed the story. I have had to apologize to this officer, and he has also been promoted for his fierce pursuit of those who would disrupt the peace of our great country. I would like at this time to introduce Major Bob Darnell, and, with the chairman's permission, yield the floor to him so that he can give you a first-hand account of this event."

"Ladies and gentlemen..." Major Darnell waited until the applause died down, his gold oak leaves shining as they proudly announced his new rank.

"Thank you, General. Ladies and gentlemen, when something supernatural happens, it takes a while for people to chew, swallow, and absorb. I cannot blame anyone for questioning what I'm about to reveal. It took me a while to realize that what I thought I had dreamt, had really taken place.

"The troops under my command were in pursuit of a small band of Covenant Keepers who had escaped our facilities through the bewitching influence of an impostor passing as a Major General. This person, calling himself General Jebosh, hypnotized our guards, and made off with the KOCs in one of our military Humvees."

"Jebosh...you old rascal! You should have taken my side when the war first started! I practically begged you to join me, but you wouldn't. Now you're involved with those losers...but just wait! I have a plan for them and for you! The Inquisition and the Holocaust were child's play in comparison." The large old figure bristled as he thought about one of his enemies.

"We set up a traffic blockade before the bridge at Umatilla, Oregon, hoping to catch them as they tried to cross into Washington. Everything was perfectly set up. I was in a helicopter supervising the operation overhead. Fifty soldiers were on the ground, heavily armed and poised to shoot upon my command. The fugitive Humvee was sighted and the troops ordered to hold their fire. But as the vehicle came into the open, instead of slowing down at sight of the blockade, it sped up at what seemed way over 200 miles per hour. I had no choice but to order fire. But, and here comes the incredible part, no one fired. Everyone was like, hypnotized, as the Humvee took off smoothly from the ground, flying like it was an air force fighter. My pilot had to maneuver out of his way, but not before I saw this impostor stick his head out of the window, waving his hat at me with a big grin on his face.

"Ladies and gentlemen, I am so glad that I was not alone, and that more than forty soldiers saw what I saw. Otherwise, I would have been laughed out of the army. Now even though it is quite contrary to military and scientific thinking, it is my solid conviction that this is a clear demonstration of the power of witchcraft. Thank you!"

"Well," the chairman spoke, "this information certainly throws a different light on this matter. The evidence presented comes from very reputable sources, and it should not surprise us that the forces of evil are working with this group. It seems that the Keepers of the Covenant could very well be the cause of God's wrath, manifested in all these catastrophes. We want to thank our mystery delegate for being first in bringing this possibility to our attention." The chairman looked toward the place where the visitor was sitting as those around him turned to thank him. But the chair was empty.

"Mr. Chairman," another delegate was recognized, "in light of the very powerful evidence presented by the military, I would like to propose that there be some plan of extermination to deal with the KOC problem."

"I second the motion!" a small chorus of voices didn't wait for the chairman to ask for a second.

"Since a motion has been made and strongly seconded, we open the floor for discussion." The chairman began to recognize different delegates who gave their opinions.

"I understand," said one, "that an extermination would be equal to a death a penalty, and that different states have different statutes. Some do not practice the death penalty. There's also the issue of due process provided by the constitution, which would rattle a lot of people in this country if not respected."

"The issue of death penalty statutes," argued another, "can be solved by transferring all of the KOCs to those states that do have the statute. As for due process, the fact that they are presenting a real threat to the health and safety of this country opens an option for the president to use his emergency powers and declare them guilty of treason punishable by death."

"Gentlemen, ladies," a grave gentleman stood up, "we are wasting our energies here. If indeed the conclusion is that these persons are causing the wrath of God, we will accomplish nothing by just executing the ones in our prisons. You must realize that there are Keepers of the Covenant in small and large cells all over the world! There is no country in the world, large or small, except for Nepal, where there are no cells of KOC's. Africa has millions, Latin America many millions more, Asia, the Middle East, China, Japan–I could go down the list until I've named them all!"

"A very accurate and wise observation, sir. The KOCs are not just an American problem; they are a world–wide problem, which demands a world–wide solution. What do you suggest, sir?"

"We need to take this problem before an agency that has the immense influence needed to persuade all the nations to act with one accord and at a given time frame, so that the problem can be eliminated once and for all," the previous speaker replied. "I believe that agency to be the one that has cradled and nurtured our religious heritage the longest, the one person that all governments respect and pay homage to by sending ambassadors to him and seeking his advice on all matters of high importance: the Great Shepherd."

"Yes…Yes! The Shepherd is the most widely accepted religious and political leader in the world. His voice is respected by all governments," some eagerly asserted.

"Mr. Chairman, I move that a commission of five recognized religious leaders and three top government officials, with the approval of the President, go to the Great Shepherd's palace and seek an audience with him in order to obtain support for a worldwide moratorium on tolerance of the KOCs, and that a time and date be established for their humane extinction."

"Second," came almost as a unanimous shout.

"There is already a motion on the floor which supersedes this one. However, since they are basically suggesting the same thing, Mr. Richardson, would you want to amend your original motion to read as the last one by Mr. Smithers?" the chairman said as he attempted to maintain parliamentary procedure. Mr. Richardson assented. The vote was unanimous, and the commission was immediately named, which included the ambitious General Gooding.

Shortly after that meeting, the approval of the president was obtained, and the office of the Great Shepherd granted the audience, to take place three weeks later. That gave the commission ample time to prepare for the audience, gathering all the evidence they could muster against the apparently defenceless Keepers of the Covenant.

Meanwhile, there was reported an unusual heat wave, which began to be felt in the Middle East, and was slowly spreading toward the east and west with a ferocity that was killing many exposed to it. People sought shelter from the direct rays of the sun, but even in the darkest shade, the heat was insufferable.

"…and in Eastern Europe, the casualties due to the heat are tabulated at bout fifteen hundred per day," the little radio blared away. "Because people are dying faster than they can be buried, bodies are piling up in designated areas around the towns and cities."

The little group of Covenant Keepers listened in somber silence to the news of one disaster after another. Guillermo opened his Bible to the book of Revelation, chapter sixteen and began to read as the others listened thoughtfully, "'Then I heard a loud voice from the temple saying to the seven angels, "Go and pour out the bowls of the wrath of God on the earth." So the first went and poured out his bowl upon the earth, and a foul and loathsome sore came upon the men who had the mark of the beast and those who worshipped his image. Then the second angel poured out his bowl on the sea, and it became blood as of a dead man; and every living creature in the sea died. Then the third angel poured out his bowl on the rivers and springs of water, and they became blood… Then the fourth angel poured out his bowl on the sun. and power was given him to scorch men with fire. And men were scorched with great heat, and they blasphemed the name of God who has power over these plagues; and they did not repent and give Him glory." Revelation 16:1–4, 8–9.

"Today," Guillermo continued solemnly, "we have witnessed the fulfilment of the fourth plague to date. Let us pray that God will continue to protect his own, not only those of us here, but all our brethren around the world, many of them in prison awaiting either death, or God's intervention on their behalf." They knelt to pray fervently, with tears of gratitude for their safety, and earnest pleading for their fellow believers. The cool air filtered through the trees and spoke to them of God's eternal love for all those who keep his Commandments out of love and faithfulness to Him, and who commit their lives to His care.

IN BABILOVIA

Brigadier General Gooding felt exhausted as he walked the streets of Babilovia. He had arrived two days before the meeting along with the other members of the commission. In spite of the intense, unbearable heat, he had insisted in seeing the small but picturesque city, being there for the first time. He rushed from shady spot, to drooping tree, to protective building until he reached his hotel. The whirr of air conditioners could be heard in the few businesses where there was a generator. His hotel, catering to the diplomatic corps, was one of them. After a cooling shower, he sat contentedly before a big window to enjoy the sights of the city from the comfort of his room. For a Brigadier General, only three months into his new rank, he felt pretty lucky and privileged to have been selected past higher–ranking officials for this special task. And an audience with the Great Shepherd! Well, not just anybody can get that!

"The morning of the audience, the commission was ushered into an elegant chamber in the palace. In spite of noisy air conditioners going at full blast, the temperature in the chamber would not dip below eighty degrees. But this was heaven, compared to the heat outside. After a while, the Great Shepherd walked in and sat before them in a very ornate chair. One by one, the members of the commission were introduced by the Shepherd's secretary, and they stepped forward, bowed before him, kissed his ring, and returned to their seats.

"I am very pleased," the aged potentate began, "to receive you this morning. I trust that you have rested well from your travel." He paused as he took a bound document from the secretary's hands.

"I have read the report and recommendations which you submitted a few days ago. I think you have done a thorough job, and I want to commend you for it." A smile of contented satisfaction was seen on the faces of the commission.

"I find myself in complete accord with your conclusions about the cause of all these terrible calamities. God expects obedience from His creatures, and these people are obviously in violation of His laws. I have been in consultation with my chief advisors and have decided to throw in our lot with yours.

"A week from this coming Sunday, I will issue an encyclical dealing with the issues of dissidence and its consequences, how God dealt with it the past, and how He directs us to deal with it in the present. All of the ambassadors have been invited as well as the top leaders of all the major religions of the world. Arrangements will be made for broadcasting by satellite to every country. Everyone who has access to a television or a radio will be able to hear my message, so that we can get a universal response of total cooperation with this unpleasant, but necessary task. Until then, you are invited to stay as my guests. There will be air–conditioned limousines available that will accommodate all of you, and you can take time to visit the historic monuments that commemorate the history of Christianity for more then eighteen hundred years. Thank you for coming and for placing your trust in my leadership."

RELENTLESS

Major Darnell didn't even bother knocking on the door but barged into Sonia's office like a Gestapo agent in World War II.

"Sonia de la Rosa?" he asked, or more accurately, declared.

"Yes, Major, and people usually knock on my door before they enter!" she answered, obviously annoyed.

"Forgive my lack of protocol, madam, but I have urgent business to attend to, and I believe you can be of great help." He was brash now that he was a major with a lot of authority to seek and destroy. But he also knew that Sonia was an important official and that he mustn't push her too far. However, this mission could be the most important in his military life and could change those gold oak leaves to silver. *Ahh... Lieutenant Colonel does sound better than Major!* was a thought frequently on his mind.

"So, what can I do for you, Major?" Sonia always felt uneasy with the military type.

"I understand that you have a son by the name of Gerry who happens to be a Keeper of the Covenant, am I correct?" Darnell asked icily. Sonia felt her heart stop and then take off pounding like a heard of buffalo.

"Yes, you...are correct, Major." She tried to project a calm exterior, but Darnell had learned to read body language quite expertly.

"No need to be nervous, Ms. de la Rosa. We just want to talk with him, You're aware, I'm sure, that KOCs are an outlawed organization, and that the state is incarcerating all those found practicing these false doctrines. However, since you are an important government worker, and in consideration of all the services you have rendered this state, I am willing to be very lenient with your boy. All we want from you is information as to where he is hiding."

"I...I don't know... where he is. I haven't seen him during the last ten months."

"Where did he go, Ms. de la Rosa? Surely he must have called or written to his own mother?" Darnell began to push harder.

"I tell you, I don't know! He left with some friends... we didn't part on good terms, so I don't blame him for not calling me or writing." Sonia was rapidly losing her composure.

"Relax, Ms. De la Rosa," Darnell changed tactics and decided the soft approach would now work. "Look, if you lead me to him, I'll be real easy on him. I'll offer him an opportunity to get out of this mess, to renounce the KOCs, and to come home safely. He's not really the one I want. The man I need to arrest and bring in is far more dangerous than your son could ever be. He is an impostor, passing for a Major General. It appears that he is a key player in this movement, and a master of witchcraft that has baffled the military establishment. Now, I'll make a deal with you, you tell me where he's hiding with this impostor, and I will personally deliver your son to you free as a bird, okay?"

Sonia remained silent for a brief moment as she thought through the generous offer before her. She waited for her heartbeat to slow down and for her anxiety to decrease before addressing the ambitious officer.

"Major, forgive me for being distrustful, but we live in a very uncertain world, and if anything happens to my son or to you, the deal is lost. Would you mind putting your offer on paper and signing your name to it?"

"Of course, Ms. De la Rosa. I'm an honourable person, and I stick to my word," he responded as he reached for his pen and the paper Sonia extended to him.

"The last time I saw Gerry," Sonia began as the major handed her the paper, "he informed me that he was going to look for work in Bend, Oregon. He told me that he had gotten married to a girl name Lisa while visiting with his friends somewhere in the Idaho panhandle, I think close to the Canadian border. I don't know the location' cause I've never been up there. So, he's either in Bend, Spokane, or up north somewhere, because he hasn't shown his face in my house. That's all I can honestly tell you."

"Well, that's not much, if you ask me. They may have gone east to Montana, perhaps crossed over to Canada. But if you hear him or get any leads, call me at the cell number on that paper. The deal will hold as long as he cooperates."

"And one more thing, Major..."

"Yes, Ms. de la Rosa."

"When you find them, bring my boy back, but please, don't bring back...the girl."

The Major nodded and walked out the door. Sonia couldn't hold back her resentment. "I know that it is that witch who turned my boy against me! Let her suffer the consequences!

 # DESTRUCTION COMMETH!

Lavish preparations had been made at the palace in Babilovia, as the world anticipated one of the most important speeches given by a religious leader in all the history of Christianity. Never had one addressed the whole world at once. every television and radio station had been directed to cease all other programming at least ten minutes before the broadcast. It would go across all time zones, so that some people would be listening during the day while others by night.

The palace was jam-packed with ambassadors and other dignitaries from all the countries in the world, along with every major religious leader, and members of the press. The streets and plazas were empty, the heat being so intense that you really could fry an egg on the pavement. Large portable air conditioning machines had been brought in to pump cool air into the palace, along with the huge generators to run them.

Electric power was down in many cities of the world due to the huge demand for air conditioning or fans. Power systems were stretched out to the limits in many places, and in others, electricity was restricted to hospitals, heat shelters, and some government offices. People with generators had the most relief, though, with black market prices of eight dollars a gallon for gasoline, they could only run them for little spurts at a time.

The moment the world was waiting for had come. The large choir, composed of some of the best operatic voices in the world, was there to set the tone for the magnificent display of pomp and power that had always characterized the Great Shepherd. And somewhere in an obscure little spot in a northwest forest, a small group of people turned on their little portable radio and listened intently while the batteries would last.

The last note died away, the choir sat, and the Shepherd's secretary stepped up to a podium, announcing in solemn tones, "To a world without borders, His Holiness, The Great Shepherd."

The man, sitting on a throne on high, in the place of God (as had been taught for many centuries), began in gracious accents the discourse that would have the last profound influence on the final events of history.

"I would like to begin with a warm greeting to all my fellow pastors of the different flocks represented here today. We are grateful for your condescension in joining us for this appellation to Almighty God for the healing of our lands, and the return of temporal prosperity to the tragic and distressed world we are living in today. We gladly welcome all the ambassadors and other dignitaries representing the nations of our globe, trusting that you will go back and persuade your governments to cast their lot with the church as it seeks to lead the world back to order and sanity in a brotherhood of all mankind. We welcome the media and thank them for making it possible for this message to reach every corner of the world simultaneously.

"The tragedy of our present world is unprecedented in history. Never before have disasters been so generalized; never before has an epidemic of disease reached such proportions as to encompass all the nations of the world; never before had the oceans, rivers, and other water supplies been turned to blood, although once, as recorded in scripture, the Nile River was turned to blood as a warning to Pharaoh to let the people of God go free from slavery. Never has the sun dared to shine with such strength as to destroy the lives of so many innocent people.

"Yet these very events were predicted many years ago. The biblical book of Revelation, in chapter sixteen, tells the story of a future outpouring of the wrath of God against a world that would rebel against his laws and against his church. The very catastrophes that have decimated a large part of our world during the last eight or nine months, are the plagues which were predicted in this holy book.

"I know that you faithful ministers and priests present here today, and many more listening to this broadcast, have endeavoured to lead the people back to God. I know that you have struggled against the desecration of Sunday, the day our Lord established for rest and worship, honouring His resurrection and the promise of His salvation through His holy church, established by His apostles after His ascension. I recognize especially the hard work and earnest efforts on the part of our Protestant brothers in America, for having led out in the restoration of God's holy day. Sunday used to be football day for Americans. Today, it is faithfully kept by that country, with an exception that I will be dealing with further on.

"The nations of Europe have dragged their feet on this issue for many years. Yet I am happy to see their ambassadors here and have heard heartwarming reports of faithful Sunday keeping there. Non–Christian denominations have expressed by their presence here their desire to join us in a celebration of universal brotherhood on Sundays, even when they wish to also retain their own cherished traditions.

"We have finally come to a point in time when the whole world is at peace with each other, and cooperation is a *fait accompli*. We have every reason to expect the blessings of heaven in terms of peace, health, temporal prosperity, and an end to the violent events caused by nature running out of control.

"Yet–and here we make a decided emphasis–yet… we are currently under the fierce judgements of God, with people dying of painful, putrefying sores, suffering extreme thirst, subjected to drinking the most abhorrent drink in order to stay alive and suffocating to death in a heat wave that seems to have no end.

"One would think that with the vast majority of the world's people obeying His law, keeping Sunday holy, and seeking peace with their neighbors, that God would smile on us and take away all of this suffering. But the world needs to understand that God is not conformed to the majority being good. God is a God of all–inclusiveness, and does not tolerate individuality when it comes to obedience to His directives.

"And there are groups of people spread out throughout the whole world who have taken it upon themselves to disobey what the Lord has ordained. I am certain that most of you have heard of an organization called the Keepers of the Covenant. They are a dissident group that insists that Sunday is not the Sabbath. Instead, they insist that the original Sabbath, which is kept by the Jews on Saturday, is still the Sabbath of the Lord. We will not go into arguments about who is right and who is wrong, for God's true church defined that many centuries ago. The Sunday Sabbath has been sustained all these years by the only institution that the Lord established to feed His flock, and that institution is the worldwide Christian Church.

"The Sunday Sabbath upheld by this church and by every other God–fearing church represented here today is based on the New Covenant established by our Lord after His resurrection from the dead, on that glorious Sunday morning. It is the same Sunday Sabbath kept by the early Christian church, and even Saint John wrote the book of Revelation on Sunday, when the Lord appeared to him as he worshipped.

"The so called Keepers of the Covenant would be better served if they called themselves the Keepers of the Old Covenant, rather than pretend that they are keeping the New Covenant. With all due respect for our Jewish brethren present here today, the old Sabbath was done away with on the cross of Calvary when the Lord died. Now, we have no objection to the Jews continuing to keep their traditions and their folk lore. We have always respected that right. And we appreciate and laud you for your willingness to join us in this Sunday celebration of universal brotherhood when we can all worship the same god.

"But, returning to the Keepers of the Old Covenant as a dissident organization, it has been the conclusion of the world's leading theologians and government leaders, as expressed through their ambassadors present here today–that it is their stubborn refusal to submit to the teaching of the church and to the laws of the land that has resulted in the insufferable calamities lashing the good and obedient people of the world today.

"So what are we to do? Do we, out of charity to a relative handful of humans with a different point of view, tolerate the outcome of their lunacy? What about charity toward the vast majority, which is struggling under the most disheartening circumstances to be faithful to God? These same respectable leaders utter a definite no! We cannot risk the future of this generation for the sake of a small group of misinformed and misdirected dissidents. The destruction of this whole civilization is at stake.

"It has been suggested that the most reasonable and expedient action to be taken is the humane extermination of these groups, so that none remain to invoke the wrath of God on the rest of mankind. I know this sounds awful. I myself recoil from the idea of destroying a life, no matter how odious or abhorrent it may be. Yet the present situation calls for a careful analysis of our options.

"This word 'expedient' is a biblical word. A noted Jewish leader used it in a council similar to this one. In the Gospel of Saint John, chapter eleven and verses forty–nine and fifty, Caiaphas said, 'You know nothing at all, nor do you consider that it is expedient for us, that one man should die for the people, and not that the whole nation should perish.' Now we all know that he was wrong as to the person because he was talking about the death of our Lord. However, the principle of sacrificing some for the good of others does stand.

"A deeper study of Scripture confirms this as we look at how God himself killed some for the good of others. In Noah's time, He destroyed the whole world for the sake of Noah and his family. In the time of Abraham, He destroyed Sodom and Gomorrah for the sake of Lot and his family. When the Jews were liberated from Egypt, the Egyptian people were severely punished and their army destroyed for the sake of the Jews.

"Furthermore, many times God ordered the Jews to destroy people who were considered wretched pagans, for instance the people of Jericho and other nations who refused to submit to the Jewish system of worship, until the Jews finally conquered all of Canaan.

"In conclusion, I find support in the Bible for the idea of the humane extermination of the Keepers of the Old Covenant. It does not have to be painful, nor prolonged, nor violent. I truly believe that this is what God is waiting for before restoring our planet and our people to health, longevity, and temporal prosperity.

"I urge all you ambassadors and religious leaders, to return to your countries and persuade your governments to acquiesce to this solution. I know that some governments have changed hands several times over the distressful political struggles they are facing, trying to solve the internal problems resulting from these catastrophes. Work with all, pray with all, and act with one accord. Let us bring back the fervent worship of the one and only true God, and of His Holy Mother Mary, the mother of us all. For Christ came in the flesh, becoming one of us, that we may become one with Him and with His gracious Mother. Amen."

Awesome! the general exclaimed to himself. *He is truly the man for this time! Incredible mind… how can anybody contradict such wonderful logic?*

"What do you think, General, do you think we can do it?" his thoughts were interrupted by a gravelly voice behind him. The voice sounded familiar. He'd never heard anyone else with such a tone. He turned to look. Sure enough, it was the huge figure of a man, with the deep–set eyes and the penetrating look, wearing the same black suit he had worn at the convention weeks before.

"Why…yes! Yes, we can! By the way, you seem to know me, but I still don't know who you are or where you're from."

"You'll know soon enough. But I'm not the important one. Keep you eyes on that man. As you said, he's the man of the hour," was the deep response.

General Gooding turned to look at the Great Shepherd. The incredible pomp and homage and power in one man left him full of wonder. He turned to continue the conversation, but the strange–looking figure was gone, even though the room was so packed that passing through the crowd was impossible.

Guillermo turned off the radio. The long speech had almost worn the batteries down. Everyone was speechless. "What an incredible misuse and misinterpretation of the scriptures was cast at the people of the world! It would almost seem as if Satan himself had written the speech or been there to dictate it. He is a very clever angel, though a fallen one. He has had time to practice deception and twisting of the truth for many, many centuries. And he has been, tragically, quite successful, too. Beginning with our first parents in the Garden of Eden, he twisted God's original words and intent so as to deceive Eve, thus unleashing a cascade of sin on this world for the last six thousand years."

"I'm a little confused about some of the things that he said. He make it seems like it's okay to kill in the name of God, or if you think God has ordered it. Guillermo, if God ordered people killed in the Old Testament, why would it be wrong for the people today to kill us if they think that God has ordered it?" Rita asked rather perplexed.

"Let me try my best to explain what the Bible teaches on this, Rita. First of all, God is the only one who has the right to end a life, because He is the only One who can create and give life. Furthermore, He is the only One who can judge whether a person is worthy of life or death. No one except God and that includes the Father, the Son our Prince, and the Holy Spirit can judge the mind and conscience of any individual–not even an angel.

"Life or death are the final rewards for mankind, based on God's judgment of his fitness to live in the Holy City Jerusalem, and eventually, on the beautifully restored Earth after the Millennium.

"Having said that, when God created mankind, He started a relationship based on the Covenant. It was established with every generation after that, as we see in Genesis six where

God does so with Noah, and He has established it with us today. At one point in history, God chose a family and their descendants to represent him on the earth, Abraham, God's friend, and his descendants, the Jews. In the book of Exodus, God establishes an earthly government, called a theocracy because God was the head and the Jews were his subjects.

"At times God used his people to execute his judgements on people who had passed the limits of his forbearance with their sin. However, they were never to exercise this responsibility without His direct command. One time, as the story goes in the book of Numbers, chapter fourteen, the people of Israel tried to make war against the Amalekites contrary to God's orders, and they suffered a stinging defeat.

"When Jesus, the Prince, came to this earth in order to carry out the plan of salvation, He was rejected by the Jews and crucified by the Romans at Jewish instigation. A few years after His resurrection, the Jews signalled their final rejection of Christianity by the stoning of Stephen the evangelist, and the gospel was then preached to the Gentiles, or non–Jews.

"Jesus the Prince, as God the Son, did not establish another theocracy, that is a direct government by God, but rather he set up a spiritual kingdom for his church. He established leadership in Apostles and Prophets, elders and deacons. But the goals and objectives of this spiritual kingdom was not to exercise temporal power, but to lead people into a voluntary acceptance of the Prince as their Lord and Saviour and to prepare them for the establishment of His kingdom in the latter times. Force was never to be a tool of the church, but rather the persuasion of God's love and sacrifice for every creature on earth.

"If the people of the world do not want to enter into this life–saving covenant which God has offered to all generations since the beginning of time, we are not to use the least bit of force or coercion. Faith in and submission to the Prince and

His kingdom are strictly voluntary actions. It always has been that way.

"But Satan, that wily enemy of God and His Son, has influenced mankind to reject the true principles of His kingdom, twisting His word and coming up with counterfeit principles and doctrines to confuse and misdirect those who do not seek God for themselves nor study His word with humility and prayer. The Apostle Paul warned that this would happen at the end of the time in his first letter to Timothy, chapter four and verse one and two, which says, 'Now the Spirit expressly says that in latter times some will depart from the faith, giving heed to deceiving spirits, and doctrines of demons, speaking lies in hypocrisy, having their own conscience seared with a hot iron.'

"Jesus Himself was dismayed with the twisting of God' word. In the Gospel of Matthew, chapter fifteen and verses eight and nine, He reproached the Jews of His day saying, 'This people draw near to Me with their mouth and honor Me with their lips, but their heart is far from Me. And in vain they worship Me, teaching as doctrines the commandments of men.'

"And so, Rita, if the scriptures could convince us that we are wrong in keeping His covenant, we need to recant and ask forgiveness of the church authorities. But all the evidence I find in the Word of God is that the New Covenant does not do away with the Ten Commandments nor the seventh–day Sabbath, their Saturday. On the contrary, the New Covenant puts the law, not just on paper, but even more so, it is written on the mind and in the heart, if what the Apostle Paul said in Hebrews 8:10 is true."

"Thank you, Guillermo. I'm so grateful that God has given you a clear understanding of His word. And I praise Him for his goodness in providing such a clear path for us to walk on, all the way to the Heavenly City."

FRUSTRATION

Major Darnell was a very busy man these days. He was now in command of a large contingent of troops, committed to hunting down the hated KOCs. As they diligently sought them out, they were transferred to Hanford where they were watched from a distant perimeter in order to protect the troops from too much exposure to radiation.

It was easier to capture the KOCs now, since the Shepherd's encyclical had polarized the whole world against them. Snitches were everywhere, reporting all suspicious persons and movements, But the cause of his greatest frustration was constantly eluding him. Sonia's information left him up in the air, going on a wild goose chase all over Washington, Idaho, Montana, and southern Canada along the U.S. border.

"*When I get a hold of that General Jebosh, I'm going to bust him down to buck private, then I'm going to strip his uniform off, tie him on a big spit, and roast him over a big pile of hot coals, then feed him to the dogs!*" he thought as he studied a map of the Northwest.

Suddenly something caught his eye that caused him to think creatively for the first time that year. Not too far from highway ninety-five, nearing the Canadian border was a branch of the Kootenai River, alongside the Kaniksu National Forest.

"Wait a minute... wait just one cotton–pickin' minute! How stupid could I be? Wherever they're hiding, they need water! And I just bet that they are near some river! The fact is that this cursed group is able to get purified water out of this bloody goop. I've seen it at Hanford and at other prisons. Their keepers can't explain it. They've even tasted the water and say it is the best they have ever tasted! Their witchcraft gets them anything they want... anything, that is, except freedom."

"Carson, come in here," the major barked out.

"Yes, sir, Major, what's up?" the lieutenant was eager to be helpful. He was up for captain in a few months, and was trying to be as efficient as possible. He felt that he still needed to redeem his blunder in Bend.

"Order the chopper and get ready to accompany me on a little air hunt." He said with an air of anticipation.

"Yes, sir, Major. It will be ready to go in half an hour."

The helicopter lifted up from the major's temporary command center in Sandpoint and headed north along highway ninety–five. Soon they veered to the left, looking for the Kootenai River. Once they reached it, the major pulled out his special binoculars and began to scout along the banks. He found the river deserted, the water a red to Purplish muck with practically no current. The situation didn't change along the course of the rest of the river as they neared the Canadian border.

"Never mind, Mr. Olsen. Take the chopper back, I don't see anything worth pursuing. Carson, prepare a contingent of ten troops and two Humvees for tomorrow. I think we'll have better luck on land," the major said with disappointment in his voice.

A SCARY DEVELOPMENT

The ambassadors and religious leaders had returned to their countries full of enthusiasm for the Great Shepherd's proposed solution. After some discussion, one country after another agreed to go with the plan. The situation in the world was hopelessly desperate, and there seemed to be no other option. One by one, they returned to the palace at Babilovia to confer with the officials as to the details of the operation. It was ten in the morning when the Shepherd opened the session with expressions of gratitude for the loyalty of the world.

"I greet you in the name of the Lord, anticipating His grace shed upon all the governments represented here. I am deeply grateful for the support you have all brought to my presence for the agreed-upon solution to the ills of our world. It appears that the solution can be executed simultaneously so that the return of God's grace can also take place simultaneously all around the world. I understand that some of your governments are still trying to gather their dissidents. Therefore, I think it would be prudent to wait another thirty days, and set the time at midnight on the thirty-first of October, as we celebrate and commemorate All Saints Day." A rousing round of applause progressed into a standing ovation for the Great Shepherd that seemed to never end. After about three minutes of clapping and cheering, the crowd finally heeded the Shepherd's plea for silence, and they sat down.

"I commend all of you–" the discourse was suddenly stopped by an astonished Shepherd. First, a powerful bolt of lightning hit the main power distribution station, resulting in power outages throughout Europe. Then, the light coming on through the windows, formerly bright and hot, suddenly began to fade and was replaced with a creeping darkness that intensified rather quickly. Within minutes, it seemed like the sun had been completely wiped out, as a dense fog–like darkness envelope that part of Europe.

The Shepherd's face blanched, and his aides rushed to his side as they also felt a chilling fear. Soon the black fog was so thick that people on the street could not see their hand when placed right in front of their eyes. People were crying on the streets and holding on to anything they could grab– to lampposts, to buildings, and to each other. Headlights of all intensities were no match for the thick fog. Cars were crashing into each other in a desperate attempt to pull over to a place of safety. After a few hours, some people began to walk again, feeling their way along the walls, or crawling on the ground, hoping to find their way home.

In the palace, the Great Shepherd had recovered from the shock and was conducting a special ritual under the light of hundreds of candles, which barely penetrated the darkness inside. The ambassadors and religious leaders were numb with fear and hoping that the Shepherd's prayers would be heard.

For three days, the strange and mortal darkness persisted, and people could not eat, drink, nor sleep. Some were so powerfully affected by the darkness, that they lost their sanity and ran screaming through the fog until they were hit by a car or slammed into a wall.

When the fog began to lift, hope sprang again into their terrified hearts. About ten o'clock of the fourth day, there was sufficient light to walk safely, though carefully so as not to step on the cadavers lying on the sidewalks and streets. Soon thereafter, city workers were out picking up the bodies and tossing them on trucks for burial. Tow trucks were seen clearing out the tangled mess on the streets throughout the city. The following day dawned with the same bright, scorching sun, but the people were never happier to welcome it.

HAPPY HUNTING!

Major Darnell was up early that morning. He whistled a tune as he dressed for an exciting adventure. He was going hunting for a general! He figured if he found nothing that day, he would at least do a little deer hunting while he was at it. A little venison would be great after army rations the whole week, though he didn't see how anything could have survived on bloody water.

Soon they were driving up Highway 95. As they were approaching the road toward the national forest, he noticed a dirt road he hadn't seen from the helicopter.

"Huh. That's interesting. Carson, take that dirt road on the left. Let's see where it'll lead."

They entered the road and travelled for about an hour, seeing nothing but a dehydrated forest and no wildlife in sight.

"Say, did you see that, Major? I thought I saw a house set back in the woods off to the right," the Lieutenant observed.

"You're right, Carson. Let's stop and ask if the folks there have seen any movements lately, or a Humvee with a would–be–general in it."

The two Humvees pulled into the clearing, right up to the steps. The major jumped to the top step and knocked on the door. No answer. Louder knock; still no answer.

"Major, this place looks abandoned. Notice the layer of dust throughout the whole porch. No one had stepped here for quite a while, until you made some prints."

"Let's check it out, Lieutenant. Have some troops knock the door down." The major wiggled the doorknob, and, to his surprise, the door opened.

"This is a nice house. Would make a great weekend retreat. I wonder who left this place... looks like they left in a hurry." Major Darnell talked half to himself and half to his lieutenant, as they went from room to room.

"Major! Come back here and take a look!" the lieutenant shouted excitedly from the back bedroom.

"What is it, Carson?" the major answered intrigued.

"You've hit the jackpot, Major! Look at this catch!"

There on the bed, neatly folded were two military uniforms: one a major general's, and the other a captain's. The nametags read in capital letters, JEBOSH and JERROD.

"Carson," the major said astounded, "do you know what this means? It means that this house probably belongs to KOCs and that they probably all escaped together!"

"The cars are in the garage, sir, which means that they hiked their way out of here. They couldn't have gotten too far."

"This is it, Carson! We are so close to these misfits, I think I can smell their stinking sweat! All we need is to bring them in with their general, and my promotion is around the corner. Oh, I love the title Colonel! It has a good sound, don't you think, Carson?"

"Yes, sir, it does! Just as sweet as the rank of captain does to me!" the lieutenant answered with a grin.

"All right, all right, Lieutenant. We've got work to do. First, have the troops set up camp here. We'll make this fine house my base of operations. Second, request some hounds and their handlers up here on the double. I'd like to get started by this afternoon."

The dogs didn't arrive until seven o'clock, so the major opted for a good night's sleep that would adequately prepare the troops for a good search tomorrow.

The sun was not yet showing its face, but dawn was here, and the troops chomped down their C–rations as the major fried some eggs and veggie patties left by Elizabeth in the refrigerator. As the sun rose over the withered forest, they headed out, the dogs wandering all over, since there was no trace of a scent left by the Keepers of the Covenant. They followed along the river at first, but the stench was so strong that they followed at a distance from the bank, stopping every so often due to the unbearable heat.

They reached the end of the trail, and nothing was before them but heavy, dried, prickly brush. But that was not stopping Major Darnell. He was a man possessed with ambition, and Major General Jebosh was the key to his dreams!

Darnell realized that the task could take much longer than at first anticipated, so he had his soldiers equip themselves for a few days of search and capture adventure. He had no idea what lay beyond the trail, but he pushed on until it was too dark to safely tread through the heavy brush. Then they made camp for the night.

This went on for three days, and he could sense his men's discontent at the roughness of the dry brush combined with the heat. But they dared not challenge his authority and plodded on until, suddenly, they reached a green patch of gentle forest. It was like finding an oasis in the middle of the Sahara, and they paused to feel its strange coolness. A cloud was over the oasis, and a cool breeze seemed to blow among the trees, bringing relief to their overheated bodies. A small stream of cool, clear water flowed among the trees, and the soldiers dove their heads into it just to feel the luxury of the water they had missed for months. They drank until they could hold no more and emptied their canteens of the junky filtrate they were carrying to refill them with the beautiful stuff so often taken for granted.

This is really strange, the major thought. *An oasis here in the middle of nowhere! I could make a mint selling fresh water right now. But how could this be, unless… wait a minute! There's only one explanation that I can think of! The KOCs! They must be near!*

"All right, men! That's all the rest we have time for. I think we are close to what we came for. Let's go downstream and see where it takes us," the major ordered with great anticipation.

He led the men and the lieutenant brought up the rear. Soon they came to the end of the green oasis, and noticed that at that point the water turned to blood and continued its downward flow off a cliff. He turned the search party around, sure now that he would soon find his quarry. They crept very carefully, since they didn't want to give advance warning through the least noise. The gentle forest soon opened to a clearing with a well–organized garden of beautiful fruits and vegetables. Darnell's heart accelerated to a fever pitch as he realized his find. He ordered the troops to make a circle around the clearing, and at his signal, they would rush the camp.

By this time, Guillermo's dog was barking loudly and running to the edge of the clearing and back, and the little group, which had gathered for evening vespers, stopped their singing and looked all around them to see if anything in particular had aroused the animal to such intense behaviour. Then they heard the major's voice coming from the vegetable garden: "Charge!"

The troops charged into the clearing just as the little group had finished praying for guidance and protection from the persecution they knew their fellow believers were also going through.

They were startled to their feet from their kneeling position, and for the moment were confused as to what was happening in their, otherwise, peaceful corner of the world. They immediately recognized Lieutenant Carson, and they knew this was the end for them…he would finish now what he had failed to do near the road in Bend.

"All right, you misfits! Thought you were going to get away with all your shenanigans, didn't you? Well, it's all over, and the fat lady sang! Now, where are your General Jebosh and your Captain Jerrod?" the major asked in a jeer.

"We haven't seen them since the same night you saw them, sir." Ahmed stepped up to the plate on behalf of the group.

"You're lying!" the major grew furious. "Now you just stand right where you are while the lieutenant and I look around. C'mon, Carson. I want you with me' when we find this impostor!"

They went into the cave and turned everything upside down but found nothing. Then they looked around the forest in the immediacy of the clearing, but found no trace of the object of their hatred. Finally, they returned to the clearing. "Carson, who's the spokesman for this batch?"

"I think it's the dark one," the lieutenant replied. "He's the one with the smart mouth."

"You! Come here! What's your name, son?" the major asked him a little more gently as Ahmed walked toward him.

"The name's Ahmed, sir!"

"Now, look, Ahmed," the major dropped his voice to almost a whisper so the others wouldn't hear, "what's a good young guy like you doing mixed up with a group like this?

Listen, I am going to offer you the chance of a lifetime. If you tell me the secrets of how you people turn the water to blood and back to fresh water, not only will I set you free, but you will be rewarded beyond your dreams!" *If this guy tells me the secret, man, I will be the most powerful general in the world! Just think! The power to return blood to fresh water again! This could be opportunity knocking at my door!"*

"We, sir, are Keepers of God's Covenant and He, in turn, is our Keeper. Only He has the power to turn water into blood. These are His judgements. He has promised deliverance and—"

"Shut up!" the major shouted. "I don't want to hear it! Now get your stuff together and start walking back to the trail. Carson, you lead the way back. Stagger the troops among the rebels."

"Yes, sir!" Lieutenant Carson looked directly at Ahmed. "You, smart mouth! You walk in front of me, where I can keep an eye on you."

"Where are you taking us?" Ahmed turned to the major.

"That's none of your business! I'd like to leave your carcasses here in your little paradise…but I need you as a bait for that infernal Jebosh and his Captain!"

"You'll never catch him," Ahmed smiled as he warned the major.

"Shut up and march!" the major snapped as he slapped Ahmed across the face with his heavy leather gloves.

Ahmed took the lead of the column back to the trail, where the Humvees were waiting for a bumpy ride back to Guillermo's house. The helicopter had been summoned, and it took most of the troops back to Sandpoint, since they all wouldn't fit in the Humvees. But the major and his lieutenant rode back with the despised KOCs. He didn't want to take a chance on another recue by Jebosh. They stopped at Guillermo's house so the major could pick up his personal belongings. The little group reminisced silently on the good times they had spent there. But they knew that it didn't come anywhere close to what the Prince had promised them. They looked to the future with great hope in their hearts.

Once in Sandpoint, they were fingerprinted and loaded into a small civilian bus headed for Hanford.

THE CORONATION

The glorious coronation ceremonies continued in the Heavenly City. At the foot of the throne was a radiant Sea of Glass, beautiful to behold down to its crystal clear depths. Upon the sea were cascading rows of empty seats, designated for the official ambassadors from the different inhabited worlds. In the middle, and facing the throne at a small distance, were twenty-four elegantly carved and upholstered chairs, twelve on each side of an exquisite red carpet runner that ran from the beginning of the Sea of Glass all the way up to the throne.

The last in a spectacular series of events was the entrance of a flock of ten radiant peacocks, flying through the air in a triangular formation. Their long tails shimmered in the lights as if studded with diamonds, sapphires, and emeralds. They approached as on a runway, at a perfect distance from each other, aligned like a stealth bomber, and coming at a very high speed, they suddenly opened up their tail feathers like dazzling fans simulating a half parachute, which broke their speed, and they landed gently before the throne. They remained still for a few moments before the throne, their elegant heads bowed before their Maker, until their angel trainers came and led them away, and they flew off, no longer in formation, to play in the green fields beyond the Sea of Glass.

Then the long-awaited moment came. The Royal Brass lifted their instruments to their lips, and played a most exalted theme. The procession began! Beautiful beings from worlds afar, each costumed in his dress of state in indescribable colors, and styles, marched triumphantly down the royal carpet, bearing a palm leaf of the most vivid green, carried in their right hands and resting across their shoulders. Each one bowed in deep respect and adoration before the throne before continuing on to his seat on the Sea of Glass. They stood before their seats, awaiting the entrance of the Prince.

Once all of the ambassadors were in their places, the Royal Brass began a new anthem for a special group coming down the center aisle. Four creatures, beautiful to behold, but difficult to describe in human language, walked in and, bowing deeply before the throne, took their places right just below it.

The music changed again, and the innumerable crowd of visitors heard a song that had the tracings of human experience. An elegant anthem with pieces of tragic sadness, exalted at the end with a triumphant grand finale, was played as twenty-four elders, the first fruits of the Prince's earthly ordeal, marched in with a look of exuberant joy on their faces. They bowed joyfully before the throne, praising the Father and the Holy Spirit for their willingness to send Jesus to save them and their brethren still on the suffering planet. Then they stood at their places before the throne on either side of the royal carpet.

There was a great silence; a joyous tension permeated the vast assembly as they turned expectantly toward the distant entry to the Sea of Glass. The Royal Brass suddenly burst into a flurry of harmonious blasts, which continued on to a very dignified, yet triumphant march. A wonderful, harmonious choir joined the brass in verses of praise and congratulations to the Prince of Peace, their Creator, their Friend, and now to be their King forever.

Down the long aisle, a young man walked in cadence with the anthem, an earthling of those who had risen from the dead when Jesus rose on the glorious morning of the resurrection. His cheeks shining with the glow of eternal health, and while holding a beautiful palm frond in his right hand, he led an immaculate little lamb. This was the most poignant symbol of the Prince, who, as a lamb to the slaughter, went to the cross for the sake of His universe. He bowed deeply before the throne, but though he smiled broadly, he couldn't hold back the tears of abundant gratitude for what all that glory had cost.

Next came the rest of the redeemed who had risen with Jesus. They all wore white robes of the most exquisite linen with colored borders and golden belts. They all carried palm branches in their right hands, and beautiful small harps in the other, The Royal Brass stopped playing once they reached the front of the throne and bowed in silent adoration. Then the redeemed tucked their palms in their belts, and began to strum a tune on their golden harps as they sang an anthem of gratitude:

"To Him who loved us, and washed us from our sins in His own blood, and has made us priests and kings to His God and Father, to Him be glory and dominion forever and ever. Amen!" (Revelation 1:5–6).

As they finished that anthem, there came the most beautiful angel of all, Gabriel, the covering cherub, the most exalted leader of all of the heavenly hosts. He held a silver frond of palm leaf in his right hand, while with the left he held the beautifully adorned harness of a pure white stallion, indescribable in his elegance. But all eyes were on the Prince mounted on the stallion, the beauty of His presence causing great awe to all who beheld him. He smiled broadly to the multitude as He passed, and they, like a continuous wave, down before Him. The group of the redeemed, bowing before their Prince, parted to both sides, as the stallion approached the throne, and Gabriel halted the handsome horse. The man with the lamb picked it up into his arms, symbolic of the Good Shepherd, and, bowing before the Prince stood while a new and glorious anthem exploded in enthusiastic harmony. The twenty-four elders and the redeemed joined together in rapturous song, saying, "Worthy is the Lamb who was slain to receive power, and riches, and wisdom, and strength, and honor, and glory, and blessing!... For You were slain, and have redeemed us to God by Your blood out of every tribe and tongue, and people, and nation, and have made us kings and priests unto our God; and we shall reign on the earth" Revelation 5:12; 5:9–10.

And the multitude shouted, "Amen. Hallelujah!"

Jesus dismounted from the stallion, and an attendant angel led it to one side. Gabriel put out his arm, and Prince Jesus put His hand on it as the exalted angel walked him up the steps to the Father and the Holy Spirit. They both stood and embraced the Prince as He came up the last steps. Then They led Him to the throne in the middle and sat Him down.

Gabriel returned down the steps as a grand orchestra played a beautiful background piece, which set the mood for the solemn ceremony of the placing of the crown. He walked over to a beautiful, ornate altar where the kingly crown lay. It was made up of the most gorgeous stones set in a diadem of pure gold. The stones did not reflect any light but generated a light of their own, giving an almost blinding brilliance for a human but well received by the redeemed and the vast multitude present.

As Gabriel marched upward with a deliberately paced step, the vast multitude and the group of the redeemed continued to stand with grave respect. Gabriel bowed reverently, as he placed the crown into the waiting hands of the Father and of the Holy Spirit. They turned toward the Prince and uttered the precious words of the crowning act,
"A crown of thorns once bruised Your brow,
as pain and sorrow swelled Your voice;
so, let the universe rejoice
as King of Kings, we crown Thee now!"

They gently laid the crown on Jesus scarred brow. The Father and the Holy Spirit turned back and took their seats, as the orchestra played the introductory notes of that glorious anthem. The Four Creatures bowed, and the twenty–four elders took off their crowns and laid them on the steps at Jesus' feet, as, with the redeemed, they fell on their knees.

The vast multitude kneeled in humble adoration, and the angel choir, led by Gabriel himself, began to resound in all the corners of the universe,

"Hallelujah! Hallelujah!
Hallelujah, Hallelujah, Hallelujah!
For the Lord God Omnipotent reigneth!
The kingdom of this world is become
The kingdom of our Lord, and of His Christ!
And He shall reign forever and ever!
King of Kings, Hallelujah, Hallelujah!
And Lord of Lords, Hallelujah!"

And He shall reign forever and ever! Hallelujah!"

The ceremony ended joyously. And then King Jesus bid all to turn and focus their attention on the final events that would close the great controversy on planet Earth. The Keepers of His Covenant were the objects of his most tender care and affection. He called Jebosh to Him from the choir ranks.

"How can I serve you, my King?" Jebosh bowed reverently.

"Go down, my good friend, and stay close to them.

As a commander in the heavenly host, see to it that all guardian angels are on watch. You know how vicious Satan can be and he will use any weapon or any of his subjects against our people," the King said with concern in His voice.

"I am truly honoured to go, Most Gracious Majesty," he bowed deeply and turning toward earth, pointed his wings backward as he went into flight, many times faster than the speed of light. In approximately eight minutes of human time, he was in outskirts of Hanford, hidden in the shadows of that visual dimension that is inaccessible to human sight.

REUNION

Each one was lost in his own thought as the bus rumbled along Highway 90 westbound toward Hanford.

"Gerry," Lisa interrupted his meditation, "I feel sick… I feel like throwing up."

"It's called motion sickness, honey. Here, let's move to the front of the bus where you'll get less sensation of motion." Gerry responded kindly.

"No, Gerry. I don't think it's related to motion. I've been feeling this for a week, while at our hideout," she went on. "I didn't want to alarm you, so I didn't say anything. But I guess you also should know that I have missed two periods in the last two months. Do you understand what that might mean?" she asked apprehensively.

Gerry looked dumbfounded for a moment then smiled as he half shouted, "Yeah, you're going to have a baby!"

Everybody snapped from their half slumber and looked at Gerry as if he were out of his mind.

"What's all this commotion about?" Mother Griggs asked, coming back to life.

"It seems that Lisa is pregnant, Mother Griggs," Gerry announced excitedly.

"No kidding?" Joyce asked as the whole group gathered around Lisa. Everyone wanted at once to make her comfortable and at the same time hug her and show their delight at the news.

"Gerry," Ben pulled his friend to the side, "how are you gonna manage this situation? Where we're going, there's probably no medical care, and the atmosphere is poisoned with radiation!"

"Ben, my good friend," Gerry replied with a reassuring smile, "We have seen the Lord's care for us in spectacular ways. I have no doubt that He will see us through this also."

"You're right, Gerry. I should know better."

The chitchat continued for another hour until they arrived at the main gate of the Hanford military reservation. Two Humvees, with their drivers in fully protected helmets and protective clothing, were waiting to take them into the compound. Once there, the passengers got out, the drivers also dropped off some supplies and high-tailed it out as fast as they could.

The little group was quickly surrounded by fellow believers who greeted them with joy, extending the hand of fellowship. But then a young couple with a little girl in tow broke through the group and grabbed Guillermo and Elizabeth in a tight, laughter-and-tears embrace.

"Dad, it's so good to see you," Isabella cried as she held tightly to her dad, as Shawn did the same for Elizabeth.

"I'm so glad to be able to hold my little girl again," Guillermo replied as he returned the hug with great emotion. Then they switched places and Isabella hugged her mom, unable to speak for a little while, as they wept with joy over being together again.

"And who might this little princess be?" Guillermo picked up the little girl holding on to Shawn's hand.

"This is your mischievous granddaughter, Hadassah, Dad," Isabella grinned, "I'm sorry about not giving you the promised grandson Willie, but I hear Rolando did. So I hope you're happy with that."

"I'm delighted, Isabella. Thank you for holding on to your faith and for your support of Shawn's ministry."

"Folks, let's bow our heads and thank the Lord Jesus for bringing this group here safely and for His continuing care of all of us, as we await the final outcome of history," Shawn invited all to pray.

That evening the inmates gathered together after a simple dinner to watch the news on a small T.V. that someone had smuggled in without the guards noticing. What they saw was so appalling that they removed the children and other sensitive persons from the large room. People wasting away with the awful sores, drinking filtered blood in order to stay alive. There were thousands of tons of dead fish along the beaches and rivers due to the bloody water. Cadavers of people dead from disease and the extreme burning heat were piling up outside the cities because there weren't any caskets or space in mortuaries to prepare the bodies.

The most current news, however, was the buzz of activity at the palace in Babilovia, where ambassadors and religious leaders from all over the world had gathered for the purpose of developing the plans for the final solution to the ills of the planet. The consensus was that God was punishing the earth because a part of the population was breaking His laws and not worshipping in accordance with church doctrine. The Christian church had already made allowance that all Moslems who wanted to worship on Friday could also do that, and Jews who wanted to still worship on Saturday could do the same, as long as everyone came together on Sunday for the official World Worship Day. It was the desecration of Sunday that was the driving issue. Universal control of all Sunday activities had been achieved. There were no football games, golf tournaments, nor beach volleyball competitions.

Theaters were closed, as were amusement parks. Churches, though, were wide open and everyone was expected to attend one, as was reported in the latest news bulletin.

"The latest development is that all the nations, through their ambassadors, have agreed to the final solution suggested by the Great Shepherd. The Keepers of the Covenant will all be executed at midnight on the night of October 31 of this year. Everyone is looking now to that date as the day of relief from the heat and liberation from the other plagues. It is expected to be the return to normalcy and temporal prosperity.

"A new and explosive report has just reached our desk. There are rumors circulating in Europe that Christ has returned to the earth. It is claimed that many people have already seen Him and are rejoicing at the fulfilment of His promised return. Wherever He goes, they say, he heals the sick, especially those suffering from the dreaded flesh–eating sores.

"We are doing our best to confirm this stupendous story and will give details as soon as we have them." The reporter sounded ecstatic.

THE DIE IS CAST

General Gooding was elated to be present at the definitive meeting at the palace. During his speech, the Great Shepherd had announced that the general had been recommended to him as the most qualified person to direct the worldwide effort at the eradication of the Keepers of the Covenant. After his speech, the Great Shepherd had introduced him to thunderous applause.

Now the news that Jesus had returned to earth boosted his desire to serve Him by eradicating all opposition to His law of the Sunday Sabbath. He would remain in the Golden Palace for the next few weeks to coordinate the work with military leaders from other parts of the world. Once everything was set, he would return to his home turf in Spokane to visit with friends and relatives and, more exciting still, to take part in the extermination at Hanford.

A week later, as he sat with his colleagues, a junior officer practically burst into the room.

"With your permission, sir," he almost shouted with excitement. "Jesus Christ is here, in the Golden Palace, visiting with His Holiness. You are specifically invited to attend this audience, sir!"

The general was beside himself with nervous excitement. He took a quick look in the large mirror on the wall to check his tie, to smooth the creases on his trousers, and to shine his two stars, soon to be three when he returned home.

As he entered the Sapphire Hall, he encountered a dazzling light shining from the front of the room by the Great Shepherd's throne. The place was packed with dignitaries, secular as well as religious. Once his eye accommodated to the bright light, General Gooding could discern a tall figure dressed in white linen, but he was too far to get a good view of his face through the golden glow.

"Come closer, General," a gravelly voice was heard clearly resounding across the large hall. *That voice sure sounds familiar,* he thought. *But it can't be! I've never seen or heard Jesus Christ!*

Everyone in the hall turned to see who was being addressed and opened a virtual aisle for the general as he marched smartly forward. He approached the apparition slowly, looking in its face, as if uncertain about something. When he was about five feet from it, he suddenly stopped, turned pale and stuttered, "It… it's…you! Can it be? You were… among us all along… and we didn't know!" Then he fell on his knees with his head bowed to the ground.

"Didn't I tell you that you would know soon enough?" The apparition smiled, the deep–set eyes looking upon the general, the gravelly voice now with a sweet tinge to it.

"And now, my dear General, I want to publicly express my gratitude for your committed service to me in helping to re-establish order in the world and promoting peace and prosperity for all people who love me enough to follow my ways. So, be of good courage! Carry out your duties with faithfulness, for a great reward awaits you and all who, with you, strive to honor my Father, my Holy Mother, and the church that I have established on earth. Sunday, the first day of the week, the day I set apart for all to worship in before I returned to heaven, will forever commemorate the glorious resurrection that makes possible eternal life for all the loyal people of the world."

As it finished the last words, the apparition began to fade and the glow dissipated from the vast hall. The general was deeply moved and could not speak for a few minutes.

"Your Holiness," he finally addressed the Great Shepherd, bowing deeply before him, "I am ready for the task at hand. I will be leaving tomorrow for a whirlwind tour of key places in the world, to make sure all preparations are as reported by my military colleagues. Once the task has been completed, I will return here to give you a complete report."

"You've already received the greater blessing, my brave general. Now, go with mine," the Shepherd replied as he laid his hands on General Gooding's head. It was October 22, a memorable anniversary for the Keepers of the Covenant. Many years before, their pioneers had awaited the return of Christ on such a date. But Jesus had not come, and there was a great disappointment. It seems that an erroneous conclusion, as to the event to take place, had led them to believe that Christ's promises in John 14:1–3 would be fulfilled then. Now the date had a different, yet still glorious meaning– on that date, in the year 1844, Jesus had entered the Most Holy chamber of the Temple in heaven to carry out the final judgement of mankind until the end of time should come. The prophecies of Daniel had led them accurately to the right event. Now, as they dwelt on the meaning of that prophecy, they looked toward the event to take place in just nine days, as announced on television–their final eradication. They spent the time in very private meditation, pleading their lives with God, that all their sins be forgiven and that they might be found worthy to rise in the resurrection, should their lives be ended. It was a most solemn and painful time, as they recalled their past lives and searched their hearts for purity and integrity.

October 23 came, and the people of planet Earth were ready for action. Many didn't want to wait until the thirty-first. They figured the sooner the job was done, the better off they would be. According to the news reports, Jesus was already going around to different places, healing the sick and providing fresh-looking water. Now, if the KOCs could be eradicated then everyone would be healed and the sea and rivers would return to normal water. But the military authorities forbade them on pain of arrest. They had to cooperate with the plan for a major, one-time effect. So the people, those few not affected by the disease, partied in great anticipation every night that week until the wee hours of the morning.

On October 31, Halloween, the crowds began to gather early around Hanford. They were not permitted to enter the quarantine area, but they had been promised that they would witness the execution, as the KOCs would be brought out within view. People brought their picnic baskets with food and drink, their folding chairs, and their binoculars. Except for the absence of flower floats, it appeared as though they were preparing for the yearly Tournament of Roses Parade at Pasadena, California.

There was a large band playing music to entertain the crowd. An elevated stage had been set up for church and government dignitaries. At the very center in the first row, Lieutenant General Gooding proudly displayed three silver stars on each shoulder, evidence of good favour with the President and with his military superiors.

THE RESCUE

Suddenly, totally unexpectedly, the ground began to shake in California, Oregon and Washington: a nine point three on the Richter scale. The panic was indescribable. There were, simultaneously, seven epicenters–three in California, one in Oregon, one in Washington, and two in British Columbia. It shook for about ninety seconds, enough to devastate most of the coastal cities. Buildings of all sizes were toppling everywhere. Fires broke out wherever gas lines were broken and sparks from crashing steel ignited the gas.

An hour later, the tsunami came in–a wave of water about 180 feet high washed the millions of tons of debris and bodies all the way to the base of the Sierra Madre Mountains in California and to the Cascades in Washington and Oregon.

The news of the big disaster in the west coast spread rapidly. General Gooding was alarmed as his adjutant filled him in on the details. It was just a few minutes to midnight, and he knew he had to fulfil his duty immediately. So he stood on the provisional stage and ordered the troops stand ready to fire on the helpless line of Keepers of the Covenant, who were standing ten deep before the firing squads.

"Ready! Aim–" But the order was interrupted by a thunderous blast followed by a second and a third blast originating anywhere between 100 and 150 miles away. Mount Hood near Portland, Oregon, went first, blowing about half of the mountain off with the sound of a nuclear explosion. The ground shook violently and all the soldiers fell on the ground, many of them setting off their weapons wildly, not hitting their targets. Mount Rainier followed seconds later, blowing an American Airlines jet, which was flying over the crater on its way to Dallas, to pieces the size of toothpicks. Mount St. Helens had been building up for another ugly spectacle, and its moment came about thirty seconds after Rainier. This time it blew another third of the mountain into the air, with such ash and smoke as to smother any survivors of the tsunami in the Northwest. The Three Sisters in Bend, Oregon, didn't want to be left behind. As they blew their tops, the giant bulge, which had been building up near them suddenly, deflated and opened up a huge cavity, swallowing up Bend and neighboring communities. Terror reigned everywhere as the earthquakes spread east across the continental shelf. General Gooding fell hard off the tottering stage and rolled on the ground. Newly promoted Lieutenant Colonel Darnell and Captain Carson ran back toward the stage in terrified confusion as the fence surrounding Hanford became electrified by lightning strikes. They helped the general to his feet, for he had suffered a broken leg, and rushed to one of the Humvees parked nearby. But they didn't get too far. The roads were all broken up, and even the tough, all–terrain Humvees were no match for the huge obstacles and the impossible visibility.

But the worst was yet to come. It began to hail. Baseball size at first. But they kept getting bigger, and Captain Carson pulled over next to a building behind the stage. The Humvee's roof was getting really battered, and they knew they had to find shelter very quickly, they wouldn't even make it to the door, so they got out and dove under the Humvee. Colonel Darnell caught one on his upper arm, which was shattered by the blow, while Captain Carson did his best to shove the general quickly under the vehicle. Just as he got his boss in, his head received a glancing blow from a baseball–sized hailstone, which knocked him unconscious. Gooding and Darnell dragged him under, and the three soldiers huddled in panic, as the hail grew bigger and the banging louder. Fifty, sixty, even seventy–pound chunks of ice were finishing off anything left standing by the earthquakes and the volcanoes. Anyone not in a concrete–fortified building was as good as dead.

At the end of thirty minutes, the banging ceased. Carson had regained consciousness but was moaning over a severe headache. Still, he crawled out first, and then helped Darnell and Gooding out. They too were in severe pain but considered themselves fortunate to be alive amidst such utter destruction and desolation. Many of the spectators who had come to see the demise of the KOCs lay on the ground, battered to death along with their picnic baskets.

They looked over where the KOCs had been awaiting their fate, and to their shocked surprise, they were still standing there! Not one was injured and despite the darkness surrounding the officers, there was a bright light shining over the entire group.

Suddenly, General Gooding felt a presence behind him. He heard a gravelly voice and felt a gentle touch on his broken leg. Instantly, the pain was gone! He turned and saw the apparition of Jesus as he simultaneously touched the colonel's arm and captain's head. These stood in amazement at the appearance of the miracle worker and the sudden absence of pain.

"My faithful servants," he said with an urgent gravely tone, "you still have a task to do! This continuous destruction will not cease until the dissident KOCs are eliminated. There are plenty of weapons! Do your faithful work for me! Your reward awaits you!" And then, the apparition faded away in a bright whirlwind.

"Darnell, Carson! Get those machine guns and bring one to me! We've got to finish this right now!" General Gooding yelled at his officers, above the roar of the elements of nature gone wild. The officers obeyed instantly and also beckoned to a few troops who had survived in the shelter of a concrete bunker. They rushed toward the Keepers of the Covenant, the General yelling, "Fire at will! Don't let anyone escape or you'll pay with your own life!"

Just as they were within range, they knelt to steady their weapons, but a thunderous explosion ripped the sky apart and opened a vast clear space, luminous with the light of the stars. In the middle of this space, there suddenly appeared two giant tables of stone with the Ten Commandments. A bright halo of light surrounded the fourth commandment that commands the universe to observe the seventh day of the week as God's holy Sabbath. All the noise from the volcanoes stopped, and the howling wind suddenly died down. There was an awful, painful silence.

"What does this all mean, Darnell?" a badly shaken general asked his colonel in desperation.

"I think it means that we have been wrong about the Sabbath and about the Keepers of the Covenant, sir," a trembling Lieutenant Colonel Darnell responded. The sight of the Fourth Commandment shining among the Ten, and of the untouched and uninjured KOCs had left him with no other conclusion. They looked with horrified amazement as the tables of stone were withdrawn through space until they at last disappeared from sight. They looked at each other and then at their weapons, still in their hands. The barrels were melted and were drooping down. They turned their eyes toward the Keepers of the Covenant. There they were still, now kneeling with their hands stretched out toward the sky, their faces aglow with joy and excitement, bright with a beautiful light falling on them.

They turned to the sky to see where the light was coming from and saw a sight that really melted everything inside them. A bright cloud was coming toward them, and music began to be heard as the cloud approached. A powerful orchestra was playing as an angelic chorus swelled a joyful anthem. The sound increased and the soldiers were awestruck as they beheld the beauty of the person on the throne. The King of Kings was arrayed in his radiant robes, and the crown on his head was so dazzling, that it lit the whole cloud with a glorious light.

"This is Jesus, Darnell! The apparition lied to us! We have been fighting against his people! We are lost!" General Gooding cried in horror and anguish. "Let's get out of here!"

They turned to run from the light and headed back under the Humvee. But as they headed for shelter, they ran straight into a tall, handsome person with curly black hair, wearing a bright, shinning white robe with a silver band around his waist. He stood there with a sad, somber look at what was left of three human beings who made the wrong choices in life. Darnell fainted as he gasped the name, "General Jebosh!" The encounter with the person he had come to hate was too much for him, and his heart gave out. The general and the captain were just as frightened, but made it to their supposed place of safety.

On the cloud, there was a moment of silence as the King turned and gave the signal to General Jebosh, the commander of all the heavenly hosts assigned to planet Earth. As he stood by the throne, he raised a gleaming silver trumpet to his lips, and a richly melodious reveille was heard around the world. Then a seemingly loud thunder rolled across the skies. Gooding and Carson didn't understand it, but to the Keepers of the Covenant it was the sweetest sound heard on the planet since Jesus had walked its streets, two thousand years before. Lazarus, Jairus' daughter, the son of the widow of Nain, and many others had heard the words, "Arise, come forth!" as they slept the sleep of the redeemed. Now that same Almighty voice rumbled around the terrestrial globe, "Awake! Awake, you that sleep in the dust and arise!"

A powerful earthquake shook the whole planet at once. Mountains crumbled and islands disappeared; and in graveyards all over the earth, the graves of God's covenant–keeping people through all the ages, from Adam and Eve to the Last Keepers of the Covenant who slept in the dust of the ground, opened up to let out their occupants, now in the glow and happiness of people totally restored to physical wholeness and beauty. An angel was standing by every grave, with a beautiful white robe of the finest linen, and a sash woven with the finest silk humans have ever seen. The clothes of the sleeping saints had rotted away in their graves, but they would never miss them, no! Not now, dressed in the robes of heavenly royalty! Once dressed, their guardian angels, who accompanied them throughout their lives, took them by the hand and, against the powerful forces of gravity, easily led them up to the cloud to meet their king.

But at Hanford, the scene was different. The mighty earthquake that opened the graves of the redeemed also destroyed everything that was still standing. The powerful, fortified walls of the military bunker, crashed down on what was left of the Humvee, bringing to their end the lives of Lieutenant General Gooding and Captain Carson.

The guardian angels also arrived at the side of each of the eagerly expectant Keepers of the Covenant and, in an act of sublime privacy, surrounded each individual with a circle of light that allowed each one to shed their worn–out earthly rags and don the beautiful white linen robe and gorgeous sash. They took the hands of their equally joyful guardians and were led upward toward the throne of the eagerly awaiting King.

HOMEWARD BOUND

Once all the redeemed Keepers of the Covenant were on the humongous cloudy chariot, it began to move upward at immeasurable speed. The scene of rejoicing was indescribable. Gerry and Lisa couldn't stop hugging each other, almost as it they were in a dream and couldn't wake up.

"Oh, Gerry! In my wildest dream, I never thought it would end like this. Oh, how I love Jesus! I can hardly wait to meet Him, but the line is long. Oh, well, we have eternity, don't we?" she said as she laughed and cried at the same time.

"Lisa…I can hardly speak… my joy is so strong that I can't express it! I was just thinking, Lisa… we're not going alone! We are going to have a baby in heaven, and the excitement overwhelms me!"

Rita was standing off to one side, anxiously looking in every direction. Her heart was beating so fast, she thought it would take off running right out of her body. Just then, a familiar face stood in front of her.

"Jerrod! Oh Jerrod, I'm so glad you're here! I'm worried! I don't see somebody so dear to my heart! What if he didn't make it?" A few tears began to flow, but Jerrod put his hand on her shoulder, and they stopped.

"Now, now, Rita, just look behind you, "Jerrod said with the most radiant smile. Rita turned around excitedly, and her guardian angel stood there with another angel and a handsome young man between them.

"Ricky!" she exploded with such joy, that everyone around her had to turn and look. "Oh, Ricky, Ricky, my love! Oh, thank you! Thank you, dear angels, for this wonderful surprise." She clung to his neck as he clung to her in a long and tearful embrace. This time, Jerrod and the guardian angels did not interfere with the tears. In a minute she was aware that a small crowd had surrounded her because of the applause and the cheers. So she had to let go of Ricky and begin the introductions.

"Ricky, these have been the best friends anyone on Earth ever had. This is Guillermo and Elizabeth, their children, Rolando and Melinda and Shawn and Isabella, and their grandchildren, Willie and Hadassah; my childhood friend Joyce and her husband, Ben; our faithful and dear friend Ahmed, who comforted me so many times when I needed it; my very dear friends and fellow classmates on earth, Gerry and Lisa, and Lisa's parents, Mr. and Mrs. Griggs–and listen to this, Ricky, cause this is really precious–Lisa is pregnant and she's going to have her baby in just one month… we are all so excited! I also want you to meet Don and Deena, and you'll meet their kids when they come around…I think they're in line to meet the King. And, finally, at least for the moment, here's Pastor Fred who baptized us on the same day, and his wife, Rosa."

They all expressed their delight at having Ricky join them and then moved into line for the greatest moment so far in their lives, meeting the King of Kings and Lord of Lords–once the loneliest, most heartbroken sufferer the whole universe ever saw, the Lamb of God, slain from the foundation of the world, now the glorious, most majestic King the universe ever beheld.

EPILOGUE

The last millennium had begun, and in the Regions of Darkness, six miles below the now shattered, utterly destroyed crust of Planet Earth, there was an immense cavern, once the pride of the spirit world, now the ruin of their once powerful alien empire. At the far end of the massive throne room, bits and pieces of the finest ivory were scattered around the huge boulders that crashed through the ceiling.

At the entrance, a tall stately figure stood looking in, his deep-set eyes burning with hatred, his wide forehead wrinkled, his once silky hair disheveled, a smashed and broken gold crown in his left hand. To one side, General Algarroba, General Beelzebub, and Captain Vesuvius sat in silent grief, reviewing in their powerful minds what they once had given up for this.

The Prince of Darkness turned away, as if unable to come to grips with the final reality. Stretching out his huge wings, their once beautiful feathers now tattered and discoloured, he glided out into the open skies, and began to survey what was left of his usurped planet. *"My enemy is gone, and he took all the hated KOCs with Him! Left behind is nothing but the stinking corpses of the rejecters of His Covenant!*

No humans left alive for me to rule over! What am I going to do for the next thousand years...

Suddenly, a loud, mournful, greatly anguished, gravelly wail filled the air and was carried by the winds around the little smoking orb, reverberating upon all the ruins of mankind's dreams and ambitions. Algarroba, Beelzebub, and Vesuvius heard it, and wept bitterly, but the end was yet to come...

APPENDIX

1. Angels. Angels are beings created with special features and powers so that they can execute the special tasks of caring for God's universe. Many of them are assigned to serve the inhabitants of planet earth, providing for their needs, protecting them from harm, and helping to guide them in doing what is right.

   A third of the original host of angels were persuaded by their once loyal, now rebellious, leader, to reject God's lordship and leadership, accusing God of being selfish and arbitrary. He had no evidence, of course, but was able to deceive this large contingent of angels, leading them into a war against God's government which ultimately resulted in their exile to planet earth (see Isaiah 14:12–20; Ezekiel 28:11–17; Revelation 12:7–10). The warfare against God was continued on this earth, Satan and his angels deceiving mankind into taking sides with him and rejecting the covenant.

   Therefore, this world has been involved in a great controversy between Christ and Satan for about 6,000 years, and will continue until Christ returns again (see John 14:1–3)

   At that time, Satan and his angels will be bound to this earth for a 1000 years (see Revelation 20:1–3).

At the end of the 1000 years, Christ will return to the earth with the Keepers of the Covenant and the Holy City, New Jerusalem, and Satan and his angels will finally be destroyed (see Ezekiel 28:18–19; Isaiah 14:15; Revelation 20:7–10).

2. Ascension of the redeemed. Upon the resurrection, the redeemed of all the ages will be lifted by angels off the earth to join Christ in His cloudy chariot to travel to the Holy City, New Jerusalem, in Heaven (see 1 Thessalonians 4:17). This ascension will be similar to Christ's ascension when He left the earth after His resurrection (see Acts 1:9–11).

3. Baptism. Baptism is the ceremony of entrance into Christ's kingdom. John the Baptist is recorded as being the first one to practice it, but it received the approval and seal of God when Christ Himself came to be baptized at the Jordan River (see Mark 3:13–15). The Bible teaches that baptism is performed by submerging the total body under water (see Mark 3:16) while invoking the blessing of the Father, the Son, and the Holy Spirit (see Matthew 28:19–20). The Purpose of submerging the whole body under is to represent a death and burial of the old, sinful life, and rising again to a new life in communion with and obedience to Christ.

4. Christ's ministry on behalf of mankind. When Jesus returned to heaven, He went into the first compartment of the heavenly temple to carry out His ministry of intercession on behalf of all who would accept Him as their Lord and Savior, asking forgiveness for their sins, and submitting their lives to the guidance of the Holy Spirit. He remained in that compartment until the time of judgement predicted by Daniel in the prophecy of the

2,300 prophetic days (or 2,300 literal years) (see Daniel 8:14). This is a major prophecy which requires a broader explanation beyond the scope of these notes.

However, to state it simply, just as the services in the earthly temple were divided into two stages–the daily sacrifices, and the sacrifices of the yearly Day of Atonement, each with a specific function and meaning representing the sacrifice of Christ on the cross, the temple in heaven also has a two–stage ministry of intercession and judgement. Since He arrived back to heaven upon His ascension, Jesus spent the years until 1844 (the year the prophecy of Daniel predicted) in the work of intercession of behalf of all sinners who sought forgiveness. In 1844, He entered the second compartment of the temple, designated as the Most Holy Place, to begin the final judgement of all mankind, determining who will be saved when He returns to the earth as promised in John 14:1–3.

5. Christ's nature. The Bible clearly teaches that the nature of Christ is exactly that of the Father's in terms of their omnipotence (all powerful), omniscience (all knowing), and innate eternal existence (see Philippians 2:5–8; Isaiah 9:6). There is another characteristic of God's person that Christ also shared before He became a human through the miracle of incarnation made possible by the Holy Spirit (see Luke 1:30–37). That characteristic is omnipresent– the ability to be present everywhere at once. When Jesus chose to take a human body for our sake, to carry out the plan of redemption, He gave up that privilege, and remained the God–Man. He returned to heaven in a physical, human body (see Acts 1:9–11), and will remain that way throughout eternity. What a marvellous

condescension to us unworthy human beings, that God the Son should be our blood brother!

6. Christ, the Prince. Jesus Christ is identified in the bible as the Prince of Peace (see Isaiah 9:6), and as the Messiah, the Prince (see Daniel 9:25). Since Jesus is the only Messiah, we have to conclude that Daniel is here talking about Jesus Christ. Further on, the prophet Daniel identifies Jesus as "Michael your Prince" (see Daniel 10:21). Daniel closes his prophetic book in chapter 12, stating that at the end of time, "shall Michael stand up, the great prince which stands for the children of thy people…" (see Daniel 12:1). Daniel knew that until the end of time, Jesus would take the role of Prince until His work would be finished in the heavenly temple. Then, the coronation will take place, making Him, "King of Kings and Lord of Lords" (see Revelation 18:11–16).

7. Coronation of the Prince as King of Kings. The author here takes poetic license to imagine what the coronation of Christ, the Prince of Peace could be like. Everything in Heaven is so sublime, that the human imagination falls extremely short of even attempting to describe it! So, one can expect a lot more beauty and glory when, in heaven, one hears or even sees a playback of what takes place at the coronation of the King of Kings and Lord of Lords! (see the verses quoted in that event in the book).

8. Christ's return to Earth. One of the greatest certainties of the gospel is the assurance that Christ is going to return to this earth to gather the Keepers of His Covenant throughout the ages, and take them home to heaven. Perhaps the best known scripture on this topic is the promise made by Christ Himself to the disciples while at the Last Supper (see John 14:1–3). The disciple and apostle John, in the book of Revelation, states clearly

that his coming will be visible to all the world–no secret rapture implied or intended! (see Revelation 1:7; Revelation 19:11–16). The return of Christ is going to be a monumental happening. It is described in Revelation as a series of supernatural events witnessed by every human being found alive at the time of the end (see Revelation 6:12–17). The wicked who will be lost at the end, will see Christ and try to hide in terror. I repeat: No secret Rapture!

9. Commandments. Most people believe that the Ten Commandments were first given to the Jews on Mount Sinai through Moses. This, however, is very far from the truth. God's law has existed throughout eternity. It has always been the basis of government in Heaven, and became the basis for government on earth from the very beginning. If this were not so, then sin would never have existed, for sin is the transgression of the law (see 1John 3:4). Lucifer, the first to sin, coveted the position of God (see Isaiah 14:13, 14). Eve coveted the forbidden fruit (see Genesis 3:6). The pre–flood people sinned in every way possible, and were destroyed by the flood (see Genesis 6:7). And so, sin, the transgression of the Ten Commandments, existed on earth for almost two thousand years before Moses was given the law on tables of stone on Mount Sinai (see Exodus 20). And in the last book of the Bible, Christ reminds John in vision of the reward awaiting those who keep His commandments (see Revelation 22:14), for they shall continue to be the basis of his government throughout the universe and throughout eternity.

10. Covenant. This agreement consisted of at least five (5) gifts that God would give His creatures: Life, Love, Freedom, Happiness, and a Law to guide their behaviour

and duties. His creatures were in turn to respond with at least five (5) gifts of their own: Love, Loyalty, Trust, Reverence, and Obedience to His laws. Only as they received God's gifts could they exist, and only as they returned gifts of their own could they enjoy that existence. We refer to this exchange as "gifts" because in both directions, they are given under the absolute freedom to deny them. Supreme love is here the determining factor in this relationship.

11. Creation. This is the mysterious process through which all things that exist came into being. It is widely challenged in the world today, particularly by evolutionists and atheists, but also by many who choose to ignore the offer of the Covenant. How God does it is something that humans cannot figure out, but its two main pieces of evidence are the Bible and the immense beauty and complexity of all objects, beginning with the mysterious ordering of DNA. (see Genesis 1; Genesis 2; Psalms 19; Hebrews 1:2)

12. Crisis and trouble. As we approach the end of time, Satan knows that he has a very short time in which to do the most damage (see 1Peter 5:8). So he influences people to wage war, commit hideous crimes, lie, cheat, kill, and practice all kinds of immorality (see John 8:44). He moves on some of the wealthy corporations to extort high prices for the most basic needs, such as gasoline, diesel, heating oil, and medicines (see James 5:1–8). He works with many preachers as they distort the Bible's doctrines, confusing people as to what is truth (see 1Timothy 4:1; Matthew 15:8–9; 2 Timothy 2–4). The world has a history of trouble and crisis. However, it was predicted that at the end of time, there would be an intense sequence and variety of catastrophic events what

would wake up the people to the signs of Christ's soon return (see Matthew 24 and 25).

13. Death. This is a subject over which there is a lot of confusion in the world today. The Bible is pretty straightforward on this teaching. When the inert body came into contact with God's original breath, man became a living soul (see Genesis 2:7). When, due to disease, trauma, or old age, the breath leaves the living body, it returns to an inert form of biological matter, that eventually decomposes back to the dust of the earth. The breath returns to God, who originally gave it (see Psalms 104:29; Psalms 146:4; Acts 17:25). He ceases to be a soul, for the soul is the union between body and God's breath of life. The state of death can only be reversed back to a living soul when God, by his power of resurrection, reconstructs the dead person to his/her original form (replicating the original DNA) and infusing his breath again into the newly reconstructed body (see Genesis 2:7 again and then 1Thessalonians 4:13–18).

14. Death decree against the Keepers of the Covenant. The Keepers of God's Covenant have been persecuted throughout history, because they are the main object of Satan's hatred. He has seduced many against the Covenant itself and against those who cherish it. The most widely known persecution of innocent Christians who attempted to be faithful to the Covenant, took place in Europe during and after the Protestant Reformation by the office of the Inquisition. Read history, people! Know what took place then! So will it be at the end (see Revelation 12:17 and 13:15). The Keepers of the Covenant will be the fly in the ointment of popular acquiescence to the demands of apostate Christianity. History will repeat itself, but this time, God will intervene in a powerful way.

15. Demons at work. Quite often, we find Satan himself at work in deceiving or attacking human beings: Adam and Eve, Job, Saul, and even trying to tempt Christ himself. Whenever he needs to handle a specially wicked task, he seems to take it on himself. We find, however, that most often he works through his agents, the millions of angel he deceived in heaven and led to rebellion against God. They were cast out of heaven, as seen above, and are bent on the deception and destruction of all human beings (see 1Peter 5:8). While Christ was on earth, much of His ministry was devoted to casting out devils out of demon-possessed people (see Mark 5:1–15).

16. Disappointment of 1844. The year 1844 was a year of intense religious awakening in the U.S and throughout the world. People from across the spectrum of religious denominations had discovered Daniel's prophecy of the 2,300 years, and decided that an event of immense importance was to take place that year. The excitement had been building up since the 1830's, and the movement was finally galvanized under a preacher by the name of William Miller. He taught and preached that the event to take place was the second coming of Jesus Christ to this earth. A large group left their former denominations and prepared to receive the Lord. But it didn't happen, and most abandoned the movement and either returned to their churches or lost faith in Christianity altogether. A small group continued to study the Biblical prophecies intently, and discovered that the date was accurate, but they had figured on the wrong event. Their study of the books of Daniel and the Revelation led them to the conclusion that what had taken place was the entrance of Christ as our intercessor from the first apartment of the Heavenly Sanctuary, or the Holy Place, into the second

apartment, or the Most Holy Place, to carry out the work of final judgement of the people of the world before His return.

17. Earth, its final convulsions. When Christ returns, the world will go into intense convulsion, as the earth breaks up, the graves open, and the resurrection of God's people take place (see Revelation 16:17–21 and 2 Peter 3:10; Malachi 4:1; Revelation 6:12–17). When Christ leaves with His saints, the world will be left in total chaos (see Jeremiah 4:23–29).

18. End time. The time Earth has existed as an inhabited planet is fast approaching its end. God Himself, in the person of Jesus Christ, contributed to the predictions of the prophets Daniel and John (see Daniel 2:44; Revelation 10:6). Jesus Himself, in his prophetic sermon predicted the catastrophic events that would precede the end of earthly time, and the simultaneous beginning of his kingdom in heaven with the Keepers of the Covenant (see Matthew 24 and 25).

19. God's character. Lucifer, who later became known as Satan, was the first to lie about the character of God. Those on earth who later came to know God, learned that He is a God of infinite love and compassion. He wants the very best for all who will enter into the Covenant (see Genesis 6:5–6, 18; Ezekiel 18:20–32), who repent from their wickedness and live right. But justice demands death for the impenitent, something we understand even in mankind's imperfect judicial systems.

20. God's provisions for the final struggle. As the crisis in the world deepens, God's people are to remember that He is on their side, and that He has made provisions for their survival (see Psalms 91; 27:5–6; 31:19–20). Even when

the plagues fall on mankind, they are to trust in their God and walk by faith (see Habakkuk 3:16–19). Just as sure as He is the Good Shepherd, they are His sheep, and the promise is that He will continue to lead, even though the valley of the shadow of death (see Psalm 23). In the end, they will hear the glad words found in Matthew 25:31–45: "Come, ye blessed of My Father, inherit the kingdom prepared for you from the foundation of the wordl!"

21. Holy Spirit and His work. The exalted title of God refers to only three persons, God the Father, God the Son, and God the Holy Spirit. This is the trinity (see Matthew 28:19). The Holy Spirit is a sacred person, entitled to the same respect, reverence, and worship as the Father and the Son. He took on the special task of making the communication between human beings and God possible, through His special intercession. When we hear the voice of our conscience telling us that we are doing right or wrong, it is the voice of the Holy Spirit guiding our choices (see John 16:7–11; Ephesians 4:30). He also made possible the specially mysterious miracle of Jesus' birth from the virgin Mary. He is a person sensitive with joy at our acceptance of Christ as our personal savior and with grief at our rejection of His Covenant.

22. Justification. This is the process through which a person is found sinless by his faith in and by the grace of Christ (see Romans 5:1; Romans 3:24). When we confess our sins with a heartfelt desire to be forgiven and our minds renewed and transformed (see Romans 12:2), God gives us a brand new, clean page to begin our life anew. We appear before the courts of heaven as though we have never, ever sinned. That is a very precious gift that enables us to enter heaven when Jesus returns for us.

23. Keepers of the Covenant. Since eternity past, God has made a covenant, an agreement with all his creatures that defines their relationship with Him and with each other. It was made with all the inhabitants of other worlds (Hebrews 1:2 and Job 1:6), with all the angels, and, lastly, with mankind on earth (see Genesis 1 and 2; Genesis 6:18; Genesis 9:9–17; Genesis 15:18, etc.). This covenant, being of an eternal nature, has been subsequently offered to every person on planet earth throughout the ages of time. Most have rejected it, but many have accepted it and lived within its provisions and privileges.

24. Lucifer. A very powerful angel created by God and made leader of all the angelic hosts of heaven. He was created with special characteristics, given special talents and powers, and the highest rank and angel can hold: that of covering cherub. He was so beautiful and so gifted that it went to his head, resulting in an insurrection against the government of God. (see Isaiah 14:12–20 and Ezekiel 28:11–19).

25. Mankind's fall. God placed a tree in the Garden of Eden that represented His sovereignty and ownership of all that He had created on this planet. Although everything else on earth was created for mankind, this tree was off limits, and would always remind them of their Creator's balance of law and freedom. It was to be their test of loyalty and obedience in light of the covenant he had made with them (see Genesis 2:16–17).

26. Marriage. Marriage is one of the two institutions created by God in the Garden of Eden upon the creation of mankind. The first institution, of course, is the sanctification of the seventh day of the weekly cycle as the Sabbath of the Lord (see Genesis 2:1–3). The second

one is established as God joins Adam and Eve into a family (see Genesis 2:21-24). One man for one woman: that is the original order established by God, and is to last through eternity.

27. Millennium. There's a lot of speculation today about the millennium mentioned in the book of Revelation. There is no room for confusion or speculation. The bible clearly talks about a 1000 year period between the second coming of Christ and His final return to earth with the New Jerusalem (see Revelation 20:2-3).

28. New Jerusalem. One of the most beautiful passages in the Bible is the stunning description of the Holy City, the New Jerusalem, which God has built in Heaven as the dwelling place of the redeemed people of earth (see Revelation 21:1-3 and 10-27; Revelation 22:1-5). God runs the universe from His throne in the midst of the city. When the great controversy between Christ and Satan is over, and Satan and his host are destroyed along with all of the wicked at the end of the millennium, Christ will renew the earth through the original process of creation, and bring the New Jerusalem down from heaven to earth, this planet then becoming the capital of the universe (see Revelation 20:7-10, 14-15; 21:1-5; Isaiah 66:22, 23).

29. Persecution. Persecution is the attempt by some to deny others their freedom. There is persecution for political, ideological, or religious convictions. This has been a practice throughout history and it will repeat itself. Christ predicted that it would be so (see John 15:18-21; John 16:1-3 and 33). Because Satan hates God's commandment-keeping people, especially because they keep the seventh-day Sabbath, a day he hates and, thus, influenced church leaders to change it to Sunday; he will

also seek the physical destruction of every Keeper of the Covenant (see Revelation 12:17; Revelation 13:7).

30. Plagues. The plagues described in Revelation 16:2–21 are the final judgements to fall on a rebellious world that has rejected God's extreme patience and loving mercy. They will fall upon mankind once Christ leaves the Heavenly Sanctuary to intercede for man no more.

31. Planet Earth. During the millennium, the earth will be in a state of chaos, just as it will have been left by the convulsing earthquakes and storms that will take place when Christ arrives to take the redeemed people home to heaven (see Revelation 16:17–21and Jeremiah 4:23–29).

32. Prayer. Prayer is the mode of choice for communicating with God. When we pray, we give recognition to God as Lord of our lives, as our Creator and Redeemer, and as Restorer of our souls from sinners to transformed saints (see Matthew 6:6–13). Jesus spent a lot of time in prayer, submitting to the will of His Father, seeking strength and guidance as He dealt with all the challenges to His ministry from the Jewish leaders, from Satan, and even from His own disciples. As one submits to God through prayer (see Mathew 26:41), He moves into his life to strengthen and fortify his will to do good and reject evil (see Matthew 26:39, 42). He fills us with love for one another, and with a real taste for righteousness and purity.

33. Prayer, intercessory. The Lord desires that we should pray for each other (see James 5:16). The Apostle Paul offered prayers for the brethren, and also asked for their prayers (see 1Thessalonians 5:25; Colossians 1:9; 2 Thessalonians 1:11; 3:1). Jesus taught everyone to pray even for their enemies (see Matthew 5:44). Why should one pray for other people? First, because through intercessory prayer,

one becomes a partner with God in the salvation of lost mankind. Second, because it breeds compassion and kindness in one's heart towards others. In this way, one imitates Christ in his dealing with sinful individuals.

34. Probation for planet Earth ends. God is a person of extreme mercy and love. He does not want to destroy; He does not want for one single person to perish, to die (see Ezekiel 33:11; Hosea 11:8; Isaiah 1:16–18). But He is also a God of justice, and must destroy evil and those who insist on being a part of it (see Isaiah 1:19–20). If God does not put a final end to evil, then it can continue to exist forever, making many people unhappy and miserable, and casting a stain upon His government. So, there will be a cut–off point, at which the people of this world, those who have consistently said no to the Holy Spirit's invitation to do right (see Ephesians 4:30), who will no longer receive that invitation, and will be lost for eternity. There will be a time in the near future, when Christ will cease His ministry of intercession on behalf of mankind, and leave the heavenly Sanctuary with these words on his lips:

   > "He that is unjust, let him be unjust still; and he that is filthy, let him be filthy still; and he that is righteous, let him be righteous still; and he that is holy, let him be holy still. And, behold, I come quickly; and My reward is with Me, to give every man according as his work shall be." (Revelation 22:11–12)

35. Promises for the Time of the End. As the world sees all the natural disasters taking place, the war in the Middle East, the threat of world–wide terrorism, and the shaky security of government, many are wondering, "Is this the time of the end? If so, what is beyond that? Will I and my family survive what's coming, or is there no hope for us?"

If one turns to the Bible, one finds that indeed the world is facing the final events of earth's history, and that there is an abundance of promises of protection, survival, and a fabulous life beyond this one for all who choose to enter into the Covenant (see Psalms 50:3–5; Malachi 4:11–3; Habakkuk 3:17–19; 2 Peter 3:10–13; Psalms 91, all).

36. Punishment. The consequence of disobedience (sin) is death (see Romans 6:23). Now, for God to execute direct justice, human beings would be doomed to death forever…zip… gone for good! However, God's immeasurable love is so great, that He could not stand to see His creatures destroyed forever. So, He, along with Jesus and the Holy Spirit, devised a plan that if one of His creatures ever sinned, if he would confess and repent, he could be forgiven and absolved from the guilt. However, the penalty had to be paid, and only one who had life of his own, one who could die and come back to life again could atone for the sin. An angel could not do it, for he is a created creature with no life of his own. So the plan always was that God would take upon Himself the responsibility to redeem mankind from the consequences of sin (see John 3:16; Romans 5:8; 1Peter 1:18).

37. Redemption. God's plan to restore mankind after the fall into sin centered on the atonement to take place on earth through the vicarious death of Christ. By his death on the cross, every person who would accept that sacrifice on his/her behalf, and, confessing his/her sins, accepted to live within the Covenant, would be forgiven and restored to God's favour. Until this sacrifice could take place, a symbolic system was set up with the sacrifice of a lamb to represent Christ, and the faith placed on the animal sacrifice, would eventually be applied to Christ Himself. In this way, every person, beginning with Adam, was

justified until the actual death of Jesus on Calvary. Since then, animal sacrifices are no longer necessary, since the real sacrifice has taken place.

38. Repentance and Forgiveness. Repentance is a turning away from evil thoughts and actions. This can only take place when the Holy Spirit, who is God in the third person, convinces the heart of sin, and the person feels grief for his disobedience (see Ephesians 4:30; Roman 2:4; John 16:7, 8, 13). When the person confesses his sin, God forgives it and the Holy Spirit begins the work in the heart to turn it away from wickedness (see 1John 1:9).

39. Resurrection of the Righteous. Once of the most precious promises Christ made to the disciples and to his church was the promises of the resurrection. To Mary and Martha, upon the death of their brother, Lazarus, Jesus said, "I Am the Resurrection and the Life; he that believeth in Me, though he were dead, yet shall he live," John 11:25. When one dies, he returns to the dust of the ground and his breath returns to God (see Psalms 104:29; Psalms 146:3–4). But when Jesus returns, He will gather together one's dust and breathe life into one's inert body, and one shall come back to life (see 1Thessalonians 4:14–17).

40. Sabbath misrepresented. We have already touched on the seventh–day Sabbath as an original part of God's creation week. However, we want to point out here, that the Sabbath will be the major point of contention against God's people, precisely because they are going against the current of popular sentiment and belief. In the book of Revelation, where the final events in world history are described, God clearly identifies His people as those "which keep the Commandments of God, and have the

testimony of Jesus Christ." (see Revelation 12:17; 14:12; and 22:14). The fourth commandment, clearly declares that the seventh day of the week is the Sabbath, not the first day (see Exodus 20:8–11). Furthermore, nowhere in the bible will anyone find a statement that God nor Christ, nor the Holy Spirit, nor the Apostles of the Lord, ordained a change of the Sabbath from the seventh to the first day. Yet the popular churches in the land insist that such a change took place. Well, indeed, it did! But not with God's approval, permission, or blessing! But rather in fulfilment of Paul's prophecy that in the latter times (that is, after his death), many would depart from the faith (see 1Timothy 4:1, 2). The vast majority of the Christian world does not know or acknowledge that the Sunday Sabbath is a child of ancient pagan Sun worship, and that it was adopted into Christianity after the Apostles and leaders of the early Christian church had passed away.

41. Sabbath keeping. The Sabbath was intended by God to be a day of rest, rejoicing, communion, and setting time apart from the weekly toil (see Exodus 20:8–11). When God created the world, He created it by stages, each stage supporting the next. The bible clearly states that each creation day started with the evening followed by the morning. Each evening was the beginning of a new day (see Genesis 1:1–31). The Sabbath was created on the evening of the seventh day, and is to be observed from the time when the sun sets at the end of Friday afternoon until it sets again at the end of Saturday afternoon (see Leviticus 23:32). Activities, such as gathering with other believers in church to rejoice in worshipping the Creator, visiting the sick to bring them cheer and serving their needs, sharing the good news of the gospel with those

who are interested in getting to know God better, and serving the poor and needy, will make of the Sabbath a day of joy and great satisfaction.

42. Sabbath: a sign of his Covenant. When God created the world, He did so in the time period of six days. On the seventh day (Saturday) He rested from His labors. He declared the seventh day holiday, to celebrate the creation. He set it apart from the other days of the week (sanctified it) and blessed it (see Genesis 2:1–3). Later on, when He reminds the people of Israel to "Remember the Sabbath day to keep it holy," He declares that it is a sign of His eternal covenant, not only for the people of Israel, but for all mankind (see Exodus 31:12–18).

43. Sanctification. Once a person is justified, he/she begins a new life, trusting in the sustaining power of the risen Christ to overcome inherited and/or cultivated tendencies towards sin. This is a process of a lifetime, and requires much patience on our part as we stumble and rise again through life. It is the special work of the Holy Spirit to speak to our hearts and persuade us to make choices within God's will. When we fail because of our own weakness, He leads us to confess and ask forgiveness, and to obtain a new opportunity to try again. If we continue to strive, trusting in the Lord, and turning to Him when we are tempted to do our own will, we will eventually develop a strong character, able to make good choices every time. When the Lord returns, He will finish the final perfection of our characters before taking us home.

44. Sanctuary in Heaven. When God instructed Moses to build a sanctuary on earth, He told him to build it following the pattern of the Sanctuary in Heaven (see Exodus 25:8, 9, 40). The Sanctuary was also known as the Temple of the Lord (see 1Samuel 1:9). The original

temple is in Heaven, and is the dwelling place and throne of God (see Revelation 7:15). The furniture in the earthly sanctuary, or temple, were representative of the furniture in the heavenly Temple (see Exodus 25:10; 26:37 and Revelation 4:5; 11:1, 19; 8:3). The purpose of having a sanctuary on earth after the pattern of the heavenly one was so that God's plan of redemption would always be close to people in symbols and practices that would make them look forward to the future sacrifice of Christ on their behalf, and thus fill them with hope when they confessed their sins and partook of the sacrifice of a lamb, the symbol of Christ.

45. Satan's counterfeit appearance as Christ. Satan's greatest dream throughout the long ages has been to be worshipped as a god (see Isaiah 14:12–14). This ambition caused his exile from heaven more the 6,000 years ago (see Revelation 12:7–9). But his hunger for worship and recognition has not waned. He has many followers who openly worship him already–the Church of Satan, witches and warlocks, and different forms of the occult--to name a few. The Bible teaches that Satan will even attempt to impersonate Christ, and receive the homage that only Christ deserves (see 2 Corinthians 11:14). Christ Himself predicted that this impersonation would take place at the end (see Matthew 24:5 and 23–27). Such a miraculous appearance will be a powerful deceptive delusion, and will unite the world in the effort to exterminate those thought to be the cause of the world's calamities.

46. Satan's exile. During the millennium of 1000 years, Satan will be exiled on the earth. He and his cohorts of demons will not have access to outer space or any celestial body. They will be left here to ponder on their rebellion and the damage they have caused to the earth and its inhabitants.

It in this respect that Satan will be bound–nobody left alive for him to tempt and annoy. Those *left behind* by the cloud that takes the saints, will be *left behind dead!* When Christ comes here for the third time, He will be coming back to reclaim this earth as the capital of His kingdom, where the New Jerusalem will be the center of universal culture. At that time, the wicked dead will be resurrected, Satan will no longer be bound by circumstances, and will incite the wicked to attack and take the Holy City, New Jerusalem (see Revelation 20:7–9). When they do, fire will rain down from heaven and destroy Satan, his horde of demons, and the impenitent wicked (see Revelation 20:10, 14–15). Then Christ will recreate the world all over again, destroying all the garbage left by sin, and replacing it with the beauty of the original creation (see Isaiah 66:22–23 and Revelation 21and 22:1–5). But that is another story, to be told in another book!

47. Second Coming of Christ. One of the things Christ repeatedly promised to His disciples and everyone who would subsequently believe in Him, was that He would return to take them to heavenly mansions (see John 14:1–3). In his great prophetic sermon in Matthew 24 and 25, He addressed all the events that will take place just before His visible coming. There will not be a secret rapture! (see Matthew 24:26, 27; 25:31, 32). Everyone living on earth will see Christ when he returns (see Revelation 1:7). The "secret rapture" concept was the invention of religious scholars, enemies of the Protestant Reformation (see the History of the Protestant Reformation in history books or encyclopedias).

48. Sin and probation. Sin is an intruder in an otherwise orderly and happy universe. God does not tolerate sin, yet in love for his deceived creatures, he delays his

judgement and consequent punishment until the sinner has rejected all offers of forgiveness and seals his doom by rejection of God's Covenant and grace (see Ezekiel 33:11). This prolonged period is called probation, and will come to an end for the whole world when Christ finishes His work of intercession in the heavenly temple (see Revelation 22:10–15).

49. Universe, the inhabited. Unless they read the Bible and believe in what it says, most people do not know that there are many inhabited planets in the universe. The Apostle Paul writes in the book of Hebrews that Jesus created other worlds (see Hebrews 1:3). And in chapter 11, verse 3, he continues to elaborate, stating that the "worlds (plural) were framed by the word of God, so that things which are seen were not made of things that do appear." In the book of Job, Moses wrote of convocations called by God in which were present other created beings presumably representatives from other worlds (see Job 1:6–7). Satan had the gall to appear there representing this earth, since he claimed it as his conquered territory.

50. War in heaven. After a time, having deceived a third of the angels about the character of God, and as he struggled to gain equality with God, he was finally cast out of the heavenly kingdom and exiled to planet Earth. (see Revelation 12:7–9) In his first attempt to conquer the loyalty of humans to himself and away from the Creator, Satan saw in the prohibited tree his golden opportunity to twist the truth and deceive mankind into disobedience to God's only prohibition (see Genesis 3:1–19).

51. Wicked Humans. During those 1000 years (the millennium), all the human beings that did not go to heaven with Christ are *left dead* on the earth (see Revelation 20:5) while the saints live and reign with

Christ in heaven during that same period (see Revelation 20:6). At the end of the 1000 years, the wicked dead are brought back to life by Christ to face their final judgement and punishment (see Revelation 20:5).

52. Work of the Holy Spirit. The Holy Spirit is God in the third person. His special work is to speak to the minds of people, leading them to Christ, and persuading them to give up evil (see John 15:7–14). It is the Holy Spirit who leads people to repentance and a change of heart (see Romans 2:4) and who enables people to change their behaviour and bad habits (see Philippians 2:12–13). The Holy Spirit is eternally God, and is deserving of all the reverence due to the Father and the Son.

www.ingramcontent.com/pod-product-compliance
Lightning Source LLC
LaVergne TN
LVHW021655060526
838200LV00050B/2366